Boss Off Limits

Misty Rogers

Boss Off Limits

3. Chapter 1 - Introductions
12. Chapter 2 - The Legacy
20. Chapter 3 - Pay Attention!
27. Chapter 4 - Brinley
34. Chapter 5 - What A Trip
45. Chapter 6 - Facebook & Heartbreak
52. Chapter 7 - Crushin'
64. Chapter 8 - This Emotional Rollercoaster
70. Chapter 9 - Is This A Date?
77. Chapter 10 - It's Kind of A Date
85. Chapter 11 - Trying New Things
92. Chapter 12 - Not A Murderer
103. Chapter 13 - Second First Date
123. Chapter 14 - Wrong Bar
131. Chapter 15 - Mystery Guest
138. Chapter 16 - Fall Solstice
151. Chapter 17 - Don't Kiss and Tell
158. Chapter 18 - Lunch in Philly
163. Chapter 19 - Paint & Sip
170. Chapter 20 - Falling for My Boss
181. Chapter 21 - The Note
189. Chapter 22 - Pulling It Off
207. Chapter 23 - Prohibition Era
213. Chapter 24 - Heartbreak & Unemployment
218. Chapter 25 - Confronting the Devil
223. Chapter 26 - Next Steps
232. Chapter 27 - Mountain Retreat
238. Chapter 28 - I Hope This Works
245. Chapter 29 - Four Letter Word
255. Chapter 30 - New Horizons
261. Chapter 31 - My Boyfriend, Ben

Chapter 1 - *INTRODUCTIONS* (Isabella)

My desk was tucked away from everyone else's in a quiet little corner of the office. If you took two lefts and a right through the cubicle maze, you'd find me at said desk surrounded by tall walls, invisible to the workers around me. Phones rang, keyboards clacked, and voices murmured, but I couldn't hear a thing when I popped my earbuds in, purposely distancing myself from the hum of the rest of the office.

The seclusion and silence that I chose for myself, as much as it made me a loner in the eyes of my coworkers, allowed me to focus on my work. And as the sole graphic designer for a multi-million dollar hotel conglomerate, I was happy to take all the solitude I could get.

This day was no different than usual, a never-ending list of projects and assignments kept me busy from nine to five. I hunched close to my computer screen and, using my wireless mouse, dragged the cursor through Photoshop swiftly, as if the pointer were sprinting across my screen. I was working on manipulating a text layer. It was quite easy to overlay some texture on top to make the design pop, just a few clicks of the mouse and a couple taps of keyboard keys and it'd be done.

The past hour or so I'd been working on a promotional postcard featuring one of the hotels' newly redesigned luxury rooms. It was a project that I was revisiting after I'd scrapped the first design a couple days ago. If only my bosses knew how many drafts I went through before they got a look at them. But, luckily for me and this postcard, I felt like my design was *finally* coming together.

I was just about to hit the alt key to merge two layers together when my coworker, Cindy Hayes, poked her head around my cubicle wall and interrupted my workflow. She waited until I removed an earbud to speak.

"Hey Isabella, staff meeting's in two. Ready to head over?"

I glanced down at the time on the bottom corner of my screen. Sure enough it was 10:28 am and I was due to be seated in the conference room in exactly two minutes for our weekly staff meeting. Thank goodness for Cindy or I would have certainly sat there engrossed in my work for who knows how much longer. I hit the save button, removed my other earbud, and shoved up out of my rolling chair.

"Yeah I'm ready."

Cindy gave me a warm smile and started to lead the way back through the winding labyrinth and down the hall. Cindy was a bit older than me, probably about twenty five years my senior, but then again pretty much everyone in this office was considerably older than I was. A lot of my coworkers had been with the company since the first hotel's incorporation in 1982.

Even though I myself had worked for Simmons' Hotels for a bit over two years, I was still considered a newbie. When everyone else has worked somewhere for decades, two years was nothing to them. And in a way I respected that. These men and women have seen the company through good times and bad times, and they still showed up every day, happy to do their jobs. I hoped that one day I could look back at my career and be able to recognize the same dedication and loyalty to a company as the people here held for Simmons' Hotels.

At just twenty six years old I wanted to think that I was doing pretty well for myself already, though. Securing a steady, well-paying job at an established company doing something I loved, how could it get better than that? Stereotypically, people my age didn't all have the same drive as I did. I always loved working hard, something about putting in a solid day's work just made me feel accomplished. I had fun on the weekends, sure, but in the office I was nothing-but-business.

I thought to myself about my career thus far as Cindy and I walked in a comfortable silence. That's what I liked best about Cindy; she was good at making people feel like they belonged. For example, she knew I was not much of a conversationalist and therefore allowed our quick walk to go by without the forced small-talk that a lot of coworkers tried to impose on me.

I glanced over at her, her short blonde hair bobbing as we walked. Cindy had a smile that made each person she spoke to feel as if they truly mattered in that moment. I imagined that's why she did so well in her position of Partner Relations Liaison. She was the reason we had had some of our local business partners since the beginning of the company.

We rounded the corner of a short hallway dotted with small meeting rooms and offices, and walked into a lofty conference room that was already full of the rest of our coworkers, seated around a large table in the center of the room.

There were about twenty of us in this office that made up all of executive management and administration for Simmons' Hotels. Besides the design department (me) and Partner Relations (Cindy), our office building also housed departments like Human Resources, Food and Beverage, and our CFO. There were other departments too, but I couldn't have named them all if I tried. Maybe that was one of the downsides of keeping to myself; it sometimes meant that my coworkers could feel like strangers, even after all this time.

Myself and my coworkers had the luxury of working out of our own little office building that was tucked away on the back of the lot of our oldest property, The Steamworks Hotel. It was nice not having to work inside one of the hotels; having the separation from the rest of the bustle of the hospitality industry helped keep us on track with the never-ending task of managing this company.

Despite the hard work I put in for this company over the past couple of years, I wasn't always so career driven. I had gone to college for graphic design thinking it'd be a fun way to be creative every day, not knowing everything that went into actually being a graphic designer. I took this job just a couple years after graduating with a Bachelor's Degree and quickly learned what it meant to be a professional. Luckily this position has felt like the perfect fit ever since, and I was settled nicely into my routine.

In the crowded conference room I sat down in a plush old lobby chair toward the back. Our conference room was made up of a hodgepodge of old furniture, some from decades ago and surely older than I was. The

Steamworks Hotel and our other two properties had gone through a few decor revamps over the years as the owner tried to keep up with the times, and our office building always got the discarded remains.

Cindy perched on a wobbly wooden bar stool in the front corner of the room just as our Senior Operations Manager, Ben Simmons, strode in.

If anyone was going to throw a wrench into my routine, it was him. Benjamin Simmons was a powerhouse business man who knew how to get shit done. Credit where credit was due, he was good at what he did, but something about him majorly threw me off. Whenever he was around it was like my brain melted and I forgot how to act like a functioning adult. He was quite intimidating despite his friendly nature and I wasn't a fan of the effect he seemed to have on me.

Ben had been the Operations Manager for less than a year but he had worked at the hotels on and off in different positions for probably as long as I'd been alive. Ben stepped up into the operations role when its long-time previous occupant, Jack Newton, retired last November.

Ben was this loud talking, weirdly energetic people-person and everyone here seemed to love him. He was a fine enough person and leader, although there was a part of me that couldn't help but to think that he'd only gotten the job because of his family ties.

Ben's Aunt June was the original owner and founder of all of the properties under the Simmons' Hotels name. June had retired from her full-time work a few years ago but still owned the majority of the shares of the company. She would still pop in every now and again and was always hands-on with the big decisions.

Ben stood in the front of the packed room. "Good morning, all!" He bellowed.

A few responses were mumbled back but for the most part everyone was ready to get on with the meeting. It would seem that no one could quite match Ben's energy in the morning; most of my coworkers took the *'this meeting could have been an email'* attitude toward these things.

Our weekly staff meetings began when Ben joined the team, as a way to catch him up with everything that was happening around the hotels. They continued now, almost a year later, because Ben seemed to enjoy the updates as much as he enjoyed the camaraderie of having everyone in the same room. If only everyone else felt the same, maybe these meetings wouldn't feel like such a chore each week.

"I want to make this one short and simple so I just have a quick agenda for this morning," Ben began. "First I want to congratulate everyone on our summer season, which just wrapped up last week. From June through August this year we more than doubled our booking rate, and alcohol sales were up around twenty percent at the bars thanks to Jess's PR efforts and the newly made-over bar at The Locomotive Hotel."

Jess Simmons was my other supervisor and just so happened to also be Ben's cousin. She oversaw press relations and marketing for Simmons' Hotels. Jess was fairly new to the hospitality industry, joining her family's business around the same time as I did, after having left a short career that she had had as an elementary school teacher. Despite her lack of training or experience, Jess had really come into her role in the company and I generally enjoyed working with her. We worked closely on a lot of projects since I handled all of her design work for the marketing campaigns that she crafted.

Jess was also the closest in age to me, only about five years older than I was. We built a good rapport being the 'young ones' in the office and she was probably the only person I genuinely enjoyed talking to on a daily basis.

From what I'd learned about them from office gossip, Jess and Ben grew up together here in Strasburg. Their close friendship made them great partners in the business world, playing off of each others' strengths. They certainly argued like brother and sister sometimes but their ideas built well on each other and they had some great contributions to the hotels in such a short amount of time. Sometimes I thought about how I really lucked out; my bosses could have been real jerk-wads but I really couldn't have ended up with a better duo.

Ben's deep voice snapped me back to reality. "Heading into fall now we have to shift our focus to the travelers coming to Pennsylvania for the foliage, the autumnal activities, and our annual Fall Ball." He continued, looking around the room, "I'll be meeting with each department this week to discuss the game plan for the next few months. Other than that, I just wanted to say thanks for your hard work everyone, and let's finish the rest of this year out strong. Does anyone have anything they want to add?"

This was the part of the meeting where Ben opened up the floor to us. Clark Turner, who managed a customer support team, waved a hand through the air.

"Have we decided on the theme of the Fall Ball yet? Guests have been calling in for a couple weeks now asking about it and my front desk agents are getting a little overwhelmed. Seeing how well the event went last year, I think word is spreading and customers are ready to book."

Ben nodded his head as Clark spoke. "We don't have the theme nailed down yet but that's one of my goals for this week. If anyone has any ideas, let me know. I'm thinking something kind of upscale to draw in the kind of customers who would also be interested in staying in our newly renovated rooms.

By the way, Isabella, Jess told me you were creating a promotional mail piece for those rooms?"

I realized that he was talking to me and nodded my head. Everyone turned to glance at me in my high back chair when they didn't hear a reply, and I curtly smiled at their gazes. I realized that with their backs turned to me, everyone besides Ben probably thought I hadn't responded. So to appease them I followed up with a 'yes.'

"Great, let's try to get that sent out ASAP. I'll come talk to you and Jess about that as soon as we get this theme figured out."

"Okay." I squeaked out as I gave a thumbs up.

A thumbs up? What was I, twelve?

Ben smiled and continued. "Alright then with that let's call it a wrap. I'm coming over to Partner Relations to talk with you first, Cindy, right after I grab some coffee."

Everyone stood up and shuffled out of the room as Ben told a few more department heads when to expect him to pop in to discuss the plans for fall.

As I wound my way through the cubicle maze back to my desk, I couldn't help but relive my awkward thumbs-up from moments ago. You see, I was the type of person that dwelled on embarrassing situations like those. Like, a 'can't fall asleep at night because I'm too busy thinking about every awkward thing I've ever done' kind of person. With a heavy sigh I plopped into my chair and rolled back up to my desk.

The official first day of fall wasn't for another couple of weeks but this morning I had switched out my usual blue coffee mug for a bright orange one that was dotted with pumpkins. I picked it up from my desk and took a sip of my cold tea that I'd made a couple of hours ago.

Fall was my absolute favorite time of the year. I was definitely ready to start dressing in fluffy sweaters and warm boots but the Pennsylvania weather probably wouldn't allow it for another month or so. I'd just have to settle for little touches of fall until then, like my orange mug and the festive cinnamon tea I'd filled it with this morning.

Oh well, I thought, shaking the thoughts from my head, *I should get back to work.*

After waking my computer screen back up I held down the alt key, left clicked on the text layer, and set the opacity to eighty percent. My layers were merged.

Chapter 2 - *THE LEGACY* (Ben)

I leaned back in my chair and took in the spacious office around me. I had been inhabiting Jack's old office for almost a year at that point but it certainly didn't look like it. In fact, the office looked kind of abandoned.

Besides one picture of my shepherd dog pinned to the cork board on my wall, there was nothing in that room that would tell you Benjamin Simmons worked there. I was so busy these days that I didn't really spend much time in this office, so when I *was* in there I made due with the hand-me-down furniture and bare walls.

After the staff meeting ended I was glad to have had a productive meeting with Cindy in Partner Relations. Cindy was working with our food and beverage suppliers to bring some fall flavors into the hotel's room service menus, like apple, cinnamon, and my least favorite, pumpkin spice. Really whatever it took to bring a touch of fall to Simmons' Hotels.

Taking on the role of Operations Manager meant that I oversaw pretty much every department of Simmons' Hotels. Sometimes it felt overwhelming, but the fact that everyone had worked here for so long meant that the place pretty much ran itself. I mostly had to check in with everyone to keep up appearances, and of course to keep Aunt June happy.

My next meeting turned into a less-than-inspiring budgeting session with Greg Stufanis, who managed maintenance for all of the properties. Apparently our second oldest property, The Locomotive Hotel, had been needing a lot of repairs as its 1989 bones were starting to show their age.

I had been thinking about holding our Fall Ball there due to its large, industrial-accented event space, but it looked like we would now have to either hold it at The Steamworks Hotel or at our third, smaller property, The Kettle Inn. I was debating the options with myself when my cousin Jess walked in.

Jess and I grew up together and she was one of my closest friends, as annoying as she could be at times. I only had brothers, so Jess was like the little sister I never wanted. I had to give her credit, though, she was a major help in showing me the ropes when I joined this side of the family business, and we did work quite well together despite our constant tiffs.

"Hey," she said as she plopped herself into one of the two mis-matched chairs on the other side of my desk.

She always went for the beige lounge chair over the plastic dining chair that I didn't even recognize from any of the properties. The furniture situation here was quite peculiar, seeing that much of it wasn't even office furniture. But that's what you got at the Simmons' family business.

"Hi, how's it going Jess?"

Jess loved to stroll into my office like she owned it, and did so multiple times a day just to chat. I mostly didn't mind although she did have a pension to walk in while I was in the middle of a phone call or meeting. All I had to do was glare at her from behind my desk and she knew to leave.

I wondered if today's discussion would be business or pleasure, as she was wont to discuss family drama while here at work. One day she had heard from her dad that one of my brothers was quitting his job to become a pilot even though he'd never flown a plane before in his life. It ended up being completely false information but Jess just loved the thrill of the gossip. That was Jessica Simmons for you.

"I've been thinking about themes for the ball."

So, this visit is actually about business, I thought.

"I love the industrial feel of our hotels but you're right about needing to attract some new higher-end customers. What about a twenties themed ball? Like flappers and mobsters, and we can call the bar a speakeasy for the duration of the event?"

Man, that's a good idea.

I thought about it for a minute as I picked up a pen from my desk and began to click it absentmindedly.

"Yeah, that could work." I mused. "What about making it a costume party and serving high-class cocktails like in that movie?"

"That movie?" She scoffed. "You mean *The Great Gatsby*? It's also a book, you know."

Little brat. I forgot she was a teacher and had probably read that book willingly in her spare time. I'd only seen the movie.

Regardless, Jess was good at finishing my thoughts. We made good business partners, and it didn't hurt that we had literally known each other forever. Jess was ambitious and full of ideas, whereas I was always more down to earth and realistic. We seemed to strike a good balance.

"Yes, that's the one, movie or book, it still emulates wealth and power which is the atmosphere we need to create for this event. I like this idea Jess, should we have Isabella mock up an invite, see how it looks on paper?"

I didn't have a single creative bone in my body so I was having trouble visualizing the theme's little details, but I knew Isabella would make something great out of it.

Jess giddily clapped her hands together. "Sure, I know she's been wrestling with that postcard design all morning so maybe she'll welcome another project to get her mind off of it for a bit."

I couldn't imagine Isabella Morgan wrestling with *any* project she was given. Every single thing she produced was immaculate, down to the tiny details. Time and time again I've been blown away by the work she put out; she was very skilled for how young she was, and Simmons' Hotels was certainly lucky to have such a talented and dedicated worker.

Not to mention she was easy on the eyes…

Isabella had the prettiest highlighted blonde hair that fell in waves down her back, and blue-grey eyes that she hid behind those corny blue light blocking glasses she always wore. She was a petite five foot something, small enough that she could disappear into the cubicle maze without having to duck down.

For someone as shy and withdrawn as she was, she sure seemed to love experimenting with colorful clothes. Today for example, she'd worn a red blouse with some light brown slacks, making her look like the human version of a caramel apple as she hid in the back of the conference room. She was definitely a quirky woman and she spent all of her time in the office absorbed in her own design world, back in that little corner. It was endearing.

It had only been recently, though, that I'd noticed how attractive Isabella was. It probably had a lot to do with my ten year relationship crashing to an end over the summer. A breakup like that will do things to a person, like make them check out a younger employee during staff meetings. I wasn't saying that I'd ever date someone that young, but I liked to tell myself that it didn't hurt to look.

But Isabella's looks weren't why I liked having her around. It was refreshing to have some young blood here when everyone else was close to retirement age. Not that I would consider myself a spring chicken at forty five years old, but sometimes I felt like a mere teenager compared to the people around me, so Isabella balanced that out.

My mind returned to reality and I realized that Jess had already left to go talk to Isabella about the Fall Ball. I sipped my room temperature coffee and decided that I was going to arrange a meeting with Jess and Isabella just after lunch to discuss some of the details while the ideas were still freely flowing in my head. I was just about to stand up and head to the break room to nuke my mug of old coffee when my desk phone started ringing. I glanced at the caller ID and quickly picked it up when I recognized the number as my Aunt June's.

"To what do I owe the pleasure, Aunt June?"

"Hi Ben, I'm just checking in. I got your report on last quarter's numbers and they look good. I was curious what the plan was moving forward into the fall months. You know, we usually get a huge tourist spike in October."

I decided to sit back down; this call would probably be a long one if we were going to discuss operations plans for all three properties for the next few months.

Despite retiring years ago, my Aunt June still acted as if she was running the place. I didn't blame her, though, seeing as she had built this company from the ground up. June had always been a business woman and we all knew that she'd never fully be able to step away from her baby. And in a way, this company *was* her baby. She had no children, just three successful hotels.

Aunt June's legacy was her cluster of these hotels in Strasburg, Pennsylvania. Our whole Simmons family was rooted deep in that town; I'd heard the stories countless times of great uncles and grandfathers that worked on the trains and built the rails that ran through the center of our small bustling town.

June loved to recount her childhood playing on the tracks and hanging around the station where her father worked. It only made sense that when she opened her first hotel it had to be train-themed.

It was actually pretty amazing if you thought about it. Aunt June was only in her early thirties when she took out a business loan and built The Steamworks Hotel along the tracks on the eastern side of town.

The Steamworks Hotel was a large, sprawling building that was originally modeled to look like it was built during the industrial age. Geometry was key in the building's design, with sharp angles playing off of flowing curves. It was a stunning building and a landmark of our small town.

That first hotel in Strasburg did so well that June built another one less than a decade later. The Locomotive Hotel sat on the west end of the tracks, closer to the train station which has since become a diner. The Locomotive Hotel was even more ornate, utilizing a Romanesque style modeled after old European train stations. That building was designed with elaborate masonry and arches, bringing baroque design to little old Strasburg, PA.

That hotel also took off; guests went crazy for the opportunity to stay in such a beautiful building. The outsides of both buildings stayed the same despite indoor decor changing every decade or so, and guests still came from all over the country to stay in June's hotels. Actually, June's two properties were the only hotels in town so business was easy when your only competition was yourself.

June then added The Kettle Inn to her repertoire in 1994, a cute little home-like establishment right smack dab in the middle of town. It was more of a smaller, cozier property, and was secretly my favorite location because of its quaint atmosphere.

I had worked at all three locations over the past couple of decades, after I'd come back to town after graduating college. I started out in the maintenance department of The Locomotive Hotel where I worked for a few years until I did a stint as a bellhop at The Steamworks Hotel. I had filled in a lot of different roles from delivery driver to bartender. Really, it came down to whatever Aunt June needed done, I did.

I was working the front desk and managing customer service at The Kettle Inn about a year ago when Aunt June asked me if I'd be interested in filling an operations position at the office. I jumped at the opportunity for a new adventure (and higher pay) and I could tell that June was happy to have me become a more integral part to the family business. I joined Jess at the office, and together we had been working hard to modernize aspects of the business while pulling in younger and more affluent clientele.

I know that a lot of the senior staff at Simmons' Hotels were used to things running a certain way, but the way I saw it, you can't run a business in 2022 the same way that it was run in the eighties. I do occasionally get pushback from the executive staff, and even from Aunt June sometimes, when I implement new ideas or policies, but it was all for the good of the company.

This business would outlive its creator and had to keep up with the industry trends regardless of who was in charge. When June fully retires (or let's be more realistic, when she dies), her shares in the business will be divided among her family members, ultimately making Jess and I major partners. Aunt June wasn't going anywhere any time soon, though, so there was no use in waiting around to make the changes we wanted to see.

Each change implemented rejuvenated the hotels, from new furniture in the rooms and lobby, to a more upscale bar experience at The Steamworks and Locomotive Hotels. We had been having Isabella redo everything from in-room menus and channel guides all the way down to the little designs on each guest's room card. With the fresh new looks we were phasing in I could see this chain continuing to thrive and pull in a steady stream of guests for *another* thirty decades.

Chapter 3 - *Pay Attention!* (Isabella)

I felt like I had finally gotten that postcard design right where I wanted it, and I was glad because frankly I was sick of working on it. I stared at the design sitting on my computer screen as I stuffed a forkful of caesar salad into my mouth. I could have gone and sat in the break room to eat lunch with everyone else, like I did on a rare occasion, but I felt like I needed to focus on this project. I often worked through lunch so it really wasn't a big deal.

For some reason this design was kicking my butt. I couldn't figure out where I wanted it to go, but this creative roadblock happened every now and again so I wasn't majorly stressed about it. Yet.

How do I resonate with these upscale customers that we're trying to draw in?

I was mulling this question over and crunching on a crouton when Jess popped her head around my cubicle wall. Her long brown hair was pulled back into a low ponytail, accentuating the curve of her petite heart-shaped face. I thought Jess was quite beautiful, with light brown eyes and tanned skin. I wondered how she was still single, then I remembered how small Strasburg's dating pool was.

"What do you think about flappers?" She asked excitedly.

I swallowed my mouthful of crouton. "Uh, what?"

Usually I could piece together the ideas that just came randomly gushing out of that woman but this time I was at a loss. Jess stepped around into my cubicle and sat on the corner of my desk. She did that quite often so I usually kept it clear, just for her.

"For the Fall Ball! Like a twenties theme with flappers and stuff. I ran it by Ben and I think he likes it so we were thinking you could help us visualize it better. Do you think you could work with that theme?"

"Oh, yeah totally!" My mind began racing with ideas, "I could go with an art deco feel for all of the print matter, like the invites and drink menus."

Jess' jovial facial expression told me that I was right on the money, and honestly this new idea excited me. I needed to take a break from the postcard anyway and something fun like this was the perfect thing.

"I'll start drafting something up and I'll get it over to you to make sure we're on the same page."

"Sounds good! Oh and CC Ben on that, too. Let's keep him in the loop." Jess said, before bounding away to her desk a few rows over.

Jess was an idea factory when it came to rejuvenating this company and she put a fresh spin on everything. I personally loved all the new things her and Ben were doing but I knew some of the other employees grumbled each time she had a new idea, because it meant they would have to adjust. So many people here were stuck in their ways after all those years, understandably, but change was coming swiftly at the hands of the Simmons cousins.

I spent the next hour or so, I wasn't really sure because I totally lost track of time, drafting up that invite. Who knew it was so hard to choose a singular font? I was scrolling through an online database of royalty-free fonts when Jess reappeared with a notebook in her hand.

"Are you at a good stopping point? Ben wants to meet with us in the conference room to go over fall stuff."

I made a show out of hitting save on my keyboard and stood up. "Yes I am!"

Unlike Cindy, Jess loved to engage in small talk. I didn't mind so much with her because it felt like we had more in common to talk about. Plus she had no problem doing most of the chatting, which made it easy for me to be a silent participant.

"Do you watch Bachelor in Paradise? Last night's episode was spicy," Jess said about the popular reality TV dating show.

Luckily it was one of the few TV shows that I tuned in to on occasion, and I just happened to catch the episode that aired the night before. 'Grocery Store Joe' found love in Paradise once again. *Good for him*, I thought, *maybe I should go on an island to fall in love. Lord knows I'm not going to find someone in this town.*

My current love life could be aptly described as non-existent; I really hadn't dated anyone since college, and that was four years ago now. It wasn't that I didn't *want* to find a boyfriend, I was just always so wrapped up in work that I didn't take much time to go out and mingle like a young single woman should. I kept telling myself that one of these days I would get out there into the dating world again, but it hadn't happened just yet.

Jess was on a tangent about one of the contestants on the dating show; our office building was quite small so I only had to entertain the rant for a couple minutes as we walked down the hall back toward the same conference room from before. As we walked in, Ben was already seated in a rolling desk chair, pulled up to the large wooden table that had more than a few dings and scratches in it. He was studying a piece of paper quite intently. Jess grabbed Cindy's bar stool from earlier and I pulled up a short wooden dining chair.

Ben greeted us with a friendly smile that always seemed to be plastered on his face. I didn't know how one man could smile so much. He must have strong cheek muscles. Even more confusing was how someone so friendly could be so good at business. Usually the two didn't belong together but Ben made it work.

Today Ben was wearing his signature light blue button up shirt with the sleeves rolled up to the elbows, a sign that he was ready to do business.

As soon as Jess and I were both seated, Ben put the paper down and got started right away.

"How's it going guys?" He turned to me, "did Jess tell you about the theme she thought of for the Fall Ball?" He seemed excited, like a dog receiving a new bone. I imagined if he had a tail, it'd be wagging.

"Yes, the nineteen twenties theme?"

For some reason I phrased my answer as a question, even though I definitely knew that was the answer. There was just something about Ben that always made me behave more awkward than usual, and that was *really* awkward. Whatever it was, it made me uncomfortable and I got all hot and sweaty. Attractive, I know.

"Yeah! Do you think you can make that theme work?"

I barely got a nod in before he turned to Jess, onto the next subject. "I want to tie in the new rooms, make a package deal and call it a VIP package or something like that. Exclusive rooms with access to bottle service at the ball, or something of that nature."

Jess and Ben started brainstorming about this new VIP package for the Fall Ball and the ideas bounced between them like a high-intensity ping pong ball match. I scribbled some notes in a pad that I had grabbed before leaving my desk, but for the most part I just listened. Trying to keep up with the two of them once they got going could seriously give someone whiplash. Rather than focusing on the brainstorming sesh in front of me, my mind started to wander, which was always a dangerous pastime for me.

Why does Ben make me so nervous? He was an attractive man, sure, but I wasn't *attracted* to him. He had to have twenty years on me, evidenced by the salt and pepper that was sprinkled throughout his otherwise dark hair and short beard. He was the only business man I knew that also looked like he belonged in the mountains, cutting down trees or something along those lines. He generally kept his appearance neat and tidy, although I bet if you caught him walking down the street in some more casual attire he might have looked a little more gruff.

I tried to subtly look down at his forearms, strong and firm as if he actually did cut down trees for a living. He was very tan and it seemed like he definitely liked to spend his free time outdoors; maybe I was onto something with this lumberjack thing?

My eyes wandered up to his face as he talked. His dark brown eyes were somehow mysterious and inviting at the same time, shrouded by thick dark eyebrows that waggled exuberantly as he spoke. When he smiled, which was all the time, his features lit up like a younger, jolly Santa Claus. Straight white teeth peeked out from behind his bushy mustache and deep laugh lines danced around his eyes.

Ben was certainly nice to look at but that couldn't be the reason I always acted so weird around him. He could be intimidating and intense when he was in boss-man mode, and that had to be the reason I turned to mushy jello around him. Or so I told myself.

"What do you think about that?" Jess' voice had me snapping back to reality.

Shit, I have no clue what she's asking about.

My expression must have conveyed that thought because she asked again, "What do you think about coming up with an ad design to place on social media? Do you think that could help attract some new guests?"

Ah, social media, yes.

"Yeah, absolutely." I quickly rerouted my thoughts back to work. "We can reach people from all over with the right parameters. And I can definitely come up with a digital ad design for it."

Jess smiled at my response but I knew exactly what she had to be thinking. I wasn't paying attention and it showed.

"Great!" Ben said, ignoring whatever weird tension was in the room due to my slip up. "Then let's start moving forward with that and we'll get the whole team together next week to talk game plan for the Fall Ball."

He gathered his notes that were now strewn out in front of him and stood up; Jess and I did the same.

I started to walk past Ben, out of the conference room, when he reached out and lightly touched my arm to stop me.

"Oh Isabella, can you send me the invite design when you've gotten a draft done? I can't wait to see what you come up with."

"Sure," I responded and quickly turned and headed back toward my desk.

Jess murmured something to Ben before catching up with me just as I sat down in my chair.

"Are you okay? You seemed spacey just now. We didn't mean to overwhelm you."

Leave it to Jess to try to take the blame for my little mistake. She was for sure an empath, feeling deeply for the people around her. It made her a pleasure to work with but she could also easily be taken advantage of if she didn't safeguard her emotions a little more. Or maybe that was just *my* defense mechanism.

"Yeah I'm fine," I assured her, "there were just a lot of ideas flying back and forth and it got a little hard to keep up with. You didn't overwhelm me, I just needed a minute to catch up was all."

That was a big lie. I was staring at her cousin's eyes; I didn't catch a thing either of them said after 'VIP package.' I felt a little bad lying to Jess but I told myself that it wouldn't happen again.

Jess looked a little skeptical of my excuse but nodded anyway, giving me the benefit of the doubt, and headed back toward her desk.

What was going on with me? I loved this job and didn't want to lose it over some daydreaming. I had to keep my head in the game. And with that, I grasped my mouse and focused my attention on my computer screen for the rest of the day.

Chapter 4 - **BRINLEY** (Ben)

I've had a productive day, I thought to myself as I hopped into my truck to head home.

I always liked to reflect on my days. It was a habit I'd picked up not too long ago when I decided I needed to focus on the positive aspects of my life. So as I thought about my day, I decided that *productive* was the appropriate word to sum it up.

Between department meetings all afternoon and that call with Aunt June, which ended up lasting over an hour, I had accomplished a lot. I think I got everyone on the same page for the last quarter of the year, which is always a big feat. Not to mention Jess coming up with a Fall Ball theme; that was a huge weight off of my shoulders. It was days like these that I could go home feeling proud of what I'd done.

The parking lot was empty as I backed out of my spot. Everyone else had left about an hour ago, but I'd hung back to finalize some details about The Locomotive Hotel's repairs. Working on a building like that could be tricky because of its specific architectural style, and there were only a few contractors in the area that were trusted to handle it. Greg had the whole situation pretty much under control, I just had to approve the work order and move some money around in the maintenance budget to make it happen.

It was only a short drive back home to my old farmhouse, which I bought precisely because of its proximity to town. I chose a short commute time over practicality, because *damn* that old house sure was tiny. It was an original 1930's American Farmhouse with a classic Gable roof, and a wide front porch that you'd expect to see an old lady sitting out on in a rocking chair. The interior, though, was a mess of walls that created small, boxy rooms. People must have been smaller back when this house was built because it definitely wasn't practical for modern-day me.

The giant yard for my German Shepherd Mollie was a bonus, though.

I rolled down the long gravel driveway that led to my farmhouse. The house couldn't be seen from the road, which I loved because of the privacy it allowed me. When I cleared the thick cluster of pine trees that lined either side, I saw a blue Jeep Wrangler parked up next to the house.

"Fuck."

I felt my heart thud in my chest like a jackhammer as I closed the distance to the house.

It would appear that Brinley, my now ex-fiancé, was at the house probably grabbing the rest of her stuff and visiting with Mollie. We'd gotten the dog together as a puppy about five years ago, but she lived with me now since Brinley's apartment didn't allow animals. I loved having Mollie stay with me because I don't think I would have been okay living alone in that house after everything. As corny as it sounded, I was eternally grateful that Mollie was still my girl, even when Brinley wasn't anymore.

I parked next to the Jeep and begrudgingly got out. I thought I had come home to this Jeep, and this woman, for the last time a few months ago when I walked into the house and was met with a breakup speech already prepared. It still stung to think about it so I usually chose not to, although seeing this Jeep parked in what was her spot made it hard to forget.

    I took one big, deep breath before I opened the front door and stepped through my comically small living room. Brinley wasn't in there so I continued into the tight kitchen. There was only so many places she could be in a house this small. I did have to say though, with Brinley taking a lot of the furniture and leaving the rooms fairly empty, they did feel a lot bigger than usual.

    There were a couple half-open boxes on the round kitchen table sitting next to Brinley's keys. I wouldn't take the house key back yet; I couldn't. We bought this house together. She may not have wanted to live there with me anymore but I couldn't lock her out like a stranger. Then again, that kind of thinking is why I now find myself now standing in a house with my ex, sweating bullets as I wait for her to appear.

    I was reminded at that moment that I had to return a call to the bank so we could finalize our paperwork; I was buying her out of her half of the house and when I did, this breakup would feel all the more real. Not that it didn't already feel real living in this house alone, or while trying to figure out how to be a bachelor after ten years of being spoken for.

    "Oh sorry, I thought I'd be out before you got home. I'm just about done.

    A brunette with an athletic build walked through the doorway from the dining room to join me in the kitchen.

    Brinley always reminded me of a stereotypical high school cheerleader (which she ironically was at one point). She was tall and slim, with strong arms and a conventionally beautiful face. She was always perfectly made up, hair done and makeup applied. She was beautiful without all that stuff, too, but you could never convince her of it.

This room felt miniscule with her in there with me, like her aura sucked all of the energy out of me. She looked good, I think she had mentioned taking up yoga just before she left. Good for her.

Her dark green eyes gave me a quick once over before she turned around and headed back to whatever room she was packing up before I came in. There was no emotion there. Cold and distant, same as the day she handed the ring back to me and shattered my heart.

I couldn't bring myself to follow her, or even attempt to make small talk as she finished up whatever she was doing. Instead, I walked back outside and around to the back yard. Arguably my favorite part of the property, the backyard was a big, flat field that covered an entire acre before it reached the treeline in the distance.

Mollie was out there sniffing at the side of the old barn where a fat groundhog had made his home. She heard me coming and ran in my direction, ears perked up at the sight of me. Now *that* was the kind of reaction I wanted when I came home to my girl. Too bad the only love I got these days was from a dog.

Mollie sat at my feet, tail thumping and mouth hanging open in what looked like a huge doggy smile. Her coarse brown and black fur had chunks of dirt and grass in it, evidence suggesting that she had found the groundhog's hole and had probably tried to become friends with him.

I squatted down to scratch Mollie's face and her hind leg started to twitch as I hit just the right spot. Her round eyes looked up at me as if she was trying to comfort me. Mollie always knew when I was feeling down.

"That's a good girl. That feels good, doesn't it?" I murmured.

Moments later her ears perked up and I heard a car door slam, and the Jeep rumbled to life out in the front yard.

I remembered when Brinley had asked me to put that loud muffler on for her. She'd wanted to be like other Jeep owners, with their obnoxious, thundering vehicles. It was a 'Jeep Life' thing, apparently. I always thought it was kind of dumb but I'd done it for her anyway, just wanting her to be happy.

I listened, and when I couldn't hear wheels on the gravel drive anymore I headed toward the back door and into the house, with Mollie right on my heels. I refilled her water bowl and grabbed a beer from the fridge. While she lapped at the water I leaned my back against the edge of the counter and sipped from the chilled bottle. The boxes were gone from the table and it felt empty in there once again.

I didn't want to think about Brinley anymore so I directed my thoughts toward work. I'd thrown myself at that job for the past few months and it did help take some of the edge off when I was forced to deal with the company's problems rather than my own. I'd prefer to deal with budgeting issues and scheduling conflicts most days rather than deal with my own feelings. I knew it wasn't healthy but it was the option that hurt the least.

Besides, I was excited with our fall plans for the hotels, especially the potential Fall Ball theme that Jess had come up with. I was pretty sure we were going to go with it, especially since no one else had offered any ideas. I was sure Isabella had already taken the theme and ran with it like she always did. She really was talented.

Quickly my thoughts drifted away from work.

I wonder what Isabella's up to right now. I bet she's already slipped out of her work clothes and into something more comfortable for the evening. What would we do if she were here with me...

And just as fast as that thought entered my head I chased it away. I didn't need to be thinking about subordinates like that, especially ones half my age.

My engagement just ended in crushing heartbreak and I was feeling conflicted. I was still having a hard time accepting it, yet I felt the yearning inside for something new.

But not with Isabella. No, that couldn't happen. But, as angry as I was with myself for letting my mind go to that place, something in my lower half seemed to be playing devil's advocate.

Why was I thinking about this woman all of a sudden? None of this made any sense, which is exactly why I was shutting those thoughts down immediately. I was probably just worked up from having to see Brinley. An icy shower waited for me in the bathroom at the top of the stairs, so that's where I headed.

Mollie followed me up the creaky narrow stairs to the master bathroom and laid outside the door as I cooled off in the shower. The ice water helped clear my mind and cool down, er, other parts of me too. I felt my body relax as muscles untensed under the stream of water.

As I toweled off in front of the vanity mirror I looked at myself. I didn't think I was unattractive. I wouldn't describe myself as sexy, but I felt like I had a certain appeal to my look. I wasn't chiseled but I still considered myself fit. I abhor exercise but I love me some hiking and boating, enough to keep myself in shape without all the definition of muscle that's sculpted in gyms with laborious workouts.

I thought Brinley loved my physique but that was one of the things she threw at me while dumping me. She said I didn't eat healthy enough and I drank too much beer. When she'd said that, my eyes rolled so hard I'm surprised they hadn't rolled right out onto the table.

While I admit that I don't have the best diet, and I *do* love beer, I don't think I'm unhealthy. I see my doctor for checkups twice a year, I get some green vegetables on my plate every now and again, and sometimes I drank water in between the coffee and the beer!

Okay, maybe I could use some lifestyle changes. But not today, I thought as I walked down to the kitchen to grab one more hoppy IPA before heading off to bed. I downed it and fell asleep thinking about department budgets, the perfect material to bore any man right to sleep.

Chapter 5 - *WHAT A TRIP* (Isabella)

At 8:30am I pulled into the parking lot at The Steamworks Hotel plaza and drove around the back of the property to my office building. Our building was located right in between an old maintenance shed and two large dumpsters. It wasn't the prettiest location but it served us well.

As usual I was early for work. I liked to take the extra time to get settled in, make myself a cup of tea, and boot my computer up. The silence of an empty office helped me ease into the work day each morning.

Just as I parked my car, a silver pickup truck pulled in a few spots down. Ben hopped out and I seriously considered waiting in my car until he walked inside, just so I didn't have to walk in with him. He saw me just sitting there, though, and waved. *Dammit*. I had to get out of the car.

"Good morning Isabella!" He bellowed as I opened my door.

I wondered if he got this energy from the coffee he drank like it was water, or if he was just naturally this lively in the morning. I've heard that some people actually *enjoy* being awake in the morning and maybe Ben was one of them. Figures.

Ben paused at the back of my car and waited for me to join him for the walk in. Luckily we were fairly close to the front door and it'd be a short stroll, so I walked up to him and we fell into step together.

Ben had another blue button up on today but the sleeves hadn't been shoved up his arms just yet. He wore no tie, always choosing to go business casual even though the office's dress code was technically business professional. *Perks of your Aunt owning the company, I guess.* He had on black loafers and his taupe slacks were a little wrinkled, a bit uncharacteristic of him. Despite his aversion to the dress code he at least always looked neat and well put together.

"Good morning Ben. How are you?" I fiddled with the strap on my purse, a nervous habit I had whenever I had to make casual small talk. Socializing just wasn't my thing, but it was for sure Ben's thing.

"I'm doing well!" He responded. "Actually, as I was leaving my house this morning my dog jumped up on me right after she ran through some muddy grass. My slacks were destroyed and I spilled my coffee."

He chuckled at himself. Ben was the only man I knew who could laugh at his own misfortune. "I had to go back in and change and make a new cup, but other than that I'm having a good morning."

"Oh wow that sucks." Was my insightful response to his unfortunate start to the day.

Ben just chuckled at my comment, unbothered by my lack of genuine empathy.

"Yeah it wasn't the best way to start my morning but it could be worse." He motioned to the building, "Are you always here so early?"

"Yeah, I like the quiet before everyone starts coming in."

"Guess I'm ruining your quiet." Ben laughed and nudged me with his elbow. He grabbed the front door and held it open for me.

"Thanks," I said as I walked through.

He nodded as he pulled his vibrating cell phone out of his front pocket and put it up to his ear, thus ending our conversation.

"Good morning Aunt June. Yes, I'm just walking in now."

He shot me a smile before heading toward his office down the hall. I walked back to my desk, flipping overhead lights on as I went. Ben didn't usually come in this early so I was mildly curious why he had done so on a random Wednesday. He probably just had some kind of meeting first thing in the morning that he wanted to prepare for, I told myself.

A couple hours later June Simmons walked through the front door and confirmed my suspicions. I couldn't see her come in over my cubicle walls but I knew the minute she was there because Clark yelled, "June! Good to see you!"

I popped my head up to see Cindy and our CFO Brenda Reinke rushing away from their desks to greet the company's matriarch. I slowly wandered toward the front of the building where all the hubbub was going down.

June still dressed sharply for a seventy year old and I admitted to myself that I'd totally rock the royal purple pantsuit she had on. June greeted her former employees warmly yet promptly and soon slipped toward Ben's office.

I walked to my desk and plopped back down into my chair. I turned my focus to the roaring twenties themed invite that had consumed me all morning. Without the details of the event there wasn't much I could put on there, but at least I think I had the color scheme and general 'vibe' down. For printing I was envisioning gold embossed lettering in a big open art deco font that I had found online. A rich red and cream background captured what I imagined the upscale hotels of the twenties felt like. I saved my draft invite and attached it in an email to Jess and Ben, and leaned back in my chair for a moment of zen before moving on to the next task.

Ping. Jess responded right away, interrupting my zen.

I love it! These are going to look great.

I smiled to myself. Jess always loved everything I sent her, rarely having any input or changes. She trusted my opinion and it was nice to have that much support from her.

My desk phone startled me with a shrill ring. For a second I didn't recognize that it was my phone because I rarely got calls at my desk. The building was small enough that if someone needed something from me they usually walked over to talk in person.

I didn't even check the caller ID before I snatched the receiver and brought it up to my ear.

"Hello?"

"Isabella," it was Ben's voice on the other end of the line, "the invite looks good! Could you come into my office for a minute?"

"Oh thanks, yes I'll be right there."

I hung up and walked across the office toward Ben's door. *Come to his office?* I'd never been in that man's office before. And June was still in there, too. *What if they're going to fire me?* That had to be what was going on.

Just as I reached for the handle to let myself in, the large wooden door swung open. Ben motioned for me to come in and have a seat. June was perched in a cozy-looking lounge chair so I took the chintzy plastic chair that was open next to her. While Ben walked back around his desk to sit down, June gave me a warm smile, making me feel more at ease. I hadn't had much face time with her since I had joined the company after she retired, but I knew enough to be respectful and polite.

"Hello June. I love your suit."

She waved her hand as if she were shooing away the compliment. "Thank you dear. You've got an eye for style! And quite the eye for design as well." June held up a printout of the invite I'd just emailed. "Ben showed me your draft of that Fall Ball invite with the nineteen twenties theme and I love it."

She turned to Ben, "I want the two of you to work together on the Fall Ball." June explained, "I have an important client coming to the ball and I want to impress them. I think your style and Ben's leadership can make this a knockout event. What do you think?" She said to the both of us.

"Of course Aunt June." Ben replied.

"I can do that." I followed up.

"Wonderful. I'll leave you to it then, and let me know if there's anything you need."

And just like that June stood up and left the office, leaving Ben and myself alone.

Okay, so I'm not getting fired. That was great news. But now I'm going to have to spend more time with the man that makes me act like I've forgotten how to function as a human being.

"The queen has spoken," Ben said with a chuckle once June was gone. "I guess we'd better get started, partner."

I felt the heat rise up to my face for the second time this week. My super pale complexion makes me look like a bright red apple in instances like these.

"So uh, where do we begin?"

"Well I think first we need to choose a location. The Locomotive Hotel will be undergoing some construction so that one's out. It's between The Steamworks Hotel and The Kettle Inn. We should probably take a look at both so we can get an idea of what we're working with and decide from there." Ben clicked through the calendar on his computer. "I'm pretty booked with meetings the rest of this week, but what about Monday morning? Does that work?"

More heat surged through me at the thought of spending so much time alone with him.

"Yes, Monday works."

"Great! I'll pencil that in then."

He gave me a huge smile and stood up from his chair. I took this as my cue to leave and in my haste to get the heck out of that office, I tripped on the leg of that stupid plastic chair. I stumbled, caught myself, and practically ran out the door back to my desk without looking back at Ben's reaction. When I was safe back behind my walls I dropped into my chair and brought my hands to my face.

OH MY GOD! I had never been so embarrassed before in my life. This was terrible.

It was only Wednesday but I was desperate for some girl time to make me feel better. I yanked out my smartphone and punched out a text to my best friend Kendra.

Isabella: Need wine and company tonight!!!
Kendra: Red or white? 6pm work?
Oh thank goodness she was available.
Isabella: Red, 6 is perfect!

At 6:30pm Kendra rolled in with two bottles of wine tucked under her arm. She was actually earlier than expected, usually when she said six she meant seven. She's notoriously late for everything so at this point it's just become something that her friends know to plan for. She must have really been in the mood for some hot tea to be spilled to be this close to being on time.

"Okay I've got a Port and a Merlot depending on how you're feeling today." She said before even shutting the front door behind her. She shrugged out of her jacket and tossed it over the back of my sofa before joining me in my kitchen.

My rental home was small but comfortable, and quite modern feeling. The open concept design allowed me to be cooking in the kitchen and still see the television in the living room, something that I found myself doing fairly often. My favorite part of the home were the tall windows that dotted every wall, letting bright light wash into each room during the day.

"Merlot. I'm not feeling sweet at all," I replied as I pulled two mismatched wine glasses from my kitchen cabinet.

All of my dishes were a mis-matched collection of clearance items and thrift store finds left over from my college days. I rarely entertained so it wasn't something I thought about until I actually had company over. I've considered replacing my dishes and glassware several different times over the past couple of years but it always came down to 'if it aint broke dont fix it.'

Kendra perched herself on a barstool at my small kitchen island and plopper her elbows onto the countertop. "Alrighty then, spill it Izzy. I've never known you to drink on a weeknight so *something's* gotta be up. Did you get canned?"

The bottle of 2019 Merlot thankfully just had a twist cap that I yanked off and tossed onto the counter. I poured two generous glass-fuls and handed one to Kendra.

She was the only one that still called me Izzy, a nickname that I had when we were growing up. It seemed childish to still use in my twenties so I had gone back to my full name to hopefully portray myself as a more serious professional.

I took a deep sip of the dark, fruity liquid before I dove into my tale of woes. "No, my job is fine. It *is* work related though. Remember how I mentioned that new boss guy a little while ago?"

"Are you hooking up?"

Kendra's light brown eyes went wide and she could barely hide her excitement at the possibility of me having a love life. She sipped her wine eagerly, leaning closer across the counter as if the gossip grasped her by the collar and held her captive.

"No! We got put on a project together."

"Oh…"

The disappointment was plain on her face. She tucked a strand of her honey-blond hair behind her ear and squinted at me as if I'd gone crazy. "So uh what's wrong with that and why did it require wine?"

"Um, I'm not sure. He makes me feel very awkward--"

"You *are* awkward, that's not him." Curiosity turned to exasperation and I could tell that she wasn't understanding where I was coming from. Kendra was my best friend but sometimes we were just on different wavelengths. Her reaction was making me think that maybe I had made a bigger deal out of this than was necessary but I kept going.

"No, even *more* awkward than usual. Like I literally can't function when he's within fifty feet of me."

Kendra took another deep swig of the wine and set her glass down with a clink. I topped it off while she stuck her tongue in her cheek as she mulled that over for a second.

"Izzy," she began, "do you remember in eighth grade when that new kid Tyler showed up halfway through the school year? He sat next to you in history class, I think. And you were a bumbling idiot every time he tried to talk to you, even if he was just asking to borrow a pencil."

I could see where she was going with this story and I didn't like it.

"Yeah, I remember. I had a massive crush on him. But that's not the case with Ben--"

"Is this Ben guy hot?"

I was becoming flushed from the wine, not from the conversation, I told myself.

"Well I guess so if you're into older guys." I tried to come off as nonchalant but Kendra's facial expression told me that I probably shouldn't try to get into acting any time soon. She was starting to see right through me.

"Older?" Kendra wasn't even trying to hide her interest in my situation now. *This* is the gossip she was expecting. "How much older?"

"I don't know for sure, but if I had to guess based on his appearance, he's got to be in his forties. But it doesn't matter because I don't like him like that!"

That was my kiss of death. She was never going to believe me!

"You're totally crushing! And on an older guy!" She squawked. She was not going to let this go.

"There's no way I have a crush on him! We work together and that would be the most inappropriate thing I could do. You know how much I love this job and I'd never do anything to jeopardize it."

"I know it's your dream job but that doesn't mean you can't make moves on the guy. It never hurts to have a little crush on someone, crushes are harmless! Well, maybe it's a bad thing for you, being the queen of awkward encounters and all..."

Sheepishly I looked down into my still very full glass.

"I tripped running out of his office today."

"You *what*?"

Kendra burst into the shrillest laughter I had ever heard from her small frame. I was so glad that my sad, awkward life could amuse her. A solid two minutes went by before she caught her breath and could take another sip of wine to calm down.

"You're doomed Izzy. You'll never make it out of this alive."

"Help me! What do I do?" I pleaded.

I guess I kind of did find Ben attractive but how would that even work? I had never tried to court a guy before, I had absolutely no idea what I was doing. Luckily I had a best friend who had way more dating experience than I did.

"Okay, okay. The way I see it, there are two options. You can either ignore your feelings and shove them down deep inside like I know you're good at doing, or you can pursue the guy."

I took a moment to consider the options. "If I wanted to pursue him... how might I go about that?"

Kendra jumped off of her stool. "Izzy, yes! Okay, so first you have to find out if he's interested. How good are you at flirting?"

"Terrible."

"This is going to take a while then. We'll need more wine!"

Chapter 6 - *Facebook + Heartbreak* (Ben)

Well that was a weird day. That was my official summary of the odd sequence of events that had made up my day.

The weirdest part being when Aunt June told Isabella she'd be working with me, Isabella looked like she was going to shit a brick. She couldn't wait to get out of my office, so much so that she just about face-planted and kept on running. What was so wrong with working with me?

I always felt like Isabella acted a little odd around me but I couldn't for the life of me figure out why. I always just chalked it up to shyness.

Does she hate me? I wondered. Maybe that was it. I wasn't sure what I'd done to make her dislike me so much, but we were stuck together on this project so she was going to have to get over it. There were only six weeks between now and the tentative date of the Fall Ball and I was sure we could manage to work together nicely until then.

As I mulled over everything from today I kept getting hung up on how Aunt June seemed *really* interested in the ball. That was the whole reason I had to go in early this morning; June had wanted to meet over a budget and general expectations for the event. She wasn't one to micro-manage me, but for some reason she was wanting to be very hands-on with this event which was very out of character for her. She cared about how the hotels operated, not about the frivolous events held within them.

Aunt June had mentioned some special guest who was coming to the ball but I wasn't sure who she was talking about, or why they might be so important. There was a big part of me that was afraid that she was going to sell the hotels to a bigger chain, and a successful Fall Ball would be a great selling point. Corporate hotel chains have tried many times to acquire the Simmons' Hotels line but Aunt June had always fought them off. Was she finally conceding?

"She wouldn't do that to her babies, right Mollie?"

Big brown eyes stared up at me from the kitchen floor where Mollie was perched at my feet. I had picked up a fast food burger on my way home and that big goofy dog was dying for a bite. I tossed her a fry out of pity and she snatched it out of midair. Mollie wolfed it down within seconds and continued to stare, waiting for more.

"I'll eat better tomorrow, I swear. But if I eat veggies then you don't get these delicious fries."

I tossed her another french fry as I finished up my meal. Then out of pure boredom, I pulled my phone out of my pocket and tapped on the Facebook app. I didn't know why I had it still downloaded onto my phone since I hadn't used it in months, but I figured it might be a good tool to kill some time. Not surprisingly, the evenings were pretty boring when you spent them alone.

I scrolled through the posts of my friends, generally uninterested in what they had going on in their lives. All Facebook was for these days was bragging about how well your life and relationships were going, and I didn't feel like celebrating others' happiness at the moment. Everyone my age was married, raising kids, starting businesses, all those milestones that one's *expected* to hit for some reason. Instead of making me feel closer to people, it made me feel alienated when I compared my life to theirs.

Sure I'm doing well for myself, but my life just didn't feel like something worth bragging about on social media. I don't think anyone cared about my career with the hotels, or about the personal record Bass I'd caught over the summer. It all just seemed so trivial and I didn't really care for it.

After scrolling for a bit I paused on a photo of an old friend from high school, posing with his wife of fifteen years and two kids at the Grand Canyon. He looked so happy. As I looked at that smiling family, I felt the slow drip of jealousy and loneliness fill my core. Deep down I knew that that's what I wanted but I missed my chance at having it.

I was just about to close the app and delete it for good when I stopped on a picture posted by one of Brinley's friends a couple days ago. It was a selfie taken at a bar in town. Actually, it looked like the bar that Brinley tended part-time. I tapped on the image to open it up and zoomed in. Sure enough in the background I could just make out Brinley, sucking face with some guy I'd never seen before. Brinley was behind the bar in her apron and the guy seemed to be a customer. *Great.* Glad to see she was nowhere near as torn up inside as I was.

All at once a new swirl of emotions surged through me. Anger, sadness, and hurt added to the jealousy and loneliness that seemed to be a constant for me. They all mixed together in the pit of my stomach making me feel hot and clammy at the same time.

We'd been broken up for months at that point so she had every right to move on, but it still stung to see just how much she was over me. We didn't talk much these days but on the rare occasion we did, she never mentioned seeing anyone new. How could she move on so quickly?

Or maybe I was the one moving slowly, hung up on a woman who clearly didn't care about me anymore.

I was once again just one more second away from deleting the damn app when I found myself typing 'Isabella Morgan' into the search bar at the top of the screen. Sure enough a few profiles popped up with the same name, and the second one down the list was undoubtedly the one I was looking for.

A welcomed distraction, I tapped on her profile and opened it up. At the top of her profile page was a picture of her standing next to a colorful painting in some museum. She had on a yellow sundress and white boots that gave her a bit of an edgy look. She looked like *she* belonged in an art museum, perfectly curled blond hair spilling over her shoulders like a waterfall in a classical painting.

Below her picture was her 'about' information.

From: Strasburg.

Studied: Graphic Design.

Relationship Status: Single. *Interesting.*

Isabella didn't post much but I scrolled a little deeper through her profile until I came across a picture of her from last fall, sitting in a pumpkin patch wearing an orange sweater. She was holding a huge pumpkin above her head and sporting the biggest smile I'd ever seen. Does Isabella smile at work? She's always so serious, I don't know that I'd ever seen her smile. Or maybe she just didn't smile around me. Either way, her smile was stunning, and I wouldn't mind seeing it in person.

Feeling a bit creepy scrolling through an employee's profile, I closed out of the app and shoved my phone back into my pocket.

Mollie perked up when I stood up from the kitchen table and headed toward the back door. She followed me outside into the still-warm evening. The sun had set already but the sky still had a little light left, enough that I could see the silhouette of my old barn against the purple atmosphere. Mollie ran past me into the yard to bark at the bats that were swooping down low to eat the few bugs that were still hanging around.

This time of year has always been my favorite. Don't get me wrong, summer is great for fishing and camping, two of my favorite things, but there's something about the fall that just makes everything feel so right. It was still too early in PA for leaves to start changing colors but I knew soon enough that the trees along the perimeter of my flat lot would turn shades of rich gold and burgundy.

This was going to be my first fall in a senior position at Aunt June's company and it excited me. I have control over aspects of the business that I never dreamed of. Oddly enough, I was most excited about transforming one of the properties for the Fall Ball. I can picture the front entrance of whichever hotel we chose decorated with corn stalks, hay bales, and gourds of all sizes. There's a local nursery that does amazing arrangements, I could bring them in to decorate.

Mollie barked again and I watched her jump at one of the bats and land with a light thud back in the grass. This time last year Brinley would have been standing next to me, laughing at this ridiculous dog who thinks she can catch something that flies. I don't know where I went wrong with her and that relationship. Ten years down the drain. The memory of the night she left me came washing over me like a cold autumn breeze, no matter how hard I fought to keep it at bay.

On that dreadful night I had gotten home from work a little later than usual after dealing with a staffing issue at The Locomotive Hotel, and Brinley was just sitting at the kitchen table staring at her hands. I hadn't noticed it but she'd already removed the engagement ring I'd given her.

I'd come in and kissed her on the forehead as I grabbed a beer from the fridge and sat across from her at the table. She hadn't made dinner yet but I assumed she had just wanted to grab something out, maybe she had a long day in class or something. She was very calm as she looked at me and said, "I can't marry you."

At that point we had been engaged for two years and I was absolutely blindsided. Up until that very moment there were no indicators that she wasn't happy being in a relationship with me. Maybe there were signs that I missed, I don't know, but I really thought we were happy.

I remembered she had gone on to say that she didn't see us lasting forever, that we had different goals in life, blah blah blah. The usual stuff that a woman says when she dumps you.

She'd also said I worked too much, which I took a bit personally considering I paid most of the bills while Brinley was in nursing school and only bartended part time for fun. I always made sure things were taken care of so she could chase her dreams of being a neonatal nurse. And when I brought that up, she simply said that I didn't need to take care of her anymore.

That part stung more than anything because it was like, what had I been working so hard for all that time? Why had I tried so hard to give her a good life if that's not what she wanted?

Hearing her words that night burned like a white hot iron and dredging up that memory now made me angry all over again. There were too many emotions running through me this evening. I decided it was probably best to just call it a night and get some rest. I called Mollie back and we walked inside, letting my mind wander one more time.

What was Isabella up to right now?

I shook my head; it didn't really matter. Aunt June had strict rules about inter-office relationships, especially between a boss and his subordinate, so Isabella was off limits. I threw out my dinner garbage and downed a beer, then headed up to yet another lonely night in bed.

Chapter 7 - *CRUSHIN'* (Isabella)

Blue or green cardigan? I held both up in my full length mirror like any cliché movie scene where a woman was trying to decide what to wear. Which one said *I totally don't have a crush on you at all*? I went with blue. Paired with my gray straight leg slacks and black bodysuit underneath I felt like I gave off a melancholy look. The exact opposite of what I was feeling inside, but that was the goal.

I think that's what I've always loved the most about clothes; they can emulate your mood, feelings, or interests based on the colors, silhouettes, and fabrics you choose. I wouldn't say I have any specific style, I just dress for my mood each day. And on this day in particular I had to spend a lot of one-on-one time with Ben, and I needed to pretend like I didn't think that he was majorly attractive.

With Kendra's help I'd come to the light (as she called it) and realized that I was, in fact, crushing hard on a certain boss of mine. But that also meant that my awkwardness would be dialed up to a hundred now that I was self aware.

I still wasn't feeling very confident about flirting despite Kendra's crash course the other night, so I'd been laying low around the office, which for me meant that I was just behaving as I normally did. Luckily the back half of last week was uneventful, as Ben apparently had a lot of meetings and I just focused all of my attention on my projects.

That damn postcard was finally done and sent to print, and I'd moved on to working on revamping the folders that go in each room to hold things like channel guides and local restaurant recommendations. I loved little one-off projects like those because they were simple yet necessary.

After a weekend of errands and house chores I was ready to get back to work that week. I'd figured, awkward Ben stuff aside, taking design point on the Fall Ball was a really cool opportunity. I didn't have any special event experience but there was never a bad time to learn, especially if it made me look good in the company's eyes.

On my drive in to work I hit shuffle on my Spotify music collection and blasted the stereo to clear my head and ease my nerves.

When I pulled into the parking lot Ben's truck was already there, sitting in its usual sopt toward the back of the lot. I parked and walked inside. I saw that Ben's office door was closed, which meant he was busy probably trying to get some work done before we visited the hotels today. So I went about my morning routine as usual, switching on lights and winding my way back toward my desk. I turned on my computer and as soon as it booted up, my email pinged.

Have a call at 9. Be ready to head out at 10. - Ben

While Ben had his call I managed to keep myself busy working *and* keeping track of time, and at 9:55 am I saved my work and headed toward Ben's office. His door was still closed and I could hear the rumble of his voice coming from inside, sounding quite agitated. I was about to turn around and walk back to my desk to wait when the door opened and Ben stepped out, just about running me over. I felt like a cartoon character teetering on my heels, about to topple over backwards.

"Oh sorry!" Ben grabbed my arms and helped steady me. "Are you okay?"

Genuine concern creased his brows as my face turned stop sign red at the feeling of his hands on me.

"Yeah I'm fine. I was just coming to see if you were ready to go."

I really hoped he didn't think I was eavesdropping on his call.

He let go of my arms and shoved his hands into the pockets of his slacks. "Okay great, I just finished up. We'll start at The Kettle Inn then come back to The Steamworks Hotel." He closed and locked his office door. "I'll drive if you don't mind."

"I don't mind," I said.

After a few seconds of silence and neither of us moving, I followed up with, "shotgun!"

Ben gave a polite half smile and motioned toward the front door of the office. "Shall we?"

I didn't have time to mull over my embarrassing remark before we were headed outside and across the parking lot to his truck. I opened the passenger door and flung myself up into the seat rather inelegantly.

The cab of his truck was very roomy and comfortable, much more so than my little car. I didn't know anything about trucks but this one felt very expensive; fitting for a Senior Operations Manager.

Ben settled into the driver's seat and cranked the engine. He flipped the radio over to the local country station and backed out of his spot.

I hadn't thought about this part until now, but the silence became heavy as I realized we should probably talk about something. Ben obviously wasn't feeling very chatty so I thought I'd take a stab at making light conversation.

"So uh what kind of truck is this?" Was my attempt at filling the silence.

"It's a GMC Sierra." Ben side-eyed me, probably trying to figure out what my game plan was.

"Oh cool. Is that a good truck?"

This time he laughed at my ignorance.

"Yeah I guess it's a good truck. It serves its purpose for me, anyway."

"That's good."

I looked down at my hands. I really wished he'd take over this conversation because I was failing miserably. No dice, though, he still seemed distracted, probably by the call he had earlier.

I took another stab at breaking through his mood and asked, "is everything okay? I'm not used to you being so quiet."

I glanced over at him and watched a small smile tug at the corner of his mouth. His mustache bustled slightly with the movement.

"I had a tough morning Isabella, I won't lie. I didn't want to reschedule on you last minute, though, so here we are. No worries, I'll be fine soon."

He had really sounded like he was giving someone the business in his office. I wondered what kind of meeting could get someone so riled up.

Trying to work on my empathy, I said, "Business is tough sometimes, I get it."

Ben shook his head.

"That's not quite it." He paused, staring out the windshield. "You're still young, but have you ever had your heart broken?"

Ben's question caught me off guard. Did his 'meeting' have something to do with that breakup he had a few months ago? I didn't know much about what was going on besides the murmurs I heard in passing, but from what I could gather it was a broken engagement.

"Um no, I haven't." I stammered. "I've never been in a serious relationship, really. Just a few dates in high school, and a month with one guy in college but I broke up with him because he spent every weekend partying."

We stopped at a red light and Ben turned to look at me briefly. He didn't say anything but he smiled softly again before turning back to the road.

"Lucky," he murmured.

We pulled up to The Kettle Inn and I hoped that meant that this conversation would be over because, talk about awkward topics! I did feel bad for Ben, though. It was obvious he was going through something, even months later. He must have really loved the woman that, I assume, broke his heart.

Ben parked and we both got out and headed toward the front door. I'd been to The Kettle Inn a few times before and I always enjoyed its antique atmosphere. The building was modeled after a sprawling Georgian style home, with tons of rectangular windows and beautiful brickwork on the outside. Columns flanked the main entrance and stepping into the front door of the Inn felt like you were walking into someone's immaculately maintained home. The rooms inside were clean and lofty with tons of natural light streaming in through gauzy white curtains.

A plump red headed woman sat behind the lobby's front desk, clacking on her computer's keyboard. She looked up and when she recognized Ben, she exclaimed, "Ben! Long time no see! How's life with the suits?"

"Good morning MaryAnn. Life's going just fine."

He motioned toward me, "This is Isabella, our designer." I waved at MaryAnn while Ben continued, "She redid those room keys you hand out."

"Hello Isabella, I absolutely love the new look you've created!"

"Thank you," I blushed.

Ben led the way toward the back of the building where the event space was. We walked up to two large wooden doors, which he pulled open to reveal a decently sized room with bright white walls and trim. As far as event spaces go, this one was a pretty blank canvas. The floors were a gorgeous dark wide plank wood and a large, ornate chandelier hung from the ceiling in the center of the room.

Some chairs and tables were stacked against the far left wall, leaving the dance floor wide open. The right side of the room was made up of tall windows that overlooked a small patio and garden. I walked across the room to look out the windows.

It was a quaint outdoor space, fenced in with thick bushes with leaves that were beginning to turn a shade of fire red. A few wrought iron tables and chairs perched on the paver patio, making it look like the ideal place for a cup of hot tea.

I turned back toward the doorway and caught Ben staring at me.

"So what do you think?" He asked me as he quickly glanced toward the windows.

"Honestly it's so much better than I expected. The Kettle Inn is small so I didn't expect to like this space very much, but this is so *nice*!"

"Yeah this space has always been my favorite," Ben cleared his throat, "I, uh, was thinking about holding my wedding here. Back when I was still going to get married."

Ouch. The heartbreak was literally oozing off of this guy today. It was unlike him to be so vulnerable, it went against his professional persona and was throwing me off big time.

I walked over to him and tried my hardest to comfort him, but all that came out was, "Sorry."

"It's fine," he shook his head as if shaking off the sadness. He quickly snapped back into business mode. "I love this space for the Fall Ball but the only issue is that there's no bar here. I don't know how we'd pull off having that speakeasy element without actually having a place to host it out of."

I was suddenly hit with a wave of inspiration.

"Okay so hear me out, that can be part of the event."

A curious expression crept onto Ben's face and my ideas started bubbling out. "Like you walk in here and you think it's a dry event because of prohibition or whatever. But we set up a bar somewhere else like in a room or something so it actually feels like you have to sneak around to get your drinks."

Ben's eyes lit up. "Or instead of having it in a room, we hold it out on the patio. We could set up a booth with a rollaway cart and bring in a bartender from one of the other hotels just for the night. Throw a few portable heaters out there to keep the October chill away, and people can 'sneak' out to the patio when they want alcohol. But that way they can still see the party going on through the windows." Ben's spark was back and his eyes twinkled as he spitballed ideas. "Isabella, this is a great idea!"

Ben wrapped his arms around me and gave me a huge bear hug. It only lasted a second before he let go and quickly backed away. "I'm sorry, I got excited."

My face and chest flushed a shade of red that matched the bushes outside.

"It's okay, I think we've come up with a really cool idea. I'm excited about it too."

"Do we even need to go back to look at The Steamworks Hotel's ballroom?" He asked.

"Definitely not, I think we've got our space here."

This time Ben just held his hand up for a high five. As I returned the five my stomach grumbled. *Loud.* It was only 11am but I had skipped breakfast because I was nervous about today.

"Message received," Ben chuckled, "we'll have to get you lunch while we're out."

"Oh no we don't have to, I have a salad in the fridge at work."

"So eat it tomorrow. I'm starting to get hungry too and I didn't bring anything. I have to stop at the bank first then we can stop somewhere," he paused. "Unless you *really* want that salad."

"No, we can stop somewhere."

He smiled and turned to head back toward the entrance. I followed after him, practically speed walking to keep up with his wide steps. Ben waved to MaryAnn as we left and we both hopped back into his truck. It was only a five minute drive to the local bank, where he parked up front and cut the engine.

"I just have to sign a form and I'll be back. You'll be okay waiting here, right?"

I nodded my head and he got out of the truck and disappeared into the bank. I took the opportunity to text Kendra. She was at work too, but she knew I'd be spending a lot of time with Ben today and I was sure she'd welcome an update.

Isabella: He hugged me...

Not even a full thirty seconds passed before I got a response.

Kendra: What kind of hug? Friend hug? Love hug?

Isabella: None of the above. Happy boss hug? Is that a thing?

Kendra: Def not a thing.

I sent her the eye roll emoji just as Ben got back in the truck with a manilla envelope in his hand. He opened up the center console and tossed it in before starting up the truck.

"So, where to?" He asked.

"Oh I don't know. I'm really bad at choosing where to eat. That's why I just eat salads, they're easy."

"Well that's boring." He teased. "Okay, we'll go to the diner then I can check in on the repairs that are going on at The Locomotive Hotel after."

Over on the eastern side of town we pulled into the diner parking lot just before noon. The old building still looked like a train station, with ticket windows and a platform still out back by the tracks. The owners that bought the station shortly after it stopped operating had turned the cement platform into a patio with tables and chairs and brightly colored umbrellas. They closed in the area with a low metal rail so guests could still look out at the tracks while enjoying their meal.

It had turned into a balmy 75 degree day with white fluffy clouds rolling slowly through the sky. Ben got us a table outside under a sunny yellow umbrella and we were unsurprisingly the only ones out there. A waitress named Sandy sat us and took our drink order before leaving us alone out on the patio.

"So, Isabella, how are you liking working for Simmons' Hotels?"

"I really love my job. It's just what I've always wanted to do."

"You've always wanted to be a graphic designer?"

He looked generally interested.

"Well, when I was little I always wanted to be an artist but that's not really practical so I got into digital art. Graphic design pays the bills and allows me to get my fill of creativity each day."

Ben rolled his sleeves up to his elbows and leaned his strong arms on the table. Sandy brought us out our drinks and took our meal orders before quickly disappearing again.

"What kind of art did you do before digital art?" Ben asked before taking a sip of his water.

I took a drink from my glass as well and responded, "I liked to paint with oils."

"Do you paint anymore?"

"Only on occasion. It's a timely process and I don't always have the patience to finish a painting anymore. I guess life's just too busy these days."

"Yeah I feel that. I'd love to see some of your work some time, though. Hell, as long as it's not a bunch of naked portraits we could probably hang some in the hotels."

While the idea intrigued me, I blushed at the thought of him, or anyone else, seeing my paintings. There's something raw about sharing a piece of art with someone.

I wanted to move the conversation away from myself so I asked, "You mentioned you had a dog the other day. What kind of dog do you have?"

A big smile crossed his face for only the second time today.

"My Mollie is a German Shepherd. And a big old love bug when she's not hunting groundhogs in the yard. Do you have any pets?"

"Not right now, just a few cats while growing up. I'd love to get a dog eventually though. They're such great companions."

"That's for sure. Mollie keeps me company now that it's just the two of us."

The topic of Ben's breakup hung heavily between us. He kept skirting around the subject but I don't want to be rude and ask about it, especially since he was obviously still so upset about it.

I scrambled to think of a new talking point when Sandy saved the day by placing our food in front of us. The act of chowing down helped to keep the conversation light for the rest of lunch. When the check came Ben pulled out his wallet and paid cash, refusing to let me chip in.

A very gentlemanly move, I thought to myself.

On to our next stop, our visit to The Locomotive Hotel was fairly quick and painless. I ran in to use the restroom while Ben talked to someone in the maintenance department about the repairs that were going on. We made pleasant enough conversation on the drive back to the office and I finally felt like I wasn't behaving like a blundering fool. By the time we pulled into the parking lot at our office it was already late afternoon.

"Why don't you call it a day? We've been very productive today." Ben said to me as we got out of his truck.

"Actually I still wanted to finish up what I was working on before we left, and I should probably make sure I don't have any missed calls or emails." I know I don't have either of those because I never do, but I did have a little bit of work to finish up before I'd consider it a truly productive day.

"Fair enough." He replied, and we walked into the building together. I headed back to my desk and tidied up my loose ends so that when I left promptly at 5pm I felt like I'd achieved a lot. It was an interesting day, that was for sure, and I couldn't wait to tell Kendra all about it.

Chapter 8 - *THIS EMOTIONAL ROLLERCOASTER* (Ben)

Tuesday morning I pulled into the lot at work around 8:30am. I didn't need to be there so early but it seemed to be around the time that Isabella got in, and there was something about us being there together that I liked, even if she hid in her cubicle and I in my office.

Sure enough, as soon as I parked and cut the engine, Isabella's blue Toyota pulled in a few spots down. I got out and walked toward her car and waited while it looked like she was debating whether or not to pretend she didn't see me in her rear view mirror.

We had a pretty decent day together yesterday and it made me rethink my hypothesis that Isabella hated me. I couldn't explain why she ran out of my office last week but I wasn't going to read too much into it. I just chalked it up to nerves; organizing this event was a pretty big deal and Aunt June did kind of spring it on her.

Isabella finally got out of her car and gave me a sheepish smile as she walked toward me.

"I had to finish the song that was playing before I could get out."

"And what song was that?"

She blushed a shade of red that I've started to become very familiar with.

"*Wasn't Me* by Shaggy."

I couldn't help but laugh at that. I didn't expect her to be listening to 2000s R&B on her way in to work.

"I'll take note of your taste in music for the next time we ride together."

"I like all kinds of music," she said as she held open the front door for me.

"Thank you. What do you say we meet about the ball after you get settled in? I was thinking of some ideas last night that I wanted to run by you, partner"

Isabella responded, "Sure."

We parted ways, I toward my office and her back toward her desk. Just as I'd asked, shortly after nine Isabella rapped softly on my open door before stepping in.

"Is it a good time?"

"Absolutely. Have a seat."

Today she chose the lounge chair over the plastic one. I made a mental note to try to get some actual office chairs in there that wouldn't trip my employees.

As Isabella sat I couldn't help but admire her choice of outfit. She wore black ankle length pants with a bright yellow shirt that matched the umbrella from our table at lunch yesterday. A crisp white cardigan covered her arms and she had on white shoes to match. I must have been staring for a second because she gingerly cleared her throat and played with a hair tie on her wrist.

"So uh, what are your ideas?"

We spent the next hour going over possibilities of decor, music, and drinks. Isabella was a really good sounding board for my ideas, I found. She wasn't afraid to tell me when something sucked but was equally good at building on my good ideas. We probably would have kept going back and forth all morning if Jess hadn't come in for her daily chat. I guess she hadn't realized that Isabella was in there with me.

"Oh sorry!" She said as she walked in and saw the blonde that was perched in her usual chair. "Sorry, I didn't realize you were having a meeting. I'll be out of your hair then. Oh but Aunt June did tell me you two were working together on the Fall Ball, how's that going?"

"It's going really well actually." I responded. "I think we've got some great ideas flowing."

Isabella smiled and nodded at Jess, confirming.

"Okay great. Well when you have solidified details let me know and I'll send out media alerts. It would be great if we could advertise on the local stations and build some anticipation for the event."

"Will do, Jess."

I didn't mean to sound so dismissive but as much as I loved my cousin she was definitely a busy body. You couldn't keep her out of other people's business if you tried, and I knew she was stalling in the hopes that I'd invite her to participate in our planning meeting. She loved to be a part of things, which is why one time she wriggled her way into sitting in on a meeting with the local township about sewage disposal. It didn't matter what it was, as long as Jess was a part of it.

She got the hint, though, and turned toward the door. As Jess left and shut the door behind her, my cell phone buzzed from its spot on my desk.

Brinley: I just got a call from the bank. House is yours. I'll leave your keys in the mailbox.

"Sorry, I don't mean to be rude. I just have to respond to this real quick then we'll get back to brainstorming." I told Isabella.

"No worries." She flashed a polite smile and took to doodling on the top of her notepad while I tapped out my response.

Ben: You can come over for dinner if you'd like. You don't have to just leave the keys.

My heart thudded in my chest. I knew it was a long shot but maybe we could have dinner, just as friends. It sounded desperate and embarrassing but I had to try.

Brinley: No, mailbox is fine.

Ouch. I wracked a hand down my face before responding. Just because I knew it was coming didn't mean that it still didn't hurt.

Ben: Ok.

I placed my phone face down on the desk and looked up to find Isabella peeking up at me from her doodles. I had a beautiful woman sitting right in front of me, yet Brinley was still there in the back of my mind, haunting me.

"Are you okay?" She asked. "We can finish up another time."

I was really hoping that I didn't look as bad on the outside as I felt inside.

"No, I'm sorry. It was my ex. I, uh, just bought her half of the house and that was pretty much all that was left of the relationship."

I can't believe I just told her that.

"Oh, is that why we stopped at the bank yesterday?" She looked apologetic as soon as she asked, as if she was afraid to bring up anything regarding my breakup. I couldn't blame her, though. I was the dumbass who keeps on bringing it up so she had every right to be curious.

"Yeah. I held out as long as I could thinking maybe we could fix the relationship, but it's been three months. I think this is officially the end."

Why am I doing this?

I worked very hard to keep my personal life separate from my work life. It could be a bit hard seeing as I worked for the family business, so the two were always going to mingle a little, but still. Bringing personal business into the office made me look more vulnerable and I never wanted anyone thinking they could take advantage of that. Yet there I was, sitting with an employee, blabbing about my failed relationship.

Isabella started to reach her hand out as if she was going to try to comfort me but snatched it back with a flush of her face.

"I'm sorry, Ben. I wish I could help."

But, I thought, *while we were being vulnerable...*

"Actually, I have a question."

She shut her notebook and nodded for me to continue, giving me her full attention. Her blue eyes stared at me, reminding me of the innocent way puppies look up at their owners. I took a shallow breath and asked the question that had been bothering me for a while.

"Are we cool? Sometimes it feels like you don't like me very much and I just want to make sure I didn't do anything to offend you--"

Isabella interjected quickly. "Oh, no Ben! You didn't do anything! I actually like you very much--"

Isabella's mouth formed a little 'o' and her cheeks burned red. She tried to backtrack, "I mean, yeah we're cool. I'm sorry I made you think otherwise, I've just been a little high strung lately trying to get my projects done."

"Is there too much on your plate? We can hire you an assistant if you need one."

"No, no, I can handle it. I didn't mean... I don't know what I meant. I'm fine."

Isabella was acting weird. I mean, weirder than normal. It felt like she was skirting around something but the poor girl looked like she was going to melt into the chair so I decided to show some mercy.

"Okay then. But seriously if you ever feel like the workload is too much, let myself or Jess know. I know we put a lot on you as our only designer and I never want you to get burnt out because of that."

I hope she knew how sincere I was. She's amazing at what she does and I wouldn't want to lose her as an employee. People like her are hard to come by.

Isabella clutched her notebook against her chest. "I understand, thank you Ben. Actually if we're done for now I have a couple things at my desk to get back to."

"Yes, of course. Go ahead, we'll resume another day."

She stood up and consciously stepped wide around the plastic chair as she headed for the door. I couldn't help but watch as she stepped out and closed the door behind her. Those slacks sure hugged her backside just right.

So she likes me huh?

I'm not usually one to read into things, and it's been *forever* since someone's had a thing for me, but I'm thinking this woman might be attracted to me? That would definitely explain the awkward encounters and excessive blushing.

I cautiously allowed myself to explore the possibility of opening up to someone new. Was I ready to move on?

I put my hands behind my head and couldn't help but to smile.

Chapter 9 - *Is This A Date?* (Isabella)

Isabella: 9-1-1 emergency!!!!

Kendra: What's going on?? Why aren't you calling actual 911??

Isabella: Oh, sorry. I may be overreacting a bit. But I think I might have just slipped up and told Ben I liked him? IDK maybe he didn't notice but I'm freaking out!

Kendra: We need to work on your emergency response techniques. But WHAT? What do you mean you told him you liked him??

Isabella: IDK, he asked if we were cool and I said 'yeah I really like you' but I meant it like I liked him as a boss. But the way I said it maybe could have been interpreted otherwise?

Kendra: How did he react?

Isabella: He didn't really say anything, he just made sure I was happy at the company. But he definitely heard me!

Kendra: Okay, relax. This guy's a professional, probably didn't want to get slapped with a sexual harassment suit or someting. But in all seriousness, just see how he acts around you the next few days. He is a man after all, what you said could have gone right over his head.

—

Wednesday came and went and I managed to hide at my desk and avoid any interaction with Ben whatsoever. I don't know what he got out of Tuesday's awkward conversation in his office but I was still embarrassed as hell knowing that I told a superior that I liked him.

Since he hadn't said anything to me about it I was starting to think that maybe I got away with it. I was praying that Kendra was right and that what I'd said hadn't registered with him. I was still laying low though, just in case.

When I recounted the whole thing to Kendra, all she could do was laugh at my misfortune, which is all anyone could do at this point. I don't know how I got myself in these situations but I'm sure it was all hilarious to everyone but me.

"I knew you were going to be a blabbering fool!" Kendra had said, referencing my middle school crush. As much as I hated it though, she was right. This was a 'Tyler from eight grade' situation all over again. Kendra had tried to tell me that it was no big deal after I got upset but I don't think she knows how embarrassing these situations are! Maybe I needed a new love coach…

I was still trying to stay under the radar when on Thursday morning my desk phone rang and I scrambled to grab it on the second ring.

"Hello?"

I really needed to pay attention to caller ID because, speak of the Devil, it was Ben.

"Good morning Isabella. I have a project today that I need your help on. Will you meet me in the parking lot in five?"

"Sure."

I knew I was going to have to face him eventually, might as well get it over with now. But that didn't help the jittery sensations originating in my stomach. I just prayed that things between us wouldn't be awkward. Or rather, more awkward than usual.

I saved the project I was working on and grabbed my purse. When I walked outside, Ben was leaned up against the back of his truck scrolling through his phone. He looked up at me when he heard my flats clacking across the blacktop.

"You look nice today," he said.

The weather forecast had predicted warmer than usual temps for the day so I had worn a burnt orange midi-dress with a black cardigan and flats. I was channeling major autumnal vibes when I got dressed this morning, imagining carved jack-o-lanterns perched on dark front porches. I was totally feeling my outfit but it was kind of weird and unexpected that Ben would compliment me. It was very out of character for someone who was usually all-business. Then again, I felt like he had been acting very out of character lately.

"Thank you." I replied, trying not to mull on it. "What are we doing today?"

"We have some event planning to do. First we have an appointment with the owner of Shaw's Nursery to pick out fall decor for around The Kettle Inn. Then we have to go to Crave Catering to decide on the menu. And, I know we're on the clock, but I've had the bartenders at The Locomotive Hotel coming up with some possible signature drinks that we'll then have to sample."

"Wow, that's a lot to do in one day." I felt my palms begin to sweat. Another day where I had to spend copious amounts of time with Ben. Kendra would say it was a good thing but I could only think of all the ways

I could mess it up and make a fool of myself.

"Yes it is, so we better get going." Ben walked toward the driver's side and called out over his shoulder, "you going to call shotgun again?"

He laughed at his own joke as he opened the door and got in. I honestly didn't know what to say; Ben was acting like a completely different person. He seemed lighter, almost. The sadness from the past few days seemed as if it had dissolved into thin air and I was kind of digging the new Ben.

I got into the truck and almost immediately burst out laughing despite myself. I don't know how he worked so quickly, but by the time I'd climbed into the passenger's seat Ben already had his phone connected to his truck's stereo and was playing what I could only assume was a 2000s hit playlist.

"Did I get the tunes right?"

This time I did laugh. Ben's eyes were wide and he had a toothy grin plastered onto his face. He looked like an eager puppy dog who'd learned a new trick.

"Yes, these are good 'tunes.' You didn't have to pick a playlist for me though." I told him.

"I told you I would!"

He did, didn't he. I was honestly surprised that he remembered that little interaction we'd had in the parking lot a few days ago. The jitters were replaced with warmth as I realized it meant he was thinking of me.

Once I was in the truck, we made the short drive to the next town over where Shaw's Nursery was located. We spent the drive listening to the best of Britney, Justin, and Usher.

I had never been to this nursery before, but when we arrived it was a glorious sight. Pumpkins, hay bales, and Mums were everywhere on the property. It was a fall wonderland! My amazement must have been written all over my face because when Ben looked over at me, he grinned and said, "I thought you might like it here."

We got out of the truck and walked toward the small shop at the front of the property. I was feeling absolutely giddy with excitement; that's what fall did to me. The only thing stopping me from frolicking through the rows of pumpkins was the meeting we were headed to, and the attractive man by my side that would think I was an absolute loon.

"Peter Shaw is amazing at seasonal decorations." Ben told me before we walked inside. "Aunt June has hired him a few times to decorate the hotels and even her own front porch. This guy just knows the right ways to arrange pumpkins and corn stalks, if that's even a thing."

We walked in and Ben introduced me to a tall spindly looking man. He was dressed in work pants and a sweatshirt, totally unassuming for a man that was supposedly amazing at putting together displays. But as soon as we began talking I understood; this man knew what he was talking about. And apparently there *was* a right way to arrange pumpkins and corn stalks.

After a short but productive planning session with Peter Shaw we had all of the details figured out. He was going to decorate all three hotels the following week, paying special attention to The Kettle Inn for the Fall Ball. We gave him artistic freedom to do what he pleased and all Ben had to do was set a budget for the project.

After the meeting Ben asked me if I wanted to walk around the nursery a bit. We had about an hour before we had to be at the catering company's office and I couldn't say no. Fall and all fall-related things just made me feel all warm and fuzzy inside so I made a beeline for the big orange gourds.

We walked together down an aisle of pumpkins in all shapes, sizes, and colors.

"Do you decorate for fall?" Ben asked after a few minutes of silence and wandering.

I looked up at him and he was watching me earnestly, waiting for an answer.

"Usually just a few pumpkins or some Mums. My house is a rental so I don't want to make my landlord upset." I paused, recounting last fall's debacle. "Last year I left a rotting pumpkin out on the front porch a little too long and he almost had a conniption fit when he drove by and saw it. But I still forgot to get rid of it and a deer ended up getting to it and smashing it all over the porch. It smelled *so bad* and I had to have my landlord come clean it off because I couldn't stop gagging."

Ben laughed at my story and I joined him, thinking about the ridiculousness of some of the situations I get myself into. *Only me*, I thought.

"I may have to come back here and grab some things, though. I never knew this place was here!" I cooed as I ran my fingers over a huge oblong pumpkin. I imagined my front steps covered in pumpkins and flowers; my house could look as festive as I felt!

I looked up at Ben and felt a surge of butterflies in my stomach as he smiled, showing those perfect teeth underneath his mustache. This day was certainly not helping my crush. If anything, wandering through lanes of pumpkins with Ben made me feel like this is what it'd be like if we dated. Dangerous thoughts for someone so awkward who was set to spend all day alone with her boss.

Ben bent over and picked up a small lumpy gourd and held it up next to me.

"It's the same color as your dress," he said.

It seemed like he was going to say something else when his cell phone began to ring. Pulling it out of his pocket, he looked at the screen and back at me.

"It's my Aunt June, I should take this. Meet you back at the truck?"

"Sure thing." I said, as I turned toward the entrance to give him some privacy. Ben walked in the opposite direction down the pumpkin lane, still holding the gourd in one hand. I was a little sad to be leaving empty handed, but now that I knew such a magical fall place existed, I was going to make it a point to come back.

I wandered slowly toward the entrance. The morning sun was peeking through tufts of pine trees that stood over on one side of the nursery. Some of the Mums still had dew drops on their petals that caught the sun rays and glinted like prisms. As I walked I took in a deep, calming breath and let the scent of the earth and the hay and the flowers erase any nerves that still had a hold on me. *It's just business*, I told myself.

Ben's truck was unlocked when I got to it so I let myself in and pulled out my phone while I waited.

Isabella: What qualifies as a date?

Kendra: I need more context... did your boss ask you out??

Isabella: No, but pumpkin picking, lunch, and drinks sure sounds like a date, doesn't it?

Kendra: Um YES!

Isabella: OK I'll fill you in later then...

Ben got in the driver's side right as he ended his call. "Ready for the next stop?"

Chapter 10 - *It's Kind of a Date* (Ben)

I had spent the past day and a half planning for today. I wanted to spend time with Isabella and get to know the real her so I figured getting her out of the office and doing something fun would accomplish that. My goal (besides completing tasks for our very real and very important work project that was creeping up on us) was to make Isabella smile. I didn't know it'd come so easily in the cab of the truck when she realized I'd chosen the music for her. Or on our trip to the nursery when she took everything in, but there it was, spread across her face as she stood surrounded by pumpkins and Mums.

It was quite a beautiful sight, actually. Her at the nursery in her orange dress with the morning sun reflecting off of her golden hair. She looked like an autumn angel, if such a thing existed.

So I *may* have orchestrated a day of meetings that would feel more like a date to possibly suss out exactly how Isabella felt about me, and I about her. Was that so wrong? We *were* working after all. Just following Aunt June's orders, I told myself.

I was hoping that, by the end of our day, I'd know better how Isabella felt about me. I was fairly certain that I was reading the signs right, and that she *did* have a thing for me, but it'd be a terrible mistake if I was wrong. I know all too well the fate of the boss who makes moves on his subordinates, only to end up hit with a sexual harassment suit because the interest was not consentual. So I needed to play it safe and make sure that Isabella was definitely interested before I figured out my next move.

Despite the good time we'd had so far, there was still a nagging voice in the back of my head that told me this was all wrong. I knew how Aunt June felt about relationships within the company, yet there I was, testing the waters anyway. It was scary and exciting and a little nerve-wracking. I hadn't felt anything like this in a long, long time.

The drive back into town from Shaw's Nursery went quickly and we got to the catering office right on time. Crave Catering was fairly new to our town, so new in fact that it had the logo of the restaurant that was there before them still on their sign. I had heard great things about their food and service, though, and I was happy to give this new local business a try.

When I initially called in, I had given Rachel, Crave's owner, our theme and told her to run with it for our tasting today. She'd seemed very capable and competent so I was looking forward to seeing what she'd put together.

Opening the door of the large building, Isabella and I stepped into a lofty seating area that was empty except for a couple tables and some chairs. The lights were dimmed and I remembered that this used to be a fancy Italian place that was popular for romantic dinner dates because of its atmosphere. While the furnishings were now all gone, the atmosphere still stood, and I wondered why Rachel hadn't changed out the light fixtures yet.

Rachel came out from the kitchen almost immediately and greeted us with a huge smile.

"Welcome guys!" She said.

Rachel had curly red hair that was pulled back behind her into a loose pony tail. A few stray strands had escaped and framed her face, making her look a bit like a wild lion. A white apron was tied around her, accentuating a tiny waist and wide hips.

Rachel wasted no time and sat us at a table closer to the kitchen entrance and placed a printout between us with a list of foods we'd be trying. I skimmed down the list, not really sure what any of it was. My curiosity was piqued for sure.

"To go with your twenties theme, which sounds super fun by the way, I decided to opt for more appetizers and finger foods as opposed to a formal sit-down meal. The thought was you want people to be up and dancing, not bogged down at a table with heavy foods. I tried to come up with a menu that took aspects of classic nineteen twenties dishes and mixed it with some upscale twists."

I didn't know about Isabella but my stomach was audibly growling at the menu, despite still not knowing what most of it was. I looked across the table at my date.

I meant, my partner. My event-planning partner. *Damn*, I think I was smitten with her already.

The soft lighting of the empty dining room lit her face in a way that made her pale blue eyes look electric. She flushed as usual when she noticed me looking at her, but I realized for the first time that the bridge of her nose was dotted with light freckles. Long dark lashes fluttered as her gaze darted back down to the menu.

Following the menu, Rachel started us out with mini shrimp cocktails on crackers, Oysters Rockefeller, and devilled eggs garnished with black olives. The colorful appetizers were arranged on a large circular platter that was placed between us, and my stomach once again requested I feed it immediately.

"Ladies first," I motioned for Isabella to choose what to try first.

"Oh. My. God." She swooned.

She had just slid one of the oysters into her mouth and her eyes practically rolled back in her head as she swallowed. After a few bites of my own I agreed with her reaction, this food was amazing and we were just getting started. I was especially taken with the deviled eggs; who knew eggs could taste so delicious?

We cleared a good amount of the platter between the two of us before Rachel swept it away back into the kitchen, leaving Isabella and I alone in the dining room for a few minutes. Isabella was dabbing her mouth with a napkin when she looked up at me with those innocent eyes.

"Way better than your salads, huh?" I teased, trying to lighten the mood. I didn't know about her, but the ambiance of the room was feeling fairly salacious. I was secretly hoping that she felt it too. I didn't want this to be one-sided.

Another smile flashed across her face, this one a bit wicked looking. "Mildly better," she said as she subtly licked her lips.

I felt a slow heat course through my body and I found myself looking over at the kitchen door, hoping Rachel would come to break the tension. I felt the heat moving lower and I was grateful at that moment that we were seated. Luckily my telepathy worked and the door swung open with Rachel carrying another platter piled up with food.

The next round of finger foods consisted of an artichoke and smoked salmon sandwich, and grilled codfish cakes. This time I was the one experiencing visible ecstasy with my first bite. The smoked salmon was so salty and mouth-watering that it was almost sinful. As we feasted, Rachel described the notes and flavors that went into each dish.

The two of us demolished the majority of the food placed in front of us in record time and as I swallowed my last bite, I slapped my palm on the table top.

"Rachel, this is unbelievable! I feel just like I'm at a party hosted by Gatsby himself. I just can't believe you got flavors this rich to fit into such small portions!"

Our chef looked giddy at my praise. This woman was talented for sure and she had to know it. I quickly peeked at her hand to see if she had a lucky someone at home who got to enjoy her cooking every day. No ring; I had no doubt someone in Strasburg would snatch her up quickly.

"Spot on, Ben, and thanks!" She said, "I want people to feel as if they've dined on a meal fit for the social elite, without stuffing them up like pigs. If they're too full they won't drink, and if they don't drink they don't dance!"

She had a really good point. And smaller portions meant a smaller bill, something Aunt June would be happy about.

We ended our taste test with lemon mascarpone cheesecake bites for dessert. Simple, to the point, and still amazingly delicious. In unison, Isabella and I groaned as we took our first bites. Within minutes we'd both cleared our plates of the fresh, light desert. I *had* to give more compliments to the chef.

"Well Rachel I think you absolutely nailed this menu. I know our guests will love it all. What do you think, Isabella?"

She nodded, swallowing her last forkful. "I don't think you could have done any better if you tried. It was the perfect arrangement of finger foods!" She leaned back and patted her stomach, "I'm still fangirling over those oysters."

"Thank you both so much! I have some leftovers that I'm going to box up and send back with you. Feel free to share with everyone at the office...or not," she said with a wink. "I'll be back in just a minute."

Rachel left Isabella and myself alone again while she dashed back to the kitchen. I really liked Rachel and I could see us working well together; she certainly knew what she was doing which was always a plus in the business world. You'd be surprised how many people were actually just faking it until they made it. The hotels were always needing events catered and if the Fall Ball went smoothly, I'd feel confident making Crave Catering out go-to vendor.

I looked at Isabella across the table. She played idly with her napkin while staring at her hands, oblivious to the fact that I was taking her in, studying her delicate features. I'd never met someone who could be so shy at times but it was kind of cute.

"Are you enjoying yourself?" I asked.

I hope I didn't come across too forward but I was genuinely curious. She obviously enjoyed the food, but did she enjoy my company?

She lifted her head and her eyes twinkled when they caught the overhead light. "Yes, I am. It's a nice break from my computer screen. And honestly how could I not enjoy myself when I just ate food that I'm pretty sure fell from the heavens?" She paused and tilted her head. "Are *you* enjoying yourself?"

"Yes, absolutely. I enjoy spending time with you."

This time I purposefully chose to be bold. I was never going to figure this woman out if I played it safe forever. And it was true, I was genuinely having a good time.

"Thanks," she blushed a rosy red that I'd become well accustomed to.

Luckily for Isabella, Rachel returned from the kitchen with an armful of plastic to-go containers. I grabbed them and generously thanked her before we left. I already knew I'd be calling her tomorrow to work out a contract and sign a deal.

"On to the next!" I exclaimed as we both climbed into my truck. We were both moving a little slower after stuffing our faces.

It was nice having Isabella in my space like this, in my truck with me. I looked over at her, looking out her window and tapping a finger on the door's armrest to the beat of the music that had just started playing again. When she was in the passenger seat it just felt right. Like she was supposed to be by my side, even if we were just running to and from meetings.

That thought kind of scared me. I had spent such a long time with only one woman, just to get my heart shattered. As I drove, I started to wonder again if I was even ready to move on. I was really enjoying Isabella's company but Brinley was still in the back of my mind, popping up at the most inopportune moments. The constant tug of war inside me was getting to be too much to handle; I wanted to be done with Brinley and that was that.

We drove in silence for a few minutes while I wrestled with my own emotions. I was almost too caught up in my own thoughts to hear Isabella say quietly, still facing the window, "I enjoy spending time with you too."

And for the first time in maybe forever I felt my own face flush. I knew right then and there that I was finally ready to move on.

Chapter 11 - *TRYING NEW THINGS* (Isabella)

Ben hadn't responded when I told him I liked spending time with him but I chalked it up to just not being heard over the music and the road noise. Even if he didn't hear me and I was only talking to myself, it felt great to say it out loud. I like spending time with him! I'm also lowkey falling hard for that man but I was choosing to keep that part to myself.

Next stop on our 'tour de Strasburg' was The Locomotive Hotel's bar. Ben pulled his truck into a spot and cut the engine. He turned toward me with his brows drawn together.

"I probably should have asked this hours ago, but do you drink? Like are you okay sampling these drinks with me?" He asked.

I just about squaked at the question. It was so sweet of him to ask but I had no problem drinking.

"Yes, I drink and yes I'm okay trying alcoholic drinks with you today. I don't want to brag, but I think I single handedly keep the Gordonville winery in business."

He got a good laugh at that remark and his concern dissipated.

But really, I loved me some wine. The primary way Kendra and I spent time together was over a bottle of wine, whether it was in one of our kitchens or dressed up at a local winery. I liked to think that drinking wine made me sophisticated, not that I knew much about wine other than how to consume it.

"Sounds good then. Let's go sample some drinks." Ben said before getting out of the truck.

Walking into The Locomotive Hotel was like taking a step back in time. The inside of this property really utilized an industrial steampunk design that made the atmosphere there unique in the best way possible. It drew in a lot of visitors year-round and was rated as one of the best lodging properties in all of Pennsylvania, which was a pretty big deal. June did a great job with the design of this one, and Ben and Jess had been working hard to update certain aspects while striving to keep the intended old fashioned look, inside and out.

The bar was located toward the back of the main floor. Ben led the way as we walked past a plastic laden entryway to the event space that was under repair. I could hear the faint sound of hammers and power tools coming from inside, and I hadn't noticed it right away, but a couple of construction workers ducked out from behind the plastic just after we walked passed.

A loud whistle came from behind me and I froze, instantly recognizing it as an unsolicited catcall. Ben whirred around and faced the men, who were the only ones around and most likely the source of the uncalled for gesture.

"Excuse me?" He barked. His tone emulated last week's when I had overheard him on whatever call had gotten him all riled up.

The two men looked rough, and pretty scary; not anyone I'd consider messing with if I were by myself.

"That was for the lady." One of the men replied with a smirk.

I looked down to see Ben's long fingers curl into a fist at his side that was so tight that his tan knuckles turned bone white. His face was red with an anger that I'd never seen on a real person before, only in old cartoons. I expected steam to start blowing out of his ears with the way he looked so angry.

"Do you want to try that again?" Ben said slowly.

He started moving toward the men until he was toe to toe with the worker who'd made the remark. Ben wasn't super tall, he probably just cleared six feet on a good day, but he towered over the stout man in a yellow helmet and matching vest.

"Frank, drop it. It's not worth a tussle on the job site for some little bimbo."

Bimbo wasn't a new insult for me, being naturally blonde. I'd heard it several times growing up and it just rolled off my back. It must have hit a nerve with Ben, though, because at that comment he focused his rage on the taller, skinnier construction counterpart.

"If either of you say one more word about my coworker I will have you removed not only from this job site but from your company altogether. I'm sure you have no idea who you're dealing with but you've messed with the wrong guy today. So what's it gonna be?"

Both men looked as if they were considering throwing a punch or two before they both shoved past Ben and back under the plastic barrier. Ben stood facing the empty hall for another minute or so before he turned back to me, clearly more composed than he was moments before.

"I'm sorry Isabella. I shouldn't have gotten so mad but those guys were dicks."

"It's okay, I appreciate you saying something. Usually when I'm catcalled I just keep walking. It's not worth my attention."

Ben walked toward me and looked down at me sympathetically. His brown eyes seemed to bore straight into my soul and it suddenly felt as if the hall walls were closing in on us.

"Does that happen often?"

"Oh no, not often, but it does happen. Mostly just the old guys in town who have nothing better to do than to taunt the pretty girls. Not that I think I'm pretty. I'm just saying."

He reached out and touched my arm for only a second before dropping his hand back to his side. I felt my chest tighten and my breathing sped up.

"You *are* pretty Isabella."

Ben's words hung in the space between us, as little space as there was. My heart thudded under my cardigan like a racehorse and my palms grew sweaty. Scratch that, my entire body grew sweaty. I thought for sure that I'd reached my melting point and was going to turn into a puddle on the floor but Ben broke the silence before that could happen.

"I think we're *really* ready for some drinks now."

Nervously I laughed, "yes."

Just a few yards down the hall was the bar, a sleek lofty room that looked like the ideal man cave with wrought iron and dark stained wood everywhere. The bar had only recently been remodeled and I bet Ben took point on the project, judging by the masculine touches. If Jess had her way, everything would be white, bright, and modern.

"It's so nice in here, I haven't been in this bar since before the remodel. Was this your project?" I hoped talking about the bar would help ease the electricity between us.

"Yes, this was the first big project that Aunt June let me take on and it was such a blast. Jess was a little butt hurt that I got my way on everything but the guests love it, so she couldn't be mad for long."

We sat at the far end of the bar facing a mirrored wall lined with premium liquor bottles. I didn't know much about mixed drinks but the colorful bottles lined up in rows reminded me of Pantone swatches. My mind always related things to art and design, seeing objects as shapes and colors as hex codes. I always wondered if other designers thought in the same way.

A bartender in a pinstriped shirt walked over. His garb reminded me of one quarter of a barbershop quartet and I smiled to myself thinking of him singing one quarter of a song.

"Good afternoon Ben!" The bartender crowed.

To me he extended a hand and asked, "to whom may I have the pleasure of serving today?"

What a gentleman. Of course, I blushed. I reached out my hand to shake his after I'd stealthily wiped it on my dress to rid it of the sweat that was pouring buckets from me a few minutes ago.

"I'm Isabella."

"Beautiful Isabella, it's a delight to meet you. My name is Dandy and I'll be serving the two of you today. I think you'll like what we've come up with."

Ben turned his head to me and winked. This Dandy guy sure was a character but he fit well into the space. I'm sure the customers loved him.

Dandy pulled a tray out from under the bar with four shot glasses on it. Two of the glasses held a green mixture and the other two were full of something clear with a cherry on a wooden pick.

"What is this green one?" I asked, intrigued by the bright color.

"That's my take on a Gin Rickey, a popular prohibition drink. Traditionally it's made with gin, lime juice, and club soda, but for your Fall Ball I added a dash of apple schnapps. The apple and lime play together to make a fruity version of the classic drink that was said to be loved by Gatsby himself!" Dandy winked at me and to Ben he said, "I did my homework Boss."

"Shall we?" Ben asked as he picked up one of the shot glasses.

"Now don't knock this one back like it's a shot of tequila. Sip it and take in the flavors." Dandy advised.

Good thing, because I definitely would have thrown it back like I was doing shots at a party bar. I picked up my glass and held it up to Ben's to toast.

"Bottom's up," Ben joked as we both took a sip.

Immediately I felt my face involuntarily pucker at the strong alcohol. Gin was no joke! Both Dandy and Ben laughed at my reaction and I put my glass down, still half full. There was no way I'd be able to finish that half of a shot that was left.

"Okay, so I'll go a little easier on the Gin in that one," Dandy chuckled.

"Next drink?" Ben asked as he finished off his gross green concoction.

"A traditional Whiskey Sour, with white whiskey from the local distillery. Typically this would be served on the rocks but I couldn't get any ice to fit into the tiny glasses." Dandy shrugged. "Regardless, it's another popular drink from the prohibition times."

I looked skeptically at the little glass. I'd never had whiskey, either. Did I mention I was really into wine, though? Maybe I wasn't cut out for mixed drinks.

Ben picked his glass up so I followed suit, and with another clink of our glasses I took a sip of the drink.

This one was a bit sweeter and I actually almost kind of enjoyed it. Both Dandy and Ben read the relief on my face that the alcohol wasn't too potent and they both laughed at me again.

"Someone's gotta teach the little lady to drink!" Dandy joked. "Enough of those flavored seltzers you young people keep obsessing over."

"Actually Dandy, I hear she's a wine type of gal. Can't you see her perched in a vineyard holding a glass of Merlot?"

Ben elbowed me as I threw on my best pouty face. I didn't really enjoy being ganged up on like that but there was truth to their words. When I wasn't drinking wine I totally opted for a hard seltzer. I was a Millennial through and through.

"I can see that." Dandy said.

Looking to change the subject I said, "with a little tweak to the green drink I think these are both great for the Fall Ball. I love that you chose drinks that were actually served at speakeasies!"

"Yeah these are perfect Dandy. Will you be our lead bartender at the ball? We'll bring on a few other bartenders to help manage but I'd like you to be the face of the bar if that's alright with you."

The way Ben took charge of a situation was always mesmerizing to watch. He commanded respect and dignity without being harsh or pushy. He had the perfect balance of authority and "nice guy" that *made* people want to listen to him.

"Sure thing, Ben, I'll be there."

"Thank you."

A couple hotel guests walked into the room and Dandy floated down to the other end of the bar to greet them. Ben pulled out his phone and checked the time. Somehow it was already four o'clock in the afternoon. The day flies when you're not stuck at a desk all day.

Ben put his phone back in his trouser pocket and looked at me.

"I'm not quite ready to go back to the office yet. Would you like to make one more stop with me?"

"Yes," I breathed out, a little too quickly.

Ben smiled.

"Great."

Chapter 12 - **NOT A MURDERER** (Ben)

    I hadn't had a day this good in a long, long time. Isabella was such great company and she was turning out to be a perfect partner for planning the Fall Ball. At each of our three stops she had contributed to the consultations in a way that was both useful and constructive. Her leadership abilities had shone through today and I was thoroughly impressed, to say the least. She made planning a major event feel like a cake walk despite all the moving parts.

    I hadn't forgotten about those assholes in the hallway, though. I intended to talk to the site supervisor tomorrow and make sure he was aware of the pigs on his crew. While it wasn't necessarily my place, it did happen in a hotel that I manage and I don't need that harassment happening to anybody on my watch. How a grown-ass man could catcall a young woman like that anyway was beyond me.

    I started to get angry all over again thinking about those men so to redirect myself, I glanced over at the quiet blonde in the seat next to me. I couldn't help but feel again that that's where she belonged, next to me. Isabella turned from the window she was looking out of and peeked at me, smiling and blushing before facing her gaze straight out the windshield.

    Isabella was a complex young woman, that was for sure. I couldn't figure her out. How the shy and awkward parts of her intertwined with the bold, dedicated worker parts of her within the same sexy body absolutely perplexed me, but I was determined to piece it all together.

She'd agreed to spend more time with me, which was a good sign that she maybe, probably, definitely was digging me. I knew that I was for sure into her and I hoped the feeling was reciprocated.

I hadn't told her where we were going, just that she was going to meet someone important. She seemed a bit nervous, like maybe she thought I was taking her to meet the queen. There were no queens in Strasburgs, only adorable German Shepherds.

I turned down my driveway, wondering what she was thinking as we drove through the thick trees. The sun hung low in the sky casting long, sharp shadows over the drive in front of us. Between the shadows were bursts of orange, as the evening sun pushed out its last rays of color before setting.

"You're not going to murder me, are you?" Isabella whispered, still watching intently out the windshield.

Shit, maybe I should have told her where we were going. I suppose a secret location tucked back in the woods could seem kind of suspicious.

"Oh no Isabella, no worries, I won't murder you." That sounded like something aa murder would say…

Luckily at that moment we pulled up to my house which I was starting to hope looked friendly and inviting, and not like a murderer's shack. I started mentally kicking myself, remembering that she had literally just been accosted by two gross men, so what's to say I'm not just like them? I was an idiot, that was for sure.

"Is this your house?" She looked confused and not at all relieved.

"Yeah it is. I promise you you'll leave here alive."

My attempt at humor to lighten the mood didn't work. I turned off the truck and hopped out, after grabbing our food from the back seat. I jogged around to Isabella's side and opened her door, hoping the gentlemanly act would reassure her. When I offered her a hand to help her down, she hesitantly grabbed it and slid out of the cab.

"I'll be right back," I told her. I was really hoping that I could turn the afternoon around after just making my graphic designer think that I was going to murder her. *Dumbass,* I thought to myself.

I trotted up my front steps and through the front door where Mollie met me with her tail already wagging. I tossed the food into the fridge and knelt down to greet her.

"Come on pretty girl, I want you to meet another pretty girl. Oh, and somehow convince her that this isn't going to be a chainsaw massacre, please."

Mollie looked up with big, round, brown eyes that clearly understood none of what I'd just said. I walked back down the steps with Mollie trailing behind. When Isabella stepped around the front of the truck Mollie bounded up to her at full speed, tongue flopping back and forth and ears perking up. She was grateful for a new friend.

Isabella's face immediately broke out into a wide grin and she dropped to her knees to receive the furry pup's greeting. Within minutes Isabella was completely sat on the ground with Mollie rubbing up on her. They were instant BFFs.

"What a happy girl!" Isabella said as I reached them.

"She's always such a good girl," I said, patting Mollie's butt above her tail. "This is my dog, Mollie."

"I'm sorry I thought you were going to murder me! You can take me to meet a dog anytime, but maybe just tell me that." She laughed at her own concern and Mollie licked her all over.

"Duly noted, and I'm sorry I made you *think* I was a murderer. Would you like to come in? I can probably scrounge up a bottle of wine if you'd like a glass before I bring you back to your car."

It was close to five now, our coworkers would be leaving soon and would probably realize that I'd never returned with Isabella. Oh well, we had a day packed full of meetings. It wasn't unlike me to work late so it was definitely plausible that we got held up at one of our many meetings today. I told myself I wasn't too worried about people's speculations anyway, even as I stood there making up excuses in my head.

"Sure, I'd love a glass of wine."

Isabella stood up and Mollie started sprinting around the front yard. After being cooped up in the house all day she was bound to have a case of the 'zoomies.' Isabella and I headed in the front door as Mollie finished her laps and trodded in shortly after us. I led the way into the kitchen.

With Isabella in this tiny room with me it felt like there was life in there for the first time in forever. I didn't feel suffocated like I did with Brinley. Instead, it felt like a breath of fresh air.

I dug around and in the back of one of my cabinets I found a bottle of some kind of red wine and placed it on the counter. I then scrounged through my junk drawer until I surfaced with an old metal wine bottle opener.

"This thing is probably as old as you," I said as I turned around with the corkscrew.

Isabella was looking around at my tiny antiquated kitchen. There was faded yellow wallpaper on the top half of the walls above the wainscoting that she was investigating. I think at some point it had a flower pattern on it but that was barely discernible now.

"How old is your home?" Isabella asked as she turned and ran a hand over the wooden kitchen table that had come with the house.

"It's almost ninety years old. This house was one of the first ones built in this town, actually."

"That's so cool," she responded, continuing to look around.

I wrestled with the corkscrew until I had the wine bottle popped open. I didn't know anything about wine but the older the better, right? So this bottle that's been in the back of my cabinet for the past five years should be delicious, in theory. I poured a small amount into a drinking glass, which was all I had since Brinley had taken her wine glasses with her.

Isabella took a sip from the glass I handed her and absent mindedly scratched Mollie's head as the joyful pup sat at her feet. The sight made my heart swell; a beautiful woman in my home, loving on my dog. Things couldn't get better than this.

"I'd love to see more of your home some time. The craftsmanship is gorgeous."

I was seriously shocked at her interest in my ancient farmhouse. Don't get me wrong, I liked the place, but I never saw it as more than a place to lay my head at night. I had no real attachment to the structure other than the fact that I owned it.

It was also very plausible that I felt some negativity toward the house considering it was the place where my last relationship fell apart, but

I couldn't blame that on the house. Maybe it was time to make new, happier memories here.

"Yeah, sure. Feel free to wander around. It's a bit empty in here these days."

Isabella looked at me with pity in her eyes, which has happened every time I've alluded to my ended engagement. Begrudgingly, I figured it was time to stop dancing around the subject.

I cleared my throat. "Ah, my ex ended our engagement, and relationship of ten years, back in June," I explained, hoping it'd be the last time I'd ever have to say those words out loud. "She's since moved out and taken most of her stuff with her, which is why I now have a very poorly furnished bachelor pad. She seriously crushed my heart a few months ago but I'm happy to report that I've been feeling better lately."

I smiled at Isabella, hoping she'd catch my drift that *she* was the one making me forget about the heartbreak.

"Oh, I'm sorry Ben. I could tell it was rough on you. But maybe it was for the better," she said as she turned and wandered toward the living room, wine in hand and dog following behind.

What did she mean by 'for the better?' I grabbed myself a beer from the fridge and followed Isabella into the living room where I plopped myself onto the sofa that I rarely used. Brinley had picked it out but she didn't have room for it in her apartment, so it was one of the only pieces I kept. Its sleek modern design didn't fit with the home's ancient atmosphere but damn was it comfortable.

Isabella admired the mantle piece on the large wood fireplace in the middle of the room before sitting on the other end of the couch. Her face was flushed with the wine and I was reminded that we hadn't eaten since our tasting.

"Are you hungry? I can heat up some of the leftovers."

Isabella shook her head up and down as she took another sip of the wine. "I could go for some of those oysters, actually."

"Okay, be back in a minute."

I went back into the kitchen and switched on the oven. I couldn't cook to save my life but I could reheat leftovers like a pro. I was arranging some of the food onto a baking sheet when I heard the front door open and shut.

Maybe Mollie needed to go out and Isabella obliged, I thought. I walked out to check on them and froze in the kitchen doorway when I saw Brinley standing at the front door, staring at Isabella who was still seated on the couch, empty glass in hand.

When Brinley heard my footsteps she whipped her head around to face me and nearly snarled, "Am I interrupting something?"

"What are you doing here?" I shot back.

Looking at the brunette standing in my living room was like looking at a stranger. In that moment I felt none of the love I'd had for her for all of those years, and none of the heartbreak she'd left me with. All I felt was anger. Anger that she'd left me, anger that she'd moved on, and anger that, after all that, she still felt like she had the right to pop back into my life, and into my house, whenever she wanted.

Brinley remained by the front door, like an animal trying to decide between fight or flight. "I came back to get something and thought you'd still be at work."

"You didn't see my big ass truck in the driveway and think *oh he's probably home, I should leave?*"

My voice spat out like venom, a tone I'd never used with Brinley before, but I couldn't help it. She couldn't just walk into this house like this! I owned the place now, she wanted nothing to do with me or it, which she had made abundantly clear. So what changed her mind?

Brinley folded her arms across her chest and stuck out her bottom lip.

"I thought I'd stop in and say hi."

Yeah OK, sure. And why didn't I hear her obnoxious Jeep pull in? I peeked out the front window to see a grey sedan parked next to my truck. There was a male figure seated in the front seat with his arm hanging out the window.

"Who the actual fuck is that, and why did you bring him to my house?"

I was seconds away from losing my temper for the second time today. My vision flashed red as I thought about Brinley bringing her new boy toy to my house when she thought I wasn't home. That wasn't going to fly and I was about to lose my shit.

"You know what, never mind. I don't give fuck who that is. You have two seconds to get out of my house and never come back. I'm keeping the doors locked from now on when I'm gone, so don't think about coming here ever again. Whatever it was you needed you can text me for next time and I'll leave it at the bar."

I couldn't help but raise my voice, but this woman was absolutely infuriating me by doing nothing but standing on my threshold. She couldn't kick me out of her life then stroll back in here to say 'hi.' I charged past Brinley and flung the door open.

I also couldn't believe she had some new guy drive her here, either. I popped my head out and waved at the douche in my driveway.

Brinley skirted past me and I barely waited until she was completely out on the front porch before I slammed the door shut and flicked the deadbolt lock into place. Then I turned toward Isabella, who I'd forgotten about on the couch until that very second.

Fear was frozen on her face, her mouth slightly agape, and the empty glass moments away from dropping out of her hand.

"Isabella... I am so sorry."

I rushed over to her and knelt on the floor in front of her. I was beyond mortified that she had to witness that, that she had to see me like that. Her face softened when I took the glass from her to place it on the coffee table, and enveloped her small hand in mine.

"Isabella?"

I thought for sure the evening was over after that catastrophe. Why would anyone stick around after witnessing my mess? I certainly wouldn't blame her one bit if she wanted to leave immediately and never talk to me again.

But much to my surprise, Isabella suddenly leaned forward and locked her warm mouth on mine.

Never in a thousand years did I expect that from her. I nearly jerked back from shock, but it only took me a second to auto correct myself and match her rhythm. Her soft lips on mine felt like a grounding force and I quickly forgot about the confrontation that had just brought out the worst in me.

My head spun. Without breaking the kiss I rose up to sit next to her on the couch. Her hands broke free from mine and found their way to my hair, and her delicate fingers wound themselves in. I teased my tongue in between her lips and met her sweet wine riddled tongue with a soft nudge.

I reached forward and grabbed her sides like they were the anchor that was going to stop me from floating away.

As I got lost in her kiss I realized that I had wanted this for a while. I had no idea how long I'd wanted this but all of a sudden everything in my world felt right. As corny as it sounded, finally kissing her felt like I'd just caught a prize-winning Bass out of the Susquehanna River. It just felt *so right*.

But then the rational part of my brain broke through and I got scared again. I pulled away, removing my hands from her body and breaking the kiss. In a moment of clarity I realized that I still needed to be careful, even if she was the one who initiated it.

"Are we sure we should be doing this?" I asked her, her eyes still closed and her mouth slightly parted.

Isabella pulled her hands back and her blue eyes looked up at me, flooded with want, and then quickly overtaken by hurt.

"Well if you're questioning it then maybe not."

Her face fell and her eyes dropped down to her lap at the thought of rejection. I hadn't put all of this effort into today just for me to chicken out when I finally got what I wanted. I wasn't letting our evening end like this so I tilted her chin back up toward me.

"Don't get me wrong, this is going to happen, as long as you want it to. We just have to be smart about it." I paused, thinking carefully about my next words. "Like it or not, I'm still your boss and starting something like this could have consequences."

"Consequences?"

Her brow drew together and she began to chew on her bottom lip. I could tell the shy, awkward Isabella from the office was back.

"Yeah," I sighed, "it's technically against company policy for me to fraternize with one of my subordinates. If my Aunt June found out we even kissed, unfortunately you'd be the one getting the ax."

Isabella looked terrified.

"But that's not going to happen! Not if we keep work out of this."

"How do we do that and, uh, what exactly *is this*?" Isabella asked slowly.

She was right to ask, because I didn't really know myself. I mean, yeah, I orchestrated this day solely to get to this point, but for what reason? I was slowly coming to the conclusion that I really wanted this woman as mine but I had absolutely no clue how to do that in a way that would end well.

"Well, I don't know yet. I think it's clear I like you, and I think you like me, but this did sort of happen in a weird way..." I scratched my beard, "let's start over."

"Start over?"

"Yeah, tomorrow. We'll start over. Now that I know you're interested, I'll do it the right way."

"I'm not sure I know what you're talking about."

"You'll see tomorrow, sweetheart."

Chapter 13 - SECOND FIRST DATE (Isabella)

"And then I *kissed him!*"

I held my phone away from my ear as Kendra screamed. I'm sure her apartment neighbors were loving that about as much as I was.

"*You kissed him?!*" She shrieked.

I was standing at my kitchen counter just a couple hours after attempting to make some moves on my boss. I'll admit, I felt pretty dejected when he put a stop to our makeout sesh. We obviously liked each other but then I got pretty worried when Ben informed me that I could be fired if his Aunt June found out, per some company policy I had no idea about. Regardless, I was pretty excited to see where this was all headed.

After our little talk on the couch, Ben drove me back to my car and now there I was, filling Kendra in on the whirlwind of a day that I'd had.

"Yup. We were like legit making out until he stopped and basically said I'd get fired if anyone found out."

"Wait what? He threatened to fire you??"

"No, he said his Aunt would fire me, that it was against policy to date people at work."

"Damn, Izzy. So that's it?"

"Well, no, not even!" I replied. "Because then he said he was going to start over and I have no idea what he meant by that."

"Like start over as in, pretend today didn't happen? He basically schmoozed you all damn day then said *nah nevermind*?"

"See, I don't know! I'm so confused!"

Gossiping with Kendra was one of my favorite things to do, even when it was about my own weird love life.

"Hmm," she paused, "so how was the kiss?"

My stomach did backflips thinking about that moment on his couch. His strong hands on my hips and my hands running through his thick hair. I still couldn't believe that I was the one who initiated it. I'd never done anything like that, ever. But spending all day with the man, and consuming some liquid courage, made me feel all sorts of things toward Ben.

"It was amazing. That man knew what he was doing, Kendra."

"Perks of an older man. He's had time to practice."

I rolled my eyes but I totally knew that she was right. Kissing him was like nothing I'd ever experienced before; not that I had much experience to begin with. But hot damn that kiss lit the fire *all* over.

"So what do I do now?" I asked her.

"I guess you just wait for tomorrow?"

My heart was pounding as I pulled into work. Even though it was a cool autumn morning, my whole body was covered in a thin veil of nervous sweat. I had no idea what the day was going to hold and the uncertainty was making me majorly anxious. And an anxious Isabella was an awkward Isabella.

Ben hadn't come to work early today so I figured I'd take advantage of the empty office to help myself calm down and ease into the day just like normal. I walked in and flipped the overhead lights on as I headed toward my desk. I rounded my cubicle wall to find a lumpy orange gourd on my desk.

Oh my God! It was the gourd that Ben had picked up yesterday at the nursery, the one the same color as my dress. I picked it up and ran my fingers over the rough surface. When did he buy this? He certainly didn't have it when he got in the truck yesterday. As I mulled it over I noticed a post-it note stuck to my desk under where the gourd was sitting.

Good morning sunshine.

My heart jumped into my throat. I wasn't sure what exactly was going on but this was freaking cute. I propped the gourd on my desk next to my empty pumpkin mug and stuck the note on the inside of one of my file drawers. I definitely didn't need Jess seeing it and asking questions, she wouldn't leave me alone until she got the answers.

Despite my fluttering heart, I fell into my morning routine easily and started my work day at 9 am with everyone else. I worked diligently for a couple hours, focusing all of my weird jittery energy on some small tasks that had been sitting on my to-do list for a while.

Around 11 am Jess rolled a chair up to my desk and took a seat. *Uh oh.*

"How did yesterday go?" She asked.

She looked curiously at me with her hands crossed on top of the desk and her head cocked slightly to one side. *Does she know something happened?*

"Yesterday went well. We definitely got a lot done. I can't wait for you to try the food we've picked out for the ball, that catering place was amazing!"

I started rambling on about the meetings and prayed that Jess didn't realize how weird I was acting. It seemed to be just the right amount of weird for me, though, because she never caught on.

"Well all of that sounds fantastic!" She crooned. "Aunt June made the right decision pairing you and Ben on this project. You guys are like total opposites but maybe that's what it takes to get the job done!"

Jess stood up and reached over the desk to place a hand on my shoulder.

"I'm really proud of you for branching out and learning more about the business. You know how integral this all is to my family and I sincerely appreciate you always taking it all so seriously. We definitely hit the lottery with you."

Well shit, now I feel a little bad that I made out with her cousin last night.

"Thank you, Jess. That means a lot. I really do love this job."

So please don't fire me when you find out that Ben shoved his tongue down my throat.

With a smile, Jess rolled her chair away and I was left again to my to-do list. I was plowing through my tasks when around two my desk phone rang.

"Hello?" Dammit, will someone remind me to look at caller ID first? Oh, why bother, there was only one person who called my desk phone anyway.

"Good afternoon, Isabella. Did you get your gift?"

Ben's voice was like molten chocolate lava oozing through the receiver. I'd never felt turned on at work before, but there was a first time for everything I supposed. I had to be careful with how I responded, though, because I didn't want anyone around me hearing something they shouldn't.

"I did, thank you."

"What are you doing tonight?" Ben asked.

"Um, nothing."

"Okay, can I take you to dinner?"

I answered a bit too quickly, "yes."

"It's a date then."

The line clicked dead and I hung the phone up with a shaking hand, my heart pounding in my throat. I had no time to recover when a moment later the phone rang again and I snatched up the receiver.

"Hey, so in an effort to sound cool and sexy I totally neglected to ask if seven worked for you?" It was Ben again.

I couldn't help but chuckle at the ridiculousness of the situation. Life wasn't like a fairy tale where the man showed up at just the right time and place to pick you up. Coordination actually had to happen in real life, and for some reason I just found that amusing.

"Yes, that's fine."

"Okay. Also, uh, I don't know where you live… so could you get me that address so I can pick you up?"

I broke out into a full on giggle fit. I knew the people sitting on the other sides of my cubicle walls were definitely wondering now what kind of conversation I was having.

"Yes I can do that."

"Okay cool. Now it's a date. I'll see you tonight."

    I had grabbed Ben's cell number from the signature of his emails and texted him my address before leaving for the day at five. Usually on a Friday night I'd head home, order some takeout, and spend my evening watching some obscure indie movie on Netflix. But now I was having to get ready for an actual date! I hadn't gone on one of those in years, which was pretty sad to think about.

    For my evening out I chose to adorn one of my few pieces of fancy attire, a satin maroon wrap dress with a deep v-neck and fluttery sleeves. I bought this years ago for a wedding and I just loved the way it accentuated my curves. I didn't have a lot of them, but the dress could make one think otherwise. I threw on a tan leather jacket and some suede booties and admired my look in the mirror.

    I struggled immensely with self image but there were times like this one where I felt a fleeting moment of confidence. It comes with the territory of being shy and awkward; you just assume that no one likes you and, thanks to modern media acquating perceived beauty to how likeable you were, that therefore no one finds you attractive.

    I grasped on to the warm feeling of self confidence and clutched it close. I wanted to feel this way all the time. The clothing helped some; a great outfit boosted my own self image, but not always.

    My moment of self reflection was interrupted by the chime of the doorbell. I had one of those video doorbells that my dad had installed one day when he was randomly worried about my safety. I peeked at the video stream on my phone and saw Ben standing on my front patio holding a bouquet of flowers.

Wow, he really was doing this the 'right' way, if there ever was such a thing.

I shoved my phone into a crossbody purse and headed to the door. When I swung it open Ben stood in the evening light wearing a navy blue three piece suit and shiny brown oxford shoes. He never got this gussied up for work but damn was he sexy. He held out the flowers and a toothy smile beamed out from beneath his beard.

"Isabella, you look ravishing." He purred.

I took the flowers and smiled back.

"Well Ben, you look... hot!"

He burst out laughing and shook his head.

"You'd better hurry up and get those in water, we have a reservation in forty five minutes and we've still gotta drive a couple towns over."

"Why'd you pick a place so far away?" I asked as I walked to the kitchen of my small rental home. I could let things get a little cluttered sometimes so I had speedily tidied up when I'd gotten home from work, and was grateful I'd done so.

Ben followed me in and stood by the door as I quickly grabbed an empty wine bottle and filled it with tap water. I didn't actually own a vase but the recycled bottle would do just fine.

"Because I don't want to chance running into anybody we know." He stated matter-of-factly.

"Ah, gotcha."

The logical part of me fought away the thoughts creeping in that told me he was embarrassed to be seen with me; I knew it was important to keep the date under wraps. I nodded as I put the flowers into the bottle.

The drive ended up being pleasant enough, sprinkled with just the right amount of small talk, and we made it to the restaurant with a few minutes to spare. I was glad I'd picked a fancy dress because Ben had chosen an upscale French place that seemed more expensive than anything I could ever afford. I briefly wondered how much he made working for his Aunt's company but quickly shooed the thought away because it really was one of my business.

Ben wrapped his arm through mine and led me inside, where a hostess around my age sat us at a quiet table near the back.

"The Bouillabaisse here is amazing." Ben said as I picked up my menu. I had no idea what Bouillabaisse was.

Everything on there was written in French and the one foreign language class I'd taken in high school did not prepare me for this. I drew my brows together and looked up at Ben.

"Don't worry, the waiter will help. I don't speak a lick of French but I've tried enough off of their menu that I could also recommend something if you'd like."

"You eat here often?" I asked.

"No, I used to, though."

I understood what that meant. I looked back at the menu. I knew fromage meant cheese and vin was wine, so at least that was something. I could survive on wine and cheese, right?

Our waiter came over promptly and saved me from my struggles.

"Good evening, my name is Remy and I will be your server tonight. Can I start you off with drinks?"

"Can you recommend a good Cabernet Sauvignon?" Ben asked.

A little dry for my taste, but I wasn't going to turn down a lavish bottle of wine. I wondered if he actually liked wine, or if he was ordering it for me.

"Of course," the waiter said to Ben, and turning to me he said, "and I will need to see your ID, Miss."

I was carded fairly often so I was used to reaching for my wallet when ordering a drink. I showed the waiter my driver's license and he disappeared off into the restaurant to fetch his wine recommendation. As I put my wallet back into my purse I looked up at Ben to find him staring at me with his head tilted to one side.

"Yes?" I asked a little sharply, feeling a bit hangry as it was eight at night and I hadn't eaten yet. I didn't know how Europeans could wait to eat this late at night!

"Nothing," Ben shook his head, "it's just been a very long time since someone's asked for my ID. It caught me off guard that my date might be young enough that a server would question her age."

He chuckled and crossed his arms on the table, leaning toward me. The faint yellow light above our table accentuated the sharp features of his face. It looked like he'd combed his beard and applied some kind of styling product to his hair. It was endearing that he put so much effort into his appearance tonight. Ben's eyes were dark and deep as they stared at me. The intensity frightened me a bit.

Our waiter returned with an open bottle of red wine and two sparkling clean glasses. He placed them on the table and poured a splash in each to allow us to try. For a dry wine it certainly was delicious, moving smoothly across my tongue. We opted to keep the bottle, placed our orders based on Remy's recommendations, and were left alone once again.

I took a sip from my glass so I could avoid having to be the one to start a conversation.

"So, where are you from Isabella?"

My plan worked.

"I'm from Strasburg," I replied. "Born and raised, Strasburg High graduate."

"Ah, so you were a Coal Miner, huh?" He said, referring to my high school mascot.

"Yes I was. Were you?"

"No, my Alma Mater was Gordonville High School, so technically we're natural born enemies."

Gordonville was our high school rival, full of preppy snobs from what I could remember. I was never into sports so I only remember the rivalry from our pep rallies.

"What year did you graduate?" I asked, before taking another sip of my wine. I was genuinely curious since I didn't actually know how old my date was.

"1996."

I nearly choked on my sip. That was the year I was born.

"Yeah I know," Ben said to my reaction, "I'm old."

"I'm sorry, I just wasn't expecting to hear my birth year!"

Ben took a moment to respond and I knew he was doing the math to figure out how old I actually was. He breathed out a low breath and took a big sip of his drink.

"I don't think I realized how young you were."

"I mean, I *am* a grown ass woman. Twenty six is no child!"

As I said that I felt *very much* like an indignant child trying to advocate to their parents for a later bedtime. A sly smile creeped onto Ben's face.

"Isabella, I lived through the eighties and you learned about them in school. You're pretty damn young."

He was right. I had a unit in high school history where we learned about the pop culture and politics of the 1980s. Awkward.

Remy brought our food, and the break in conversation was greatly welcomed by the both of us. We passed the remainder of dinner by making conversation about our favorite movies, hobbies, and interests. As it turned out, we were both big fans of slapstick comedies and we both enjoyed spending time outdoors.

While Ben was paying the check I excused myself to the ladies' room. I was a few glasses of wine in and my bladder was seconds away from bursting. I managed to walk pretty steadily to the bathroom despite the height of the heels on my booties, but when I sat down in the bathroom stall I felt the dizziness hit. I did my business and walked over to the sink to wash my hands.

While I washed I looked at myself in the mirror, trying to steady my vision. I had curled my hair into ringlets that ran down my back, and pinned the front pieces away from my face. My lips were red from the wine and I was flushed in the cheeks and chest. I was trying to decide if I looked too young for my date when in the mirror's reflection I saw a well-dressed woman exit a stall and choose a sink next to me to wash her hands.

She looked at me and smiled in the mirror as she lathered soap under the water.

"I love your dress," she said to me.

"Thank you."

I shut the water off and grabbed a paper towel from the dispenser next to me. The woman did the same and as she was drying her hands she asked, "did your date buy it for you?"

Her question confused me.

"Um, no, I bought it for me."

"Oh I was just wondering," she smiled. "I'm here with a daddy too."

"Oh no, Ben's not -- no he's just my boss. Er, my date. We're on a date."

The woman smiled at me curtly.

"It's okay hun. No judgment here."

She exited the bathroom and left me standing in the fluorescent lights, seriously confused. Did she think I was some gold digger? I mean, Ben didn't look that old! I walked back to our table where Ben was waiting for me.

"Are you ready to go?" He asked.

"Yeah."

Ben stood and linked his arm through mine again. Thank God, because walking around had made me realize how much of that delicious wine I'd actually had. We walked arm in arm out to Ben's truck. It was really nice, actually. Besides making out, this was the closest I'd been to him. His body was warm and strong, his arm taught around mine. The area in between my legs grew heated when I thought about Ben's body so close to mine.

He helped me in the truck and shut my door. My head felt off-balance and my stomach was heavy from all of the delectable French food we'd consumed. I really wasn't positive about what it was I'd eaten but it was good either way.

Ben started driving back toward our town, a little over half an hour away. I rested my head against the cool window as we drove through the dark night. There were no street lights in rural Pennsylvania and the cab was only illuminated by the dashboard buttons and gauges.

"Are you alright?" Ben asked after a couple of minutes. I could see his profile glance over at me in the dim light.

"Yes, I'm fine. The wine was good."

"I know."

I could hear the smile in his voice. I hope he didn't think I was a lightweight. Or a lush.

"Thank you for dinner." I said while closing my eyes to help ease the spinning.

"You're welcome, I hope you enjoyed yourself."

A couple minutes of silence passed before he asked, "is the age thing weird?"

I opened my eyes and looked at him. His eyes were on the road but I could see his brow furrowed together like he was genuinely concerned about the fact that he was nearly twenty years older than me.

"Ben, it doesn't bother me one bit. I like it, actually. Unlike guys my age you've got your shit together. You have a career and you know that life is about more than bar crawling and football games."

"I never really liked football."

"You know what I mean. I like the maturity."

"Oh you do, do you?"

The smile was back in his voice.

"Does the age gap bother *you*?" I asked.

"I'm unsure about it." He said after a minute or so.

My stomach felt uneasy and I didn't know if it was from his response or the movement of the truck. I was suddenly afraid that he thought I was too young for him.

He continued, "actually, I'm not bothered by the age difference. I'm bothered by what other people might think about it. You know, the perceived notions of someone my age going after a younger woman."

"Like people thinking you're my sugar daddy?"

He laughed, "yeah that, and people assuming I'm going through a midlife crisis thinking I need some hot young thing on my arm."

"Nobody's going to think that looking at me."

Ben's head whipped around to face me and I was worried for a second about the fact that we were hurtling down a back road at fifty miles an hour in the dark, and he wasn't looking. But after shooting me a glare he turned back to the road.

"Isabella do you really think that? I'm genuinely curious, do you not know how damn attractive you are?"

His voice was strained, like he was actually mad that I'd just put myself down.

"I don't know. I struggle with self confidence sometimes."

"Well you listen to me now because you are the hottest woman I've ever known. You're literally the complete package, from your hair down to those sexy legs. But not only that, you're damn smart, too! And talented. And just a generally really interesting person to be around. Don't listen to your brain when it tries to convince you that you're any less than that."

I didn't know what to say. No one had ever hyped me up like that. Even Kendra couldn't rally that hard. This man was something special.

"Thank you Ben."

He reached over in the dark and placed his hand on my arm, sliding it down until he found my hand. When he'd located it he brought it up onto the center console that separated us and laced his fingers through mine. I hadn't had my hand held since high school but this simple gesture was somehow erotic, now that it was my boss.

Again, the area in between my legs sparked to life, begging for me to acknowledge it. I wasn't going to make any moves tonight, though. I tried that yesterday and I got turned down. Ball's in his court now.

When we were about ten minutes outside of town Ben asked me what I wanted to do. It was nearly ten and I was tired from working all day, but my nether regions were still raring for some action.

"Would you like to come back to my place?"

So much for not making any moves. Asking someone in is almost always just code for inviting them to have sex with you. It's like saying you're going to watch Netflix and chill; everyone knows *exactly* what that means.

"Sure, I'd love to."

When Ben pulled into my driveway my heart began pounding. I was nervous as all hell to have this man inside my home now and possibly inside somewhere else. I unlocked my front door and let us in to my small living room.

"Could I have a glass of water?" Ben asked.

Happy to oblige and escape the tiny living room, I dashed into the kitchen to pour Ben a glass from the fridge. When I walked back out, he was standing by my photo gallery wall where I'd haphazardly hung dozens of photos of my friends and family in mis-matched frames. I walked over to hand him his glass and stand next to him.

"Is this your dad? You look just like him." He said, motioning to a photo of me and my dad at my college graduation.

"Yes, that's him."

"Who's this here?" He said, pointing to a picture of Kendra and me from high school.

"My best friend, Kendra. Really you owe her a thank you, because I definitely wouldn't have kissed you yesterday if it weren't for her encouragement."

"Oh, I'll definitely have to thank her," he said, his eyes growing dark and his mouth turning up into a slow grin.

Ben leaned in and pressed his lips against mine, hard. His mustache tickled my nose until we found our rhythm and the kiss deepened. He set the glass down on the side table next to him without looking and wrapped his hands around my waist, pulling me in close to his body. I linked my arms up around his neck, partially because I was afraid my gelatin legs would give out from under me at any minute

Ben snuck his tongue between my lips and met mine with a tease. I pushed my body against his, and pressed up there against my stomach I felt *him*, hard and ready, straining against his suit pants. I reached down and stroked his lengthy mound over the pants and a primal growl escaped from his throat.

"Isabella."

He broke the kiss and pressed his forehead against mine, eyes still closed. I stroked him again, watching his brow furrow, but this time in pleasure.

"You better stop that if you want anything else from me tonight."

Ben opened his eyes and pulled back. He slipped a hand in between the silk of my dress and the thin cotton of my bra. His strong hand located a pert nipple and began to idly play with it.

"Let me take care of you," he said.

That was all I needed to lead him down the hall to my bedroom. I'd never been so glad that I'd preemptively changed my bedding. Before we were even fully in the doorway Ben picked me up by my waist and placed me on the bed, making sure I was on my back. He slid his hands up my thighs until they were hovering over my wet center.

"Is this okay?" He asked as he nipped my bottom lip with his teeth.

"Whatever you're about to do, *yes*."

Ben yanked down my panties and without hesitation found my bud which he massaged with one apt hand, while the other made its way back up to my breast. His hands got to work on my body and I quickly felt the build up of heat in my lower stomach. My back arched and I slammed my pelvis into his hand as I was rocked with waves of prickling pleasure. An animalistic moan escaped my mouth before Ben covered it with his.

My climax came but Ben didn't stop. I felt another wave building up quickly when I reached down and grabbed his wrist.

"I want you." I all but panted.

I needed to feel him inside of me immediately. I frantically grabbed at his pants, popped the button open and yanked the zipper down.

"Fuck, Isabella."

"That's the goal."

Ben nipped at my neck as I freed him from his boxers. I don't know what I was expecting to find but I was impressed.

"Hold on, let me grab a condom." Ben said.

He grappled with his pants before pulling a silver packet out of one of his pockets. While he sheathed his sword I pushed his suit jacket off and unbuttoned his shirt. The man underneath was firm and toned but not overly muscular. Dark hair covered his chest and tapered to a thin line that ran all the way down to his length.

"We wouldn't want to ruin that dress, Isabella. Why don't we take that off?" Ben said.

His eyes were darker than the night sky and I saw the desire written on his face. It was as if he'd been taken over by an animalistic hunger that could only be satisfied by me. I untied my dress and Ben slid it off of me, taking a moment to take in my own physique. This is the part I was nervous about. What if my body wasn't what he wanted?

That thought was tossed aside as Ben stooped down and kissed my stomach, working his way down until he stopped just before my throbbing loins. Then he brought his mouth back up to mine and kissed me hard as he positioned himself between my legs and began to enter.

I flinched just a bit as the tip entered; I wasn't a virgin but man had it been a while, and my college boyfriend had nothing on Ben's member. He took it slow as the rest of him filled me up. We both groaned in unison when I reached max capacity, and Ben began to pump in and out, slowly at first and then building speed.

"Is this okay?" He asked between kisses.

I moaned out a 'yes' as he hit my g-spot over and over again. I could feel another orgasm just on the horizon. I grabbed onto his shoulders as I felt closer and closer to floating away in ecstasy. Ben's rhythm grew faster and harder and I knew he was getting close too. With just a few more pumps we both rode the waves out, grasping onto each other and embracing the release.

When I could think again I released my grip on Ben and he flopped onto the bed next to me. Sweat coated both of us and I considered cracking a window to let the cool night's air in, but I couldn't move my legs yet. After a few minutes of nothing but panting, Ben broke the silence.

"Damn. Isabella."

I laughed. And then I kept laughing. I fucked my boss. And it was *good*.

"You always laugh manically after sex?" He asked.

"Nah, just enjoyed myself was all."

Ben got up and located his pants. While he pulled them on I sat up and wrapped myself in my duvet. I hadn't noticed it while I was yanking his pants off, but he had the perkiest butt I'd ever seen on a man. Ben caught me looking.

"Like what you see?"

"Oh yes."

"That's good. So what are you up to this weekend?"

As soon as Ben asked me out earlier today I'd texted Kendra and requested some girl time tomorrow. I was going to want to spill the details of the night and I knew Kendra was going to want to hear all about it.

"I'm going to meet up with my friend Kendra tomorrow, but that's my only plan. Maybe get some laundry done or something, too."

"Oh yuck, can you do mine, too? That's one chore that I put off as long as possible."

I laughed. I guess it didn't matter how old a man was, he was never going to want to do his own laundry.

Ben fastened his pants and sat next to me on the bed. His hair was disheveled and he looked so incredibly sexy.

"I had a really great time with you tonight Isabella."

"I had a great time, too."

"What do you think about a second date?"

"I mean, this already felt like a second date but yeah, I'm up for another one."

"Great," he smiled. "We'll get something on the books then."

With that he stood and it was clear he had no intentions of spending the night. *No big deal*, I told myself. If he didn't like me he wouldn't have asked about a second date.

I threw on an old tshirt from my dresser drawer and walked him to the door. We said our goodbyes and goodnights and he kissed me on the forehead before disappearing into the dark night. I shut the door and stood there for a few moments thinking about the past couple of days. I just went on a date with my older boss. I had sex with him! And we have plans for a second date. I started laughing at myself.

Who was this woman and what had she done with Isabella?

Chapter 14 - WRONG BAR (Isabella)

Kendra agreed to meet me at Draft, the only freestanding bar in town. It was a little sports bar-y for us but I thought it'd be a good change of scenery from our usual winery or living room couch. I don't know why, but I was feeling a little daring lately. Could it have something to do with the confidence boost I gained from sleeping with my boss?

I got there first and grabbed a booth off to the side of the bar. Knowing it'd be a bit before kendra showed up, I sipped mindlessly on my first drink while I waited. I went with a rum and coke, something easy that I thought I'd have no trouble with. I was trying to expand my palate after my poor performance at The Locomotive Hotel's bar with Ben.

It was my first time in this bar, actually. I looked around at the couple of flat screen TVs playing what I thought might be college football; a baseball game was playing on some of the other screens. I really had no interest in either, I only knew a bit about football from my dad who was a die hard Ravens fan, but sports weren't really my thing.

The bar itself was a bit dark and dingy, and I noticed the mid-afternoon crowd was kind of sad. A couple of old guys who looked like they were permanently glued to their stools, some middle aged guys who looked like they were having some drinks after a round of golf, and a half-asleep security guard were the only ones in there besides myself and two bartenders. I was served by an older woman who I thought might be one of the owners. She was nice but a bit gruff, the kind of woman who would thrive in the bar industry.

The other bartender was hanging around the golf guys so I didn't get a good look at her. I could just hear her laughing over the blaring sports games and looked over to see her hanging off one of the men. *Real professional*, I thought.

Kendra eventually walked in past the security guard and gave me a look that said, *why?* Her face scrunched up as one of the men at the bar looked her up and down before turning back to his drink.

I shrugged. I was trying all sorts of new things lately.

Kendra slid into the booth across from me. "Interesting choice."

"Whatever. You wanna hear the deets or not?"

The whole point of getting together today was to gossip about my date last night and I had some hot tea to spill for sure!

"Let me get a drink first then yes, absolutely!"

The older woman who'd served me had disappeared into the back and the other bartender was still flirting with the golf men. Kendra waved her hand for a minute until the bartender looked up at her. The bartender rolled her eyes, whispered something to her patron, and came over to our booth.

As she got closer I felt my whole body ice over. I recognized her as the woman who walked into Ben's house the other day, his ex-fiance.

That whole thing was crazy; imagine my surprise as I sat on Ben's couch, minding my own business, when a complete stranger walked in the front door. I had no idea what to do so I just froze. And Ben was *so angry* when he saw her. Talk about awkward!

But now there she was, strolling up to our booth. I tried to hide my face with a curtain of hair as she walked up to us, pen and pad in hand.

"What can I get you?" She asked Kendra impatiently.

"I'll have what Izzy's having. What is it you're drinking? Izzy?"

Kendra nudged me with her leg under the table and I knew I wasn't going to be able to get out of this situation by hiding. Maybe she wouldn't recognize me? I tucked my hair behind my ear and mumbled, looking down at the table, "rum and coke."

"Okay then, one for me and another for the weirdo. Thanks." Kendra said, unknowingly dismissing Ben's ex so we could talk about Ben.

"Oh, I know you." The dark haired woman said slowly.

I looked up but couldn't meet her eyes. Instead I stopped at the nametag pinned to her chest which said Brinley. That was definitely her, Ben's ex-fiance. She was pointing her pen at me like she was casting a spell.

"Yeah I know you. I'll be right back with your drinks." She said, and turned on her heel back to the bar.

"I can't drink that now, thanks a lot." I whispered to Kendra.

"Why? Who was that?"

"Ben's ex."

"Okay what? Like the one who showed up to his house while you were there? Is that why you picked this place?"

Kendra peeked over her shoulder. Brinley was at the bar fixing our drinks and flirting with the men again. I felt very hot all of a sudden, like the room was closing in on me and I was running out of air. I wasn't prone to panic attacks but I thought I might have been having one.

"I didn't know she worked here." I choked out.

I felt the room spinning around me as I heard the security guard greet someone who responded with a familiar voice. That voice was the only thing stopping me from passing out onto this beat up old table.

"Hottie at twelve o'clock," I heard Kendra say through the fog in my head.

I turned around toward the door and sure enough there was Ben, standing at the doorway with a cardboard box in his arms. He was wearing faded jeans and a t-shirt, attire I'd never seen him in before. His upper arms peeked out of his sleeves, broad and strong.

Looking at him I could feel myself start to breathe again. He looked sexy, even though he was looking at Brinley with a scowl on his face as she schmoozed the golf guys. There was a moment where it felt like time stood still, where Brinley hadn't realized that Ben had walked in, and Ben didn't see me over in our booth watching the situation unfold.

After a minute or so Brinley looked up from behind the bar and across her face crept a slow, seductive smile that would probably bring any other man to his knees. She slithered out past the men at the bar and as she passed our booth, shot me a piercing glare. She knew exactly what she was doing.

Brinley walked over to Ben, reached out for the box and purred, "thanks hun."

The whole encounter made my stomach jump into my throat. Something about seeing this woman interact with Ben crushed my confidence. Brinley truly was beautiful, with short brown hair and a lean figure. She probably had five inches on me height-wise, and my petite stature suddenly made me feel like a young, dumb child. Who was I to try to date someone way out of my league like Ben?

Poor Kendra had no clue what was going on, she was just waiting impatiently for her drink. Kendra loudly cleared her throat to get Brinley's attention, causing both her and Ben to whip their heads toward our booth. I tried to duck down below the seat back but I was too slow.

"Isabella?"

Ben walked over to our booth.

"Izzy what's going on?" Kendra asked.

"Izzy?" Ben repeated, this time amused at the use of my nickname. Brinley had sulked back to her spot behind the bar to pout when she realized the attention wasn't on her anymore. You'd think I was the only one in the room, the way Ben was looking at me.

Kendra still just looked confused.

"Kendra this is Ben, Ben this is Kendra." I said, looking down into my drink.

It was always awkward when worlds collided, but this situation was especially inopportune. Kendra looked at me with her eyebrows raised and her mouth slightly agape. I guess she didn't know I could snag such a 'hottie.'

I looked up at Ben and he was beaming at Kendra with his businessman smile as he offered his hand. She took it and Ben said, "I believe I owe you a thank you."

Kendra tilted her head and asked, "why's that?"

"From what Isabella tells me, you're responsible for getting her to go out with me."

Ben slid into the booth next to me, his hips bumping mine causing me to scoot over and make room for him. Kendra looked at me then back at Ben with a wicked look on her face. I could only imagine what was going through her mind.

"And how did that go?" She asked.

"Oh, Isabella didn't tell you?"

"Izzy was going to spill the beans over a drink but your ex is a terrible server."

Kendra motioned to my empty glass. Damn, she did not hold back! Ben laughed; at least the two of them were having a good time.

I glanced up at the bar to catch Brinley peering back at our booth. It looked like she'd lost interest in her customers and was instead wiping down the bartop to look busy as she kept an eye on us.

"Yeah, weird choice of establishment, *Izzy*." Ben said to me. "I'm offended you didn't choose the bar I worked so hard on. You know Dandy would get you whatever you wanted."

He took a stab at a puppy dog look and I couldn't help to crack a smile. I was going to kill Kendra for telling him my nickname but hanging out with the two of them was kind of nice, despite the circumstances.

"I thought I'd try something new today. Obviously that bit me in the ass."

They both chuckled at my misfortune. I was surprised, though, at how nonchalant Ben was despite the woman watching from behind the bar. Just a couple weeks ago he was still heartbroken over her (which I totally didn't understand now that I'd had the displeasure of interacting with her), but today he acted as if she never existed.

"So Ben, since Izzy hasn't told me anything about your date, I might as well get it from you. Where did you go last night?"

Kendra leaned in across the table and I could tell she was swooning.

"Bonne Nourriture," he said in a perfect French accent. "Only the best for Isabella."

Ben put his arm around me and smiled. As corny as it sounds, my stomach filled up with butterflies. The way he sounded almost possessive of me was flattering. His arm felt comfortable and strong around me and I couldn't help but smirk at the thought that Brinley was having to witness this.

Speak of the she-devil, Brinley came over and plopped two drinks onto the table without even looking at myself or Kendra. We looked at each other and silently agreed that they weren't safe to drink. Instead, Brinley kept her eyes on Ben and continued to sport the pouty face that she seemed to love so much.

"Ben," she said, "can I talk to you for a minute."

I felt Ben's arm tense around me.

"No thank you."

Pouting turned to irritation as her face scrunched up like an angry cat. Ben took his arm off of my shoulders and stood up.

"Please Ben, just for a minute." She pleaded.

"No, actually I've got to get going."

Brinley reached for his arm; he sidestepped her and started heading toward the door.

"Us, too," Kendra said as she slapped a twenty dollar bill onto the table. We both got up and followed Ben out the front door; luckily Brinley didn't follow us. It felt amazing to step out into the crisp, cool air and leave the drama in the dingy old bar.

"Let's never go back there." Kendra said as we all stopped in the parking lot.

"You don't have to tell me twice." I muttered.

"Well, I have some more errands to run today, so I'll talk to you soon?" Ben started to reach his arms out as if to hug me but quickly dropped them and looked around. We *were* standing in a parking lot in the middle of our town, best to keep it professional.

"Sure," I said with a smile, "have fun running errands."

Ben headed toward his truck and Kendra walked with me over to my car.

"Get in." I said once Ben was out of earshot. "We're going to have our girls' day if it kills us!"

Chapter 15 - *MYSTERY GUEST* (Ben)

"Good Morning Cindy!"

She flashed a grin and held the door open for me to pass through.

"Morning Ben!"

Cindy was heading out the door to an early meeting with a business partner when I walked in. As I moved past the cubicle maze toward my desk, I glanced quickly toward the back corner where I knew my favorite blonde was already hunched over her keyboard. It was ten past nine and everyone was beginning to start their work for the day, while Isabella had certainly been working since 9 am on the dot after coming in early to fix herself a cup of tea.

I unlocked my office door and didn't even get a foot through the doorway before my desk phone started ringing. I shut my door behind me and slid into my leather chair.

"Ben Simmons."

"Hi, Ben."

It was my favorite blonde. Running into her at the bar in town on Saturday was a weirdly nice way to break up the monotony of my weekend errands. I had been so reluctant to drop off that box of random crap for

Brinley, but it felt like if Fate were a thing, it had a hand in that day. Isabella was just the thing I needed to keep me grounded in that bar. Her friend Kendra was nice too, but I preferred my shy Izzy.

Izzy. I liked that name. I wondered why she didn't use it here at work.

"Good morning Isabella. To what do I owe the pleasure of hearing from you first thing this morning?"

"Sorry, I know you just walked in. But the Fall Ball invites came back from the printer and I wanted to show you. If you want to see them."

I thought I might test out that nickname of hers.

"Pretty Izzy, you can call me any time. I'd love to see the invites. Give me a bit to get settled in then bring them in."

"Yes sir," she responded before hanging up.

I didn't know if the use of the word 'sir' was sarcastic or not but I kind of liked it. Damn, what was that woman doing to me? I mean, I was already working on planning out our next date. I never put this much work in with Brinley, even in the beginning of our relationship when it was all butterflies and rainbows. But Isabella was different, I wanted to do whatever I could to make her happy.

As I walked back out of my office toward the break room, empty coffee mug in hand, Jess emerged from the cubicles and fell into step with me. I noticed her mug was also empty.

"Coffee or tea today, Jess?"

"You know I'm a tea kind of girl. How was your weekend?"

I always felt like Jess already knew all of my secrets, but I decided that playing it safe was the best way to hide my budding office romance from my snoop of a cousin.

"It was uneventful. How was yours?"

"Oh it was pretty good," she responded.

Jess spent the whole time that it took the coffee pod machine to heat up to tell me about her weekend. Apparently she painted her kitchen cabinets. *Neat.*

Then she broke into a topic I could get interested in.

"So, Aunt June asked me if I'd work on obtaining press coverage for the Fall Ball."

"Oh?"

She flicked her hair off of her shoulder, knowing that she had my full attention now. She'd dangled the carrot in front of me and I chomped at it, anxious to learn anything I could about Aunt June's fixation on this event.

Jess went on, "yeah, we've never had the event covered like this before but she wants newspaper articles leading up to build hype, and I have to try to get a reporter to attend and write a story."

The coffee machine sputtered out my usual donut shop blend as I pondered this information.

"I wonder why this year's event is so important. She has some secret guest attending but she won't say who."

"Do you think it's the President?"

Jess bobbed a tea bag in her hot water and I just shook my head. At first I thought she was joking, but she stood there as if she were actually considering the possibility. Sometimes I wondered if she ever pulled her head out of the clouds.

I lowered my voice. "No, I don't, but I do think it may have something to do with selling."

"What are you selling?" Greg asked as he walked into the breakroom to join us in fixing a cup of morning coffee.

"I'm selling Girl Scout cookies if you're interested." I said sarcastically to throw Greg off. He wasn't always the brightest crayon in the box but I didn't need a rumor like this spreading around the office. I turned back to Jess before venturing back to my office.

"Jess, let's try to dig up some info."

"What kind of Girl Scout cookies?"

I was sitting at my desk sipping my coffee and clicking through emails when I heard a soft rap on my door.

"Come in."

Today Isabella was wearing a grey blazer over a dark blue blouse that looked like it was as silky as I knew the skin underneath it was. Her slacks hugged her hips and tapered down to show off slim, pale ankles. Her hair fell in ringlets over her shoulders and her glasses were pushed up onto the top of her head. She held a stack of invites wrapped in shrink wrap.

"Could you close the door behind you?"

She clicked the door closed and approached my desk, offering the stack to me. I took them without looking and continued to soak in the woman in front of me. I swear her eyes were a different shade of blue every time I looked at her, as if they changed with her mood. Today they were dark and sultry, like the depths of a lake. She was wearing some kind of gloss on her lips that reflected the fluorescent lights above us and it took all I had not to climb over my desk and kiss that taunting mouth.

Instead, I decided to behave myself.

"How was the rest of your weekend? Did you get to catch up with your friend?"

"Yes I did, and she got all of the details out of me. She won't tell anyone, though. Kendra knows I can't lose this job." Isabella finished quickly, making sure to cover her actions. She knew that this dating thing was top secret and that was good.

"That's good. She seems like a good friend." I responded.

"Yeah, she is. She offered to burn down the bar and it took a lot to convince her not to."

She laughed at that memory. Isabella was still standing in front of my desk fiddling with her jacket cuff like her usual awkward self. It was like we hadn't been completely naked with each other in her bed just a few nights ago.

"You can relax," I assured her, "no one can hear us in here if you're concerned about that."

"Ah sorry, I can't help the awkwardness. Plus, being in your office reminds me of when I tripped and it makes me nervous that I'm going to do it again."

"I don't think you could repeat that encounter if you tried." I quipped.

"You'd be surprised," she said as she finally settled into the lounge chair.

She sat with her legs crossed and her hands folded in her lap. Her pant leg raised an inch or so and I noticed a small tattoo above her inner ankle. *Interesting*, I'd have to explore that at another time.

"So what do you think of the invites?"

I looked down at the shrink wrapped stack in my hands. Even wrapped in plastic I could see the raised lettering in a bold, round font. A red and cream-colored background made the gold pop out. There were geometric shapes and a subtle elegance to the copy placement. They were amazing, if a piece of cardstock could even be described that way.

"Oh, Isabella, these are perfect!" I looked back up at her. "Are you happy with them?"

"Yes Ben, I love them, they came out exactly how I pictured them."

Pure joy radiated off of her. It was evident that she truly enjoyed what she did for a living. Many people would kill to be this happy in their careers; I really admired her love and dedication to this job.

Which is why I had to make sure she never lost it because of me. If I could just prove to Aunt June how valuable Isabella was by pulling off this Fall Ball, maybe she'd go easy on us dating. Aunt June wasn't heartless, but having never found her own love I was afraid she wouldn't understand what it meant to be in love with someone.

Woah. What? Why am I thinking about love?

"I have to run these over to the Post Office this afternoon to have them send these out. June emailed me a list of people to invite so I'm going to make up mailing labels."

"Wait, she sent you a list of names?"

"Yeah, it's pretty much the usual people who are invited, the Mayor, some business owners, you know."

"Could you do me a favor and forward me that list when you get back to your desk? I'm just curious who she has on there."

"Absolutely. I'll go do that now."

I handed the invites back to her and she left my office, hair bouncing behind her. I was dying to see who was on that list. I was pretty sure I'd be able to recognize anyone out of the ordinary, and maybe figure out who this mystery guest was that had June all tied up in knots.

A few minutes later my computer dinged with a new email from Isabella. I hit print on the attachment and waited with bated breath as my printer shot out a single piece of paper. I was hoping that this list would help answer some of the questions that I had buzzing around in my head.

I snatched the paper out of the printer and scanned it closely. At first glance the list did seem to be all of the usual suspects. But on a second read through one name toward the bottom stood out as one I didn't recognize.

Charles Penbrook.

Who are you Chrales, and why are we trying to impress you?

Chapter 16 - *Fall Solstice* (Isabella)

"Isabella?"

I looked up from my computer to see Ben peeking over my cubicle wall. It was Wednesday afternoon and I was buried in a new project, making some posters for Jess to advertise the Fall Ball with around town.

"You know it's after five right?"

Sure enough, the time on my phone said 5:25pm.

"I did not know that, I was concentrating too hard."

That's the down side of people leaving you alone; when it was time to go they just left you there. It's happened to me more than once. The worst part was having the lights turned off on you.

"Well it's just you and me left, do you want to walk out together?"

"Yes!"

I quickly saved my work and shut down my computer. Ben waited patiently while I gathered my stuff. Looking out over the cubicle maze he said, "you know, out of all the jobs I've ever had, I've never worked in a cubicle."

"Oh really? How'd you manage that?" I asked as I slung my purse over my shoulder.

We started weaving through the maze toward the front door.

"I'm not really sure. When I started here I just bounced around to whatever department needed me, then one day I found myself in my own office."

Ben held the door open for me as I stepped through. Tomorrow was the first day of fall and the air was already crisp and breezy as the sun sank low. It would still be light out for a couple more hours, but the days were already getting shorter with each sunset.

Ben walked the short distance to my car with me.

"What are you doing tomorrow night?" He asked.

"I was going to sacrifice a goat to the new moon."

I looked up at Ben and his face was frozen in a state of confusion. I laughed and said, "I was joking. I *do* know how to joke, you know."

"A rare occurrence from Ms. Morgan." He chuckled. "Well if you have time before your ritual would you like to have dinner with me? We can order something in."

Ordering in sounded nice, and one huge perk of not going out was complete privacy; no chance of prying eyes.

I hit the button on my key fob to unlock my car door and he opened it for me. As I slid into my front seat I replied, "I'd love to. Your place? The goat will be chilling at mine."

This time he laughed at my joke and nodded his head as he shut my door for me. I felt like that went smoothly, like I was finally feeling comfortable around him. No more awkward interactions for me!

As Ben headed over to his truck I put my car in reverse to leave. At least, I thought I did. I ended up throwing my car into drive and jerking forward, catching my front bumper up onto the cement parking barrier in front of me. I ducked my head low as Ben turned back at the loud 'scratch' sound that came from my car as I backed up off of the barrier.

So much for being smooth, Isabella.

After work on Thursday I ran home to get changed before my date night in with Ben. I stood in my second bedroom which I had converted into a makeshift walk-in closet, with free standing clothes racks, my dresser, and a full length mirror. I'd stripped down to my bra and underwear but was unsure about what to put on. Going out to dinner was easy because you could just get dressed up. But hanging out at someone's house was different; do I go classy casual? Is classy casual even a thing?

I dug through my dresser drawers and pulled out my favorite pair of jeans. They hugged in all of the right places and distressing on the knees made me feel trendy. I then leafed through my hanging tops until I found the burnt orange sweater I was looking for. Soft, cozy, and low cut. I pulled on some brown ankle booties and combed through my hair quickly before looking in the mirror at my finished look. I felt like the perfect embodiment of fall, warm and cozy.

A few spritzes of perfume completed the ensemble and I dashed out the door. Ben lived about fifteen minutes away on the other side of town, closer to work.

I arrived at his house shortly before six and parked my car next to his truck in the gravel driveway. It looked so little sitting next to his truck; a lot like how I felt when I was with him. Physically he was almost a full foot taller than me but I also felt little in the sense of our age. Most of the time I didn't notice the age difference, but it was always there.

Ben was standing at the front door waiting for me, he must have heard me pull in. I walked up his front steps and saw that he'd gone casual as well. Ben had put on jeans that *also* hugged him in all the right places, and on top he wore a navy blue half-zip pullover. He certainly understood tonight's dress code.

"Good evening Isabella. I hope you like Thai food."

I stepped into his living room and the smell of peanuts and spice wafted through the air. It was quite presumptuous of him to order food for me but it also smelled delicious so I wasn't mad. Lucky for him I wasn't very picky.

Takeout containers were sat on the coffee table along with an unopened bottle of wine, two glasses, and a couple lit candles. I couldn't help but smile at the effort.

"I thought we could watch a movie or something." Ben said, explaining the living room setup.

"That sounds fun. The candles are a nice touch, Ben."

He rubbed a hand on the back of his head as he shrugged. "Thanks, the lady at the department store that helped me pick out this pullover suggested them."

"Wait, some random lady helped you pick out your date night outfit?"

Ben looked totally embarrassed but I found it endearing. It was nice not being the embarrassed one for once.

"Yeah I must have looked pretty lost because *she* came up to *me* and offered to help."

I tried to picture the scenario in my head and giggled.

"You both did well because you look good." I told him.

"Thanks. Shall we?" He motioned toward the couch where I had kissed him for the first time.

I sat down and peeked into one of the containers. I'd tried phad thai once in college, but I usually didn't get too adventurous with my food. Ben saw me looking and said, "Peanut noodles, red curry, and Tom Kha Kai, a coconut chicken soup from Lotus Thai in town."

"I don't know what any of that is but it smells delicious, so I trust you."

He laughed and poured the cabernet into two very new looking wine glasses. They were wide and tall, the ideal shape for red wines. That was a nugget of knowledge that I'd picked up from one of the wineries.

I wondered if he knew he had grabbed the right glasses, or if he had help choosing those, too.

"Where's Mollie?" I asked, just realizing that the happy pup was nowhere to be seen.

"I placed her in her kennel so we wouldn't have to share our food." Ben winked at me and finished pouring. "I'll let her out when we're done, I'm sure she's excited to see you."

I smiled because I was low-key excited to see his dog again, too. I was the kind of person who went to a party at someone's house and found the pets right away.

"So what shall we watch?" Ben asked as he handed me a glass.

I took a sip and let the savory Cab flow over my tongue. It was fruity and peppery at the same time. Probably not the best pairing for Thai food but I'd take it.

"Do you have Netflix?" I asked.

"Yes I have Netflix, I'm not an old man. Hell, I'm pretty sure my dad has Netflix and he's *old*."

I rolled my eyes and set my glass down. "I was asking because you don't seem like someone who watches a lot of TV."

"Why's that?" Ben asked.

He pulled two paper plates out of a bag that was tucked under the table and started dishing out food while he waited for an answer.

"Well, you just seem like a very outdoorsy person. Like, you look like you'd rather chop down a tree than watch a TV show."

"Chop down a tree?" The corner of his mouth tugged up into a half smirk.

"You know what I mean."

"I'm not sure I do, Isabella."

His smile turned wicked as he handed me a plate.

"It's your looks. The beard, the tan, the strong arms. You just *look* like someone who spends his free time outside."

I took a bite of the noodles so I didn't have to talk for a minute or two while he pondered my answer. The food tasted as good as it smelled; the sweet peanut and hot spice mingled together in a perfect medley. I definitely didn't mind expanding my palate when Ben was the one I was doing it with.

"Do you like the beard?" Ben stroked his short salt and pepper beard and looked at me while I swallowed.

"I love it. Beards are sexy."

He flashed that wicked grin again. He was digging for compliments and we both knew it. He set his own plate down on the table and brought his face close to mine. His lips were a mere inch away from mine but he didn't close in for the kiss.

Instead, he whispered, "you're the sexy one, Isabella. Do you know what that neckline is doing to me?"

I saw his eyes drop down to my chest before he straightened up and grabbed his plate. He ate with one hand and grabbed the remote with the other. We ate in silence for a few minutes while Ben flipped the smart TV on and opened Netflix.

"Comedy? Thriller? Romance?"

I was a total baby when it came to thriller movies, and romance seemed too mushy for a second (or third?) date, so I chose comedy. We decided on something lighthearted that we could talk over without really missing anything. We finished up eating fairly quickly and killed half of the bottle of wine before Ben started clearing off the coffee table.

"Can I help?"

He was shoving the trash into the bag from under the table.

"No you relax, I'll be done in a sec."

Ben brought the remains of dinner into his kitchen and returned quickly with Mollie on his heels. He sat down a little closer to me this time and wrapped his arm around me while Mollie sniffed around looking for scraps of food. With his free arm, Ben grabbed a blanket that had been draped over the back of the sofa.

"Care to cuddle?" He asked.

"Of course."

I snuggled into his side and he spread the blanket over our legs. As the movie went on I sunk in closer to him and his arms held me tighter. He was very good at cuddling.

At a lull in the plot I looked up at his face. Smoldering eyes looked back down on me and he slowly leaned in, locking his lips onto mine. The kiss started off as gentle nips until I reached up and wrapped my arms around his neck as I loved to do, then the pace quickened and I felt his tongue shimmy its way through my lips. He tasted like spice and wine, warm and inviting.

In one quick maneuver Ben flipped me onto my back so that he was on top of me, his body crushing mine into the sofa. I must've been wriggling to readjust under him because, without breaking the kiss, he propped my torso up onto a throw pillow and I immediately felt more comfortable.

While his mouth did wonderful things to mine, I decided to let my hands wander over his clothes. First along his broad shoulders then down his strong back, then even lower to that amazing ass. I gave it a squeeze and he finally came up for air.

"New rule," he panted, "wherever you touch me I get to touch you, too."

"Deal," I breathed back before stealing another kiss.

Ben placed a soft peck on my lips before beginning a trail of kisses that started at my mouth and crept its way down my neck, and stopped at the neckline of my sweater. He slid a hand down into my bra and popped my right breast out of the cup. He lowered his head down to my nipple and gently nipped at it with his teeth. Electric shocks ran through my body with each bite. He teased it for several minutes before pulling the other one out and doing the same thing. With each pinch I felt the fire smoldering between my legs until all at once it ignited into flames. I needed him immediately.

"Ben," I gasped.

"Not yet."

He moved his attention from my chest to my jeans, which he swiftly unbuttoned and peeled off of me. My core was thudding with arousal so strong I could barely handle it. Ben slowly pulled my underwear down and the anticipation built in me like a volcano ready to erupt.

"Ben," I tried again. I needed the sweet release soon.

"Not yet Isabella." Mischief flashed across his face.

Ben lowered his head down to my entrance, where the volcanic pressure was moments away from eruption. His tongue ventured down and quickly found my bud, which he flicked mercilessly. It didn't take very long for him to push me over the edge, and I welcomed the hot relief as my body quivered.

When I'd recovered from my orgasm I realized that Ben had stood up and begun to remove his clothes. I watched as the pullover was yanked over his head, and revelled as muscles flexed in his arms and chest. He kicked off his jeans and when he realized I was watching, made a show out of slowly pulling his boxers down off of his erection until it sprung up like a jack-in-the-box. He picked up a silver condom package that had made its way onto the coffee table.

"You know, I'm on birth control." I said.

"What are you suggesting there, Isabella?" Ben's dark eyes looked like an abyss that could swallow me up.

"We don't have to use a condom as long as, you know, you're clean."

Ben chuckled. "Yeah, you have nothing to worry about there. I got tested after the witch left me because I was concerned she might've been cheating."

Oof. I did not want to be thinking about her right now. Ben tossed the unopened condom back onto the table and scooped me up into his arms.

"Why don't we move this to the bedroom," he growled.

I wrapped my arms around his neck and nibbled on his ear as he took us up the steps and into his bedroom. He gently tossed me onto the bed before climbing on top of me and stealing my mouth. As he gently nibbled on my bottom lip I felt his length slip into me. I had never had sex without a condom before and the sensation of him inside of me felt like we were melding into one. Ben thrusted rhythmically, slowly at first before speeding up.

He broke the kiss as he focused on his movements. I watched sweat bead up on his forehead and I could see on his face that he was close. I tilted my hips up and the friction on my already tender bud built up quickly until I was also moments away from release.

"Isabella," Ben groaned.

He reached climax and I followed mere seconds after. Our bodies pulsed together until there was no more movement and we stayed frozen in position, both panting heavily. Still holding himself up with his arms, Ben looked down at me. I couldn't tell what he was thinking so I reached up and caressed his cheek. His beard was soft and wirey beneath my fingers.

"Stay with me," he breathed. Ben rolled onto his back next to me.

I propped up onto my elbow to face him. "What do you mean?"

"Stay here with me tonight."

He reached over to switch on a lamp that was on his bedside table. Illuminated, I could see that the bedroom was fairly empty. Besides the bed, Ben only had two bedside tables and a small dresser in the room. I assumed that if there was more furniture, his crazy ex had taken it.

"Okay, I can stay." I kissed his nose and laid down.

A digital alarm clock next to the lamp said that it was just after nine. Usually around this time I would be crawling into my own bed and reading a few chapters of whatever romance novel I was into at the time.

"Do you actually use that thing as an alarm?" I asked, referring to the clock.

"Yes, how do *you* wake up in the morning? Please don't tell me you're one of those morning people that wakes up with the sun." He groaned.

"No," I laughed. "I use the alarm app on my phone. I don't think I even own a clock."

Ben slid an arm around me and pulled me close into his side. He wiggled the comforter up over us until we were cuddled up close and warm.

"It's little things like that that remind me how much older than you I am." He said, sounding amused.

"I'm sorry."

His arm tightened around me. "No, don't apologize. I don't see our age gap as a bad thing. I actually love it." He paused and started tracing shapes on my arm. "There are times when I look at you and it seems like you're from another planet; like when you text a mile a minute or when you use some slang word I don't know. Those are the times that I notice the age difference. But it's not weird or annoying, rather it's intriguing, to watch your youthfulness."

He continued, "then there are so many other times when I feel like I'm the younger one, like you have more experience with life than I do or something. The way you dedicate yourself to your job, and the drive that you have makes you seem so much more mature than other women. I don't know, I just really like being with you and I guess my point is I don't care what people think about the age gap anymore."

"What about June?" I asked.

He may not care about what others think of us being together, but that won't get him very far if his aunt will still fire me.

"Yeah, there's still the matter of Aunt June. But I'm working on that."

"You are?" I stared up at the shadows on the ceiling. Thinking about the future of my job made me feel extremely uneasy, even when I was wrapped in the arms of my sexy boss.

"Yes. I'm hoping if she sees how well we work together, she won't want to fire you because you're too valuable."

"Sounds like a risky plan."

"You're worth the risk."

Ben kissed the side of my face. I turned my head so that we were nose to nose, and this time he kissed my lips. This kiss was different from the other ones we'd shared; this kiss was slow and deliberate. Ben maneuvered us so I was on top of him and I straddled his hips. His hands explored my body as our lips moved together.

The slow burn continued as I felt his erection come to life below me. I decided I was going to take charge of this round and I lifted my hips up so I could position myself onto his length. Matching the pace of our kiss, I slid slowly down until he filled me up completely.

I raised and lowered my hips in a measured rhythm. Ben's hands found their way to my ass and he cupped my cheeks as I kept my pace. We weren't having sex; in that moment we were making love. That cliché act that I read about in romance novels each evening was happening as our bodies connected in a way that could only be described as *making love*. There was lust and passion, sure, but this time was just different.

In unison, we both peaked and finished together before I melted down onto Ben's chest, where I stayed for quite some time before drifting off into dreamland. Eventually I ended up on the bed next to Ben, and I didn't move until his alarm clock went off the next morning.

Chapter 17 - DON'T KISS AND TELL (Ben)

I stood in the breakroom and watched my mug fill up with my third cup of coffee of the day, which was pretty bad considering it was only 9 am. I'd had a cup while sitting at my kitchen table trying to wake up, and slammed another on my drive in. I'd stayed up way too late last night and, although I didn't regret it, I was definitely feeling the repercussions this morning.

Isabella had left early this morning to go back to her house so she could shower and change before coming in today. I hadn't seen her yet at work but I wondered if she was handling the late night any better than I was.

I should find a reason to stop by her desk today, I thought. I wanted to see her, to talk to her, anything so I could be near her.

Walking back to my office, I started thinking about the night before. Any time I spend with Isabella is a good time, but last night felt different. There was something more there and she had to have felt it, too.

Whatever it was made me feel a little uneasy. How could such strong feelings develop in such a short amount of time? I couldn't spend too much energy thinking about it while at work, though, because there were much more pressing matters at hand.

I sat down at my desk and pulled out my Fall Ball folder. Right now the only things in there were contracts with Crave Catering and

Shaw's Nursery along with one of the invites Isabella made, and the printout of Aunt June's guest list. There was still so much to plan for the event with less than a month left to get it all done. It was time for Isabella and I to kick it into high gear.

I stifled a yawn as Jess came in and sat down, mug in hand.

"How's my favorite cousin?" She asked.

"I'm telling Jim and Scott that you admitted I'm your favorite." I teased her.

"Your brothers already know that." She said matter of factly. She took a sip of her tea and peered at me over the top of her mug. "You look terrible."

"You don't look too great yourself." I tossed back, slightly offended.

She actually looked fine, but I wasn't going to tell her that. Jess still dressed like a kindergarten teacher, wearing bright hues and bold prints as if she was teaching everyone in the office about shapes and colors. It certainly matched her strong, colorful personality.

Jess rolled her eyes. "Whatever, I know you're just deflecting to try to divert my attention. The kids used to do it to me all the time so I'm immune. So tell me, why do you look like you got hit by a train?"

I could tell I wasn't going to be able to change the subject so I decided to give minimal details to satisfy her.

"I stayed up too late." I shrugged.

Jess leaned forward. "Doing what?"

"Watching a movie."

"What movie?"

"I don't remember the name."

Why didn't I just name a random movie? Rookie mistake, she was going to be on to me now.

Jess placed her mug on the edge of my desk and drummed her fingertips next to it. "So you were *so* invested in a movie that you stayed up late to watch it, but you don't remember the name of said movie?"

"Yup."

Her eyes narrowed. "So who were you watching the movie with?"

Was I that bad of a liar? I mean, I wasn't lying per se. I actually had no clue what the name of the movie was due to the fact that I was utterly distracted by the woman who'd chosen it.

"No one. Just myself and Mollie."

She picked her mug back up and took a sip. I felt like I was being interrogated by a seasoned detective. Maybe if marketing didn't work out for her she could go join the police force.

"Mhm, sure. Benjamin Simmons spent the night with someone!" She taunted me.

Jess broke out into a toothy grin. When we were kids, that shit eating grin of hers made me want to punch her in the mouth, in the most loving way possible. As an adult though, I just had to let it roll off my back since HR probably wouldn't take keenly to a cousin brawl in the middle of the office.

Jess decided to push for more details. "Do I know her?"

"How am I supposed to know who you do or don't know?"

"So you admit there's a her!"

"I plead the fifth."

"You know I'll find out Ben."

I decided to change the subject even though I knew that meant that I was admitting defeat. Deep down I knew that she was definitely going to find out, it was just a matter of biding time until after the Fall Ball. It wasn't Jess I was worried about, it was Aunt June.

"So, I have some information unrelated to my personal life that you might be interested in."

"Okay, spill. We'll circle back around to your mystery woman later."

I pulled out the sheet of paper that had the list of names from Aunt June. I underlined Charles Penbrook and handed it to Jess.

"What am I looking at?"

"A list of people that Aunt June wants invited to the ball. Do you recognize the underlined name?"

She scanned down the list and her eyes went wide.

"I do, actually. Mr. Penbrook is an investor from Gordonville who funded a new strip mall right off the highway. I remember reading about it online last year. The story was getting major press attention because of how upscale the property was, apparently that's Penbrook's thing."

"So he builds fancy buildings?"

"He *pays* to have them built, yes. He's a developer."

"Why is Aunt June so interested in him? You don't think she's going to sell the hotels to him, do you?"

I couldn't get the notion of selling out of my head. No matter what way I spun it I just couldn't see any other reason for contacting someone like that. And it was freaking me out that Aunt June was keeping this all a secret from me.

Jess didn't seem as concerned and simply shrugged. "That's a very valid concern Ben but I don't know. Hell, maybe we've got this all wrong."

"No way, this is too much of a coincidence, he has to be the mystery guest June has been alluding to."

"So what do we do now?" She asked.

"I don't know. I have to think this over a bit."

Shortly after noon I wound through the cubicle maze toward Isabella's desk. At this time of day everyone was either in the break room eating lunch, or out picking something up. The maze was silent except for the clacking of one woman's keyboard. I knew Isabella usually worked through her lunch hour so it was the perfect time to pay her a visit without wandering eyes.

"Hi pretty Izzy," I said as I rounded her cubicle wall.

Isabella's head popped up, eyes wide behind her glasses, as she glanced around to see if anyone had heard. She stood up to peek her head over her walls to survey the maze.

"Relax, everyone's at lunch." I assured her. "Speaking of which, are you going to eat today?"

Looking at Isabella you'd never be able to tell that she was up all night. Her hair was pulled back into a sleek ponytail and she wore a tidy pink button up shirt tucked into dark grey slacks. There were no dark circles under her eyes like there were under mine. I guess that's the difference twenty years makes.

"I didn't have time to fix anything this morning so I was going to skip lunch." She responded.

"Why don't we go pick something up?" I offered. I could always pass it off as an event planning lunch. No one would suspect a thing.

"Actually I've been pretty busy designing the menus that will go on each table, based on Rachel's sample menu. I wanted to get this done before I leave today so I can send it to print."

Isabella motioned to her computer screen where a big round font spelled out the first half of our menu on a cream-colored rectangle. I had no idea how she did her design stuff but it always came out perfect. I had no doubt she'd get this done today *and* it'd look great.

"Fair enough. Let me take you out to lunch this weekend, then."

This time I looked around before tilting her chin up toward me and stealing a kiss. Her lips were warm and soft, and tasted like earthy tea leaves. I felt the heat rise to her face as I kissed her harder. But, despite the requests my groin was making, I broke the kiss and took a step back.

Isabella pushed her glasses up onto her nose and cleared her throat. "I can do lunch this weekend."

"Great," I said. "Sunday?"

"Sunday is perfect."

She sat back down in her chair and looked up at me. A smile spread slowly across her face as she looked at me.

What was she thinking?

Before I could find out, Jess appeared behind me.

"Don't harass my designer!" She said while playfully punching my arm. I turned to face her and quickly scrutinized her body language to try to determine whether or not she'd seen or heard anything that had just happened in this cubicle. I decided that if she had, she wasn't going to let on, so I just had to play it off.

"Your designer is also my project partner so I have every right to harass her."

"Blink once if you're under duress." Jess said to Isabella.

My favorite blonde laughed and kept her eyes wide open. Good girl. It was time to make my escape before Jess felt the electricity flowing between myself and Isabella.

"Back to work ladies!" I flashed them both a smile before sauntering back to my office.

My cousin was unknowingly making it very hard to keep my budding romance a secret. And I really shouldn't have kissed Isabella here because now that's all I could think about. I shut the door to my office and shook my head. I was getting myself into some trouble, wasn't I?

Chapter 18 - *Lunch in Philly* (Ben)

"I looked at my kingdom, I was finally there/To sit on my throne as the Prince of Bel-Air" Isabella rapped.

I glanced over at her big goofy smile and just laughed.

We were in my truck driving down Route 30 towards Philadelphia. As soon as I told Isabella we were heading to grab lunch in West Philly, she began to rap the entire theme for the Fresh Prince of Bel-Air. And I had to admit, I was pretty impressed that she knew the whole thing, especially considering that show was off the air by the time she was born.

I figured Philadelphia would be far enough away from Strasburg that no one would see us out and about together. We'd been in the car for only twenty minutes and had another hour to go until we arrived at Booker's Restaurant, our lunch destination. It was extremely easy to make conversation with Isabella when it was just the two of us alone like this and I was enjoying my time with her.

Isabella looked beautiful today, wearing tight black jeans and a flowing white top. She'd pinned her hair away from her face and wore large sunglasses that made her look like a movie star in disguise.

"Would you like to play 'would you rather'?" Isabella asked after a short stretch of silence.

Now that's a game I haven't played in forever.

"Sure, you go first."

"Hm, okay," she said as she curled a lock of hair around her finger. "Would you rather live in a tent for the rest of your life or only be able to drink water?"

"Easy. Tent. I'll live in my tent and drink beer, and die a happy man."

Isabella snorted. "Nice. Okay tent man, your turn."

I took a moment to think before asking, "Would you rather move to somewhere that's always warm or always cold?"

"Hm, as much as I love my sweaters and boots, I'll take warm weather over cold weather any day. I hate the snow and the cold."

I should have known that would be her answer. At the moment she was taking full advantage of the truck's dual climate system and had her half of the cab nice and toasty.

"Ah see, I'm the opposite, I'll take the cold." I told her.

"Then I'll come visit you in the cold as an excuse to wear my cute sweaters, but then I'm returning to my warm and sunny weather."

"Fair enough, I look forward to your visits then. We can cuddle to stay warm inside the tent. Your turn to ask!"

Her next question came out fast; she was prepared for this one.

"Would you rather have to work every day for the rest of your life and always feel fulfilled, or never have to work again but never feel that sense of accomplishment."

"Wow, Izzy's pulling out the tough questions. That's a tough one. I don't mind my job but I may have to go with never working again." I said. "I'll spend my days fishing and camping and living in the cold tent you've banished me to."

I felt Isabella turn to look at me. "But you'll never feel fulfilled with the fish that you catch."

"This is true, but I'd also never have to wear office attire again."

"But you look so good in it." She playfully whined.

"This is also true."

I could literally hear her eyes roll. "Whatever, next question!"

I had a good one ready. "Would you rather only date men older than you or younger than you?"

And as fast as I asked, she answered. "Older. Obviously."

"So had we not started seeing each other, you would have seeked out some other older guy?"

Isabella turned back toward her window as she considered her answer.

"No, not necessarily, but in the scenario you presented I'd rather date someone older than me because of the maturity and stability. Guys my age are a mess so I don't even want to think about younger guys."

"Good point. I *know* I was a mess at your age."

"Hard to imagine business man Ben Simmons ever being a mess." She laughed.

"Yeah I'm glad you didn't know me twenty years ago. You wouldn't have given me a second look."

"You don't know that."

"Oh yeah I do." I chuckled. "It was around your age that I settled back down in town, much to my dismay. Aunt June had needed help around the hotels and she knew I was looking for a steady job after college so she offered to keep me employed. I didn't want to help with the hotels but I really needed a job."

"So why did you stay so long if it wasn't what you wanted?"

We were nearing our exit and I was almost sad that our conversation would end soon, even if it was just to walk into a restaurant.

"Because the business grew on me."

"Do you still think about moving on to something else?"

I felt like her question could have had a double meaning but I chose to keep it light and focus on our talk about work.

"At this point, no. It's a steady, well paying job that I've got there. I'm not really up to the challenge of starting new somewhere else."

Isabella was silent for a moment as she thought about my response. I think it blew her mind that I could work somewhere and not be in love with the job. We couldn't all be as content as her.

"Remember how you asked me a few weeks ago if I was happy at Simmons' Hotels?"

"Yes..." I pulled into a parking garage and rolled my window down to take a ticket.

"Well, are *you* happy?"

I found a spot large enough for my truck and parked, placing the ticket on my dashboard.

"Yes, I am. Especially lately."

That answer seemed to satisfy her for the moment so we got out and walked about a block to the restaurant. I gave the hostess our name for the lunch reservation and we were quickly seated. After we placed our orders I looked across the table at Isabella as she idly read through the drink special card that was on the table.

"Anything catch your eye?" I asked her.

"You." She said quietly, before nervously chewing on her bottom lip. She was trying to flirt and it was absolutely adorable. I couldn't help but to smile.

"All in good time, sunshine. I do have a surprise for you after lunch, though."

"Oh? Do tell." Her eyes lit up, interest piqued.

I chuckled and responded, "no, then it wouldn't be a surprise. You'll just have to wait and find out."

She stuck her bottom lip out and pretended to pout.

"That won't work on me. It doesn't work when Mollie does it and it won't work when you do it!"

I lied. I gave in to Mollie way too often and I would totally give in to Isabella if I wasn't so stoked about the surprise I'd arranged for her.

Booker's Restaurant was a local favorite, according to the reviews, and I was excited to try them out. I'd gotten the chicken and waffles while Isabella went with the salmon sliders. The food was absolutely delectable.

We enjoyed a pleasant lunch with fun conversation that just seemed to keep flowing, comparing our childhoods and laughing at the difference twenty years makes when it comes to some things. I was having such a great time with her and it was a relief not to have to look over my shoulder thinking someone would see us. I couldn't wait for the day when we didn't have to hide anymore.

I paid for lunch and as we stepped out into the sunshine I asked Isabella, "Are you ready for your surprise?"

"Yes!"

Chapter 19 - PAINT + SIP (Isabella)

As we walked up to a small gallery storefront that was just down the street from our restaurant, I saw a sign in the window that said 'Paint & Sip Today!'

"Are we going in?" I squealed.

I had always wanted to go to one of these events where you drink wine and everyone paints along with an instructor. Literally my two favorite things combined! Kendra never wanted to go with me because she was embarrassed by her lack of artistic skills, even though I told her that these things had no skills required.

"Yes we are," Ben said as he held the creaky door open for me.

Excitement absolutely overwhelmed me. I bounded into the old building's front room that had a rickety wood floor and walls lined with colorful paintings on stretched canvases. There was a woman seated at a small counter wearing sharp cat eye glasses and bright red lipstick who was sketching on a scrap of paper. She looked up when the bell on the door jingled with the movement.

"Hello there, are you here for the paint and sip class?" She asked.

The woman was looking right past me, at Ben who was standing behind me. He put his hands on my shoulders quite possessively and replied, "we're both here for the class. I called in our registration, it should be under Simmons."

The woman seemed unbothered by Ben's correction. She slid her glasses down her nose and peered at the old computer screen sitting next to her on the counter.

"Ah yes, here it is, Simmons. You can head down the hall, it's the first room on the right. Class will begin in about ten minutes." She motioned to a doorway shrouded in a tied back curtain. It reminded me of a fortune teller's tent at a carnival.

I led the way down the hall and into the room where there were six other people seated next to blank canvases or helping themselves to a delectable looking charcuterie board. Too bad we'd just eaten or I'd be over there stuffing my cheeks with those gourmet cheeses.

I walked past the food spread and picked a spot toward the front of the room with two unclaimed canvases set up on wooden easels in front of high stools. The room looked a lot like a classroom, with all of the easels facing the front, and a long folding table set up with the teacher's supplies. I noticed a couple bottles of wine chilling in an ice bucket, surrounded by mis-matched glasses. It reminded me a lot of my own collection of glassware at home.

"I knew you'd be a front of the class kind of girl." Ben teased as I hung my purse on the ledge of one of the easels.

"What does that mean?"

"It means you're a goody-two-shoes, Isabella Morgan. Haven't you ever broken any rules?" He straddled one of the stools and spun to face me.

"Absolutely." I crossed my arms. "I'm dating you, aren't I?"

Ben broke into a belly laugh that had the other class members turning to stare at us.

"Touche." He snickered.

I sat down on the stool next to him and looked over our supplies. Each canvas station was set up with one of those empty wine glasses, a few brushes that varied in thickness, a cup of water, and pots of paint that held black, brown, blue, and yellow colors. I tried to guess what we'd be painting just by the colors supplied, but before I could come up with any ideas the woman from the front room walked in.

"Good afternoon, everyone, we're going to get started here in just a minute. But first, let's get some wine flowing in here!" She grabbed a bottle from the ice bucket and ceremoniously popped the cork out while everyone clapped.

The rest of the class members settled onto their stools and our instructor walked around pouring glasses of what I guessed to be a sweet Riesling. I looked over at Ben, who was inspecting his pots of paint.

"Have you ever painted before?" I asked, nudging him with my elbow.

"Nope. Well, walls yes, canvases, no. So this is going to be interesting." He shrugged while picking up one of the brushes which he pretended to paint with.

Even doing an activity he'd never tried before, he didn't look uncomfortable or out of his element. It seemed like Ben Simmons could take on any task with ease. I felt all warm and fuzzy thinking about Ben researching painting classes just for me, especially since he had never painted before. It was a level of effort that I had never seen in a partner before. How refreshing.

The instructor came over and filled our glasses last before returning to the front of the room. She flipped around a large canvas that had been propped up against the wall to reveal an old steam locomotive, chugging along tracks underneath a dark night sky that was riddled with yellow stars. The perspective on the train made it seem as if it was going to burst out of the painting, and I could almost hear the whistle sounding in the quiet night.

"Alrighty! My name is Mindy and I'll be teaching our class. As you can see, today we'll be painting this night train piece! Don't worry, it's easier than it looks."

I turned to look at Ben, only to find he had the same reaction on his face.

"Did you choose this class on purpose because of the painting?" I whispered.

"No, I had no idea that's what we'd be painting!"

"It must be a Simmons thing, then. You guys and your trains." I rolled my eyes jokingly.

Mindy got us started painting the background, guiding us in what colors to use and where to apply them onto the canvas. I was completely in my element, painting my heart out between sips out of my wine glass. The smell of the acrylic paint brought me back to college, where I had taken a few painting classes to fill in my schedule. I remembered long nights in the studio studying still life subjects and mixing paint colors on a large, flat palette.

I have to get back into painting regularly, I told myself. Sitting there in front of a canvas, I realized how much I really missed it.

I was so absorbed in my own painting that when I looked over at Ben's to see how he was managing, I was pleasantly surprised at his pretty night sky. His brow was drawn together in concentration and he leaned close to the canvas, dotting yellow stars into his dark, streaky sky. In my mind I took a snapshot of the moment, wanting to remember it forever.

Nobody had ever put this much effort into planning a date for me and I needed to cherish the feeling.

When the background was completed according to Mindy's instruction, we all took a quick break to allow it to dry before moving onto the train in the foreground. Luckily we were using acrylic paints which dried quickly, unlike the thick and sticky oil paints that I was used to.

I put down my brush and swiveled around to talk to Ben.

"You're doing great!" I said.

While his technical application could have been better, he was doing an impressive job considering this was the first time he'd done something like this. I think he might have had a secret artistic talent hidden deep within him.

Ben turned to look at me and he had the tiniest swatch of blue paint on his cheek. I giggled and wiped it off.

"How embarrassing," he mumbled. "But look at your painting! Wow, Isabella!"

He looked genuinely impressed at my half-finished piece. I shook my head; I did not like receiving compliments for my artwork. Chalk it up to Imposter Syndrome, but I felt like my artwork was never good enough for other people to look at, despite the compliments that people paid on the rare occasion someone did see my work.

I was about to ask Ben how he was enjoying himself when our instructor Mindy came over. She put her hand on Ben's shoulder and exclaimed, "we have a true artist in our midsts!"

Ben shook his head.

"No, no," he said, "Izzy is our artist."

Mindy didn't even look at me or my canvas. Instead she replied to Ben, "have you painted before? Because you're a natural!"

He smiled politely, probably realizing he wasn't going to shake the woman that easily. "Thank you, no I have not."

"Well there's a first time for everything!" Mindy sang before returning to the front of the room.

"Do you always have women hanging off of you wherever you go?" I teased once Mindy was out of earshot.

Ben raised an eyebrow, "No, but like she said, there's a first time for everything."

Another few minutes went by before instruction started up again, and I fell back into an intense concentration while I followed directions. I personally felt like I could have done the painting without instructions, just by looking at the completed work, but this way was fun, too. It was more relaxed.

In what seemed like no time at all, we had all made a train come to life on our canvases. Flirting aside, Mindy was a good instructor and I so enjoyed my time in the class.

In the amount of time it took me to finish off another glass of wine, our paintings had dried enough that we could handle them. Ben and I thanked Mindy and walked out toward the front of the building.

"Hey Isabella?" Ben said.

"Yes?"

He held out his painting with a cheeky grin, "I made this for you."

"Oh how nice of you!" I feigned. "And I just so happened to make this for you!" I held my painting out to him and we swapped.

"I hope you had a good time." Ben said as he held the door open for me once again.

We stepped out onto the sidewalk where the late afternoon sun hung hazily in the sky. I looked up at Ben, the light falling in his eyes turning them a gorgeous chocolatey brown. I took another snapshot in my mind, wanting to remember this beautiful man that stood before me.

I smiled to myself, thinking how lucky I was, then replied, "are you kidding me? This was the best date I've ever been on!"

Ben took my hand and we began to walk down the sidewalk toward the parking garage. "I thought you might like it."

Chapter 20 - *FALLING FOR MY BOSS* (Isabella)

Ring!

I grabbed my phone receiver on the first ring, confident that I knew who was on the other end.

"Good morning Ben," I said in the most professional tone I could muster. It was kind of hard considering I'd seen him naked multiple times at that point.

"Are you ready to plan the rest of this ball with me today?"

Spend the day with my sexy boss? "Absolutely."

"I think we shall take over the conference room today. Meet you there in ten minutes?"

"I'll see you there."

I gathered up my notebook and the folder where I'd been stuffing all of my notes and projects related to the ball. The folder was fairly sparse for an event that was less than three weeks away. It was probably good that we were going to work on the event today.

I had had the most amazing afternoon with Ben yesterday, but I was still itching for more one-on-one time with him. Lately it felt like I just couldn't get enough of him. Every single one of my thoughts were consumed by that man. For the first time ever, I was finding it hard to focus on my work because my mind always wandered back to Ben Simmons.

It was quite a weird feeling, actually, and one that was completely new to me. I found myself choosing my outfits each morning based on what I thought Ben would like. I'd never worked this hard to impress anyone, ever! Yet there I was, straightening my blouse, combing quickly through my hair with my fingers, and popping a mint into my mouth in preparation for our Fall Ball planning sesh.

Ben was seated at the conference table when I walked in, his own folder of paperwork already strewn all over the table, and his brow drawn together in concentration. I pulled up a chair and sat down, making sure that I wasn't placing myself too close to him. The downside to meeting in the conference room was the plethora of windows that allowed anyone walking past to see what we were up to. Maybe that was the point.

Ben read me like an open book. "I thought the windows would keep us accountable."

I nodded in agreement and mentally noted that I needed to work on keeping my thoughts *inside*. But he was right, this event wasn't going to plan itself and heaven knows we don't get much work done behind closed doors.

"So what do we still have to get done?" I asked Ben, hoping the list was short.

His glare said otherwise. At that moment I was looking at my boss, not the man I had been dating. He was actually a bit scary, sitting across from me with a stern look across his face.

"Everything, Isabella. We have everything to get done still."

He handed me a sheet of paper with a checklist of planning to-do's. The list was broken into sections like decor, music, and staffing, with multiple bullet points under each. My eyes skimmed the list all the way to the bottom of the page.

"It's two-sided." Ben said flatly. I could tell he was stressed about the amount of things that still sat unaccomplished.

"Okay, then I guess we better get started. Should we divide and conquer?"

"That sounds like a good idea. I'll work from the top and you work from the bottom, and hopefully sometime soon we'll meet in the middle."

For the next several hours we worked nonstop making phone calls, sending emails, and successfully crossing things off of our list. We even worked through lunch, tossing ideas back and forth in between bites of food. Eventually around 2 pm we hit a midday slump and both made our way to the break room to refill Ben's coffee and my tea.

Apparently Jess had hit the same slump because she was also in the breakroom, brewing hot water in a kettle on a small hotplate for her own cup of tea. When we walked in she looked up at us and smiled.

"How's it going, planning committee?" She asked. Her tea kettle started to whistle and she removed it from the hot plate, pouring herself a cup before offering what was left in the kettle to me.

"Well, we're making good progress, but there's still a lot left." Ben replied.

"Is there anything I can do to help?" Jess asked, plopping a tea bag into the steaming water.

"No, I think just a few more hours of keeping our noses to the grindstone and we'll have the thing pretty much figured out. Although if you'd like to help with setup the day-of, I'd definitely welcome that."

Jess nodded as Ben popped a coffee pod into the machine. As it heated up and Jess and I steeped our tea bags, she stepped a little closer to Ben and lowered her voice.

"So, how's your secret girlfriend going?" Jess asked him.

His face somehow remained calm while I felt my eyes practically bulge out of my skull, and blood rushed to my cheeks. *He told her?*

Ben was careful not to look at me as he answered. "Great."

"That's all you're going to give me?" She whined. "You don't have to worry about present company, Isabella won't tell anyone your secrets, right?"

Jess turned toward me with a sweet as molasses smile on her face. *Did she know?* I was so confused and totally freaking out but decided that playing dumb would be my best bet to getting out of there alive.

"Right." I responded.

"See? So who is she, Ben? If I had an amazing boyfriend I'd want to gush about him nonstop."

Ben raised an eyebrow in annoyance. The awkwardness of the whole situation made me want to melt into a puddle onto the break room floor; Jess was unknowingly asking Ben to talk about me, *in front of me*!

"Of course you would, because you gush about everything nonstop. I'd like to think I hold myself to a more professional standard when it comes to discussing relationships at work." Ben huffed.

"Oh sure, Ben the professional." Jess teased back, completely unphased by Ben's backhanded comment. "I remember when you used to have contests with your brothers to see who could pee the farthest. You don't have to be professional around me!"

Ben's coffee sputtered into his mug, filling the extremely awkward silence. I considered leaving the breakroom but I didn't want Jess to catch on to the fact that I was the woman he was hiding. Instead I turned toward the counter to pretend I was really concerned with fixing my tea just right.

"You know what? *Fine.*" Ben huffed. "My 'secret girlfriend,' as you call her, is quite amazing. We've been having the best times together." His tone softened as he continued, "she's sweet and snarky, hilarious, and creative. She's really, really great."

And even with my back turned to him, I could feel Ben's eyes boring into me.

Jess placed her hot mug down onto the counter next to me and bombarded Ben with a hug. "Aw Ben, I'm so happy for you! I hope I get to meet her one day."

Ben shrugged her off and grabbed his full mug from the coffee machine. "Okay, okay. Izzy and I have to get back to work."

My eyes went wide, once again, but now at the use of my nickname. I turned toward the cousins to gauge the reaction.

"Izzy? I didn't know you went by a nickname," Jess said to me. "I love it!"

Ben ushered me out of the breakroom and back to our workstation. When we were safe behind closed doors he said, "I am so sorry."

He kept a straight face but his eyes showed true remorse for the catastrophe of Jess' break room interrogation.

Nervously I chuckled. "It's fine, she didn't know. But what you said was really nice."

"Even though it was definitely to get her off my back, I still meant it all."

"I know."

"We barely made it out of that one alive." Ben laughed, his facade finally cracking. "This is the first time I've been grateful for her cluelessness. Anyway, back to work we go."

I looked at our list and, working backwards, my next task was to confirm that The Kettle Inn had enough high top tables and chairs onsite already and, if they didn't, coordinate with the other hotels to get them there. I pulled the phone toward me that Ben had temporarily set up in the conference room, and had just begun dialing the number for The Kettle Inn's front desk when Ben said, "*Fuck.*"

I looked up at him, anger creeping onto his face, and followed his gaze toward the wall of windows; on the other side of the glass was Brinley, walking briskly down the hall toward us. She was dressed in scrubs and sneakers, a stark contrast to the waitressing outfit she wore the last time I saw her. Brinley flung the conference room door open and stood in the doorway, commanding our attention.

Despite the aggressive way she burst into the room, her voice dripped like sweet golden honey. "Ben, may I talk to you in your office?"

"No. I'm in the middle of something important." Ben motioned to the spread of papers all around us.

Brinley took it all in then zeroed her gaze on me. The next few moments happened in slow motion, like I was watching a scene from a movie instead of experiencing it in my own body. Brinley squinted at me, then she scowled. Disdain turned into realization as she put two and two together. Then with a wicked grin she said, "No, Ben, I think you might want to come talk to me."

Ben looked at me, then her, and his face went as pale as a sheet. He slowly shoved up from his chair with his hands braced on the edge of the table. He looked as if he was going to pass out any second.

"Excuse me, Isabella." He said through gritted teeth. "I'll be right back."

Ben hurried Brinley out of the conference room and back down the hall. I realized I still had the phone receiver held up to my ear, dial tone beeping, and dropped it back onto the base.

I was sure that Brinley had just realized who I was and that was why Ben looked like his soul had left his body. But what could Brinley want? She was the one who dumped Ben, yet it felt like she wasn't ready to let him go. I was wondering what exactly he'd ever seen in her when my cell phone buzzed in my pocket.

Ben: *Please continue without me.*

I guess I wasn't going to find out any time soon. I worked the rest of the afternoon in the conference room, alone. I got through a considerable amount of the list, securing the tables and chairs, as well as a local musician who agreed to play twenties hits, and then I ensured that The Kettle Inn's ballroom floor would be waxed two weeks before the event.

At five of five I stacked all of our papers up and carried them back to my desk, passing Ben's office. The door was closed and I couldn't tell if Ben and Brinley were in there, or if they'd left to go talk elsewhere.

"I heard that Brinley came to ask Ben to get back together."

Cindy came up from behind me and just about scared the crap out of me. I clutched the paperwork close to my chest to keep myself from flinging it across the floor. I turned toward Cindy, who had a look of deep concern etched into her forehead.

"Is that a bad thing?" I asked, curious to hear the gossip. Of course it would be a bad thing for me if Brinley successfully convinced Ben to get back together, but I wanted to know why Cindy looked so perturbed about it.

"I don't think Brinley was ever good for him." She told me while glancing around to make sure no one could hear. "I knew Ben before they got together and it just felt like, over time, the spark within him died. I've seen it come back lately, though, and I feel like it definitely has to do with the fact that she's out of his life."

I thought about that for a moment. Would it be vain of me to think that *I* had given him his spark back?

Suddenly I felt a warm feeling originate in my gut and spread to my chest, grasping it tight until I couldn't breathe. This was certainly a new emotion for me; jealousy wracked its way through me until I felt utterly consumed by it. Brinley had stolen my man away to try to win him back, and the worst part was that he just went with her! Maybe Ben wasn't feeling the same way that I was…

I wished Cindy a good evening as the clock struck five, and I quickly brought my stack of papers to my desk. I hastily gathered my things and went home, ready to hide under the covers until morning, sulking about the whole situation.

I was falling hard for Ben, but his afternoon made me question if the feelings were reciprocated. Sure, we had great times together, but was I simply a rebound? Or worse, a carrot on a string meant to make Brinley jealous? My anxious mind started playing through the scenarios as my stomach churned like an amusement park ride that never stopped.

Sadly, my plans of throwing an epic pity party were crushed very shortly after changing into loungewear and climbing into bed.

My phone vibrated with the notification of a rung doorbell, and I turned on the live stream to see who was interrupting my moping. Ben stood at my front door, wracking his hands through his hair and shifting his weight from foot to foot impatiently.

"Isabella, it's me." He said to the doorbell, fully aware that I'd be watching. "Can I come in?"

I used the intercom function to reply, "it's open."

By the time I shuffled out to my living room, Ben was already inside pacing the floor. He looked up at me and rushed over, scooping me up into a tight hug.

"What's going on, Ben?" I asked as I wiggled free.

I distanced myself to the other side of the small living room and crossed my arms over my chest. Ben still looked uncharacteristically pale, and his hair was disheveled as if he'd spent the last few hours running his hands through it nervously.

"Brinley's a crazy bitch, that's what's going on."

I narrowed my eyes at him. "Can I get a little more context?"

Ben sat down on my secondhand couch and I followed, perching on the opposite end. Ben took a deep breath before explaining the afternoon's events.

"Brinley came into the office today to try to convince me to get back together with her." He shook his head, "she tried to explain that the distance made her realize what she really wanted, and apparently it's me."

Ben rolled his eyes so hard I was sure he'd just looked at his own brain. "She's moving to Indiana to complete her clinicals for nursing school and asked me to go with her."

"Okay…" I felt my heart thudding in my chest like a hummingbird's wings. Only a second passed, but it felt like a lifetime.

"I said no, obviously, and that was met with a lot of… resistance. When she realized that I was no longer interested in a relationship with her, she started asking questions about…. You. And us."

Ben reached across the sofa and grabbed my hand in his. His usually warm, strong hands felt cool and clammy. Is this what Cindy meant when she'd said that Brinley took away Ben's spark? Because at the moment, he felt more like a cadaver than a living, breathing man.

"Isabella, I'm sure Brinley's not done trying to get me back. She seemed adamant that I should move with her."

"So what do we do? Because you're definitely not going with her, right?"

"Right. I'm done with her. But I'm not sure there's anything we can do besides wait her out. She'll be moving in just a few weeks and then she's gone for good." Ben lifted my hand to his lips and planted a kiss. "I'm sorry I've brought this craziness into your life. I'd understand if you wanted nothing to do with it."

I scooted closer on the sofa until I was practically in his lap. "I'm not going anywhere, Ben. But why does she seem to scare you so much?" I needed to know why she turned a calm and collected man into a nervous wreck.

"I'm not sure, Isabella. She just gives off bad vibes lately, and it frustrates me beyond belief that she would bring this... this *drama* into my place of work. It just sucks."

I placed a hand on his cheek and leaned in slowly, until I found his lips beneath a neatly trimmed mustache. I appreciated him keeping his lips free and accessible, even though I knew he only trimmed his facial hair to keep it from going in his mouth while eating.

Ben quickly responded and matched my movements, eventually parting his lips so I could tease his tongue with mine, stealing a trick out of his book of great kissing tricks.

I took initiative and climbed into his lap, straddling him and wrapping my arms around his neck. I felt at ease knowing that Ben was still mine. I had worried myself into a tizzy for nothing, it seemed, and now I wanted to make sure that he knew what he had right in front of him. We spent the rest of the evening tangled up together in various rooms of my house, making love and experiencing fiery lust. Ben reassured me with his own passion that he wasn't going anywhere with anybody but me.

Chapter 21 - *THE NOTE* (Ben)

T minus twenty days until the Fall Ball and I was feeling the pressure.

Isabella and I had gotten a lot done in the past week, sure, but there was so much stuff that couldn't happen until the day of the event. For example, stocking the mobile bar with ice, setting up chafing dishes for the caterer, and running a sound check for the musician we'd hired, just to name a few. These were the things that stressed me out and kept me awake at night, worrying that I'd forget something and ruin the whole event. The high stakes of Aunt June's developer guest were also weighing on me big time.

Isabella was handling everything really well, though; she was keeping detailed lists of what had gotten done and what was still left to be done. My favorite blonde was killing it at this whole event planning thing and was keeping me sane, inside and outside of the office.

Isabella was really coming into her own with this project. How she managed to balance it with all of the other stuff on her to-do list absolutely baffled me.

Maybe we expand her job title, I thought, *and compensate accordingly, of course*. We host events at our hotels all the time, it only makes sense to have someone handle the event planning.

I had another planning session set up with her for this morning to go over the last few big ticket items on our to-do list. Then I thought I might take her out to lunch. A work-related lunch, obviously. But really, everyone in the office knew that we were paired together for this project by the head honcho herself, so no one questioned the insane amount of time we spent together lately.

Shortly before nine I walked into the office and peeked over toward Isabella's corner, where I knew she was sipping on hot tea, probably already hard at work on her computer. I unlocked my office door and flicked the lights on before stepping in.

I smiled to myself as I looked at the painting that now hung behind my desk. A beautiful rendition of a locomotive, painted by the most beautiful woman I knew. I couldn't wait to see Isabella's reaction when she finally noticed the painting hanging there. I'd noticed that she had my version hung in her living room, on the wall with her family photos.

I sat down in my chair, feeling really great about where we were at in both our personal and work relationships. I almost didn't notice the folded sheet of paper sitting on top of my otherwise tidy desk until I spun around in my chair and was staring right at it.

I picked up the paper and unfolded it slowly, sort of afraid that something would jump out at me. On the unfolded page there was just one short line of typed text that read, 'I'm telling Aunt June.'

No signature, no date, just those four words. I folded the paper back up and shoved it deep into a desk drawer before letting the panic wash over me like an unwanted icy shower. My mind started scrolling through everything bad I'd ever done before I realized that the note could only be referring to my relationship with Isabella.

To me it seemed someone knew about us and was threatening me with it. That had to be it, I hadn't done anything else that woul warrant such a threat. *But who would do this?* And why was my relationship such a threat to someone? A little love never hurt anyone.

I went over those four words in my head over and over again. *I'm telling Aunt June.* Had someone overheard Isabella and I talking during a personal conversation? Or maybe someone had seen us out on one of our dates, despite our best efforts to hide.

The more I thought about it, the more sure I became about one thing. There was only one person who knew I was seeing someone; there was also only one other person here who called June 'Aunt,' and she had just walked into my office.

"Morning Ben!" Jess said, closing my office door behind her and perching in her usual spot. Her shirt was bright pink, like a piece of bubblegum, and she had lipstick on that matched.

Her sunny disposition has bugged me plenty of times in the past, but today it was driving me up the wall. If my hunch was right, I was staring at a jealous, vindictive woman.

"Good morning Jess," I said while narrowing my gaze at her.

Her brows drew together immediately at my tone and her cheery grin disappeared.

"Are you okay?" She asked.

"What do you think?" I shot back, irritation prickling up my spine and into my voice.

Slowly, Jess said, "you definitely don't look okay… what's going on Ben?"

Frustration bubbled up in my chest and I stood up from my chair, slapping my palms onto my desk a little harder than intended. How could my own cousin do this to me?

"I saw the note. What do you have against me and Isabella?"

"Against you and... what? What note? I don't know what you're talking about." Her bottom lip started to quiver and tears welled up in her eyes. Either she was a good actress or...

Shit, I think my hunch was wrong.

I sat back down and took a stabilizing breath before calmly speaking again.

"I got a note on my desk this morning, Jess. You're sure you don't know anything about it?"

She swiped at a tear before it could roll down her cheek. "No, I don't know anything about a note. What on earth did it say to rile you up like this?"

"All it said was 'I'm telling Aunt June.'" I pulled the note out of my desk drawer and handed it to her, watching closely to see her reaction. Unfortunately, she still looked upset that I had shouted at her.

"What does that mean? Ben," she said slowly, "what did you do?"

I exhaled sharply. I knew I was going to have to tell Jess everything, especially after making her cry, which I felt absolutely terrible about now.

"Isabella is the woman I've been seeing. You know how Aunt June feels about inter-office relationships, so we've been keeping it a secret to protect her job here. I think someone knows and is threatening to tell Aunt June now."

"Wow," Jess breathed before breaking into a wide-eyed grin. "I have *so* many questions! How did this happen? You're like a million years older than her!"

I rolled my eyes. "Jess, this is serious! Isabella is going to get fired if someone tells Aunt June! We can't lose her."

"You mean *you* can't lose her?" Jess folded the paper back up and placed it in front of me.

"While I am afraid of what this could do to our relationship, you're also well aware of how amazing she is at what she does. Where else are we going to get a great designer that's willing to work for a small hotel chain in the middle of nowhere Pennsylvania?"

"You have a good point there. So what do we do?"

Before I could answer there was a soft knock on my door.

"Come in," I said, recognizing the knock.

Isabella pushed the door open and popped her head in. Suddenly I worried that my shouting was heard by those out in the cubicle maze, and I grew worried that our ruse was up. Isabella didn't look concerned at all, and my nerves settled back down a notch. But only one notch.

"Are we still meeting in the conference room today?" Her eyes darted to the artwork behind me and her face flushed red.

At the sight of Isabella, Jess broke out her annoying shit-eating grin.

"*Shut it.*" I bit off at her under my breath. And to Isabella, I responded, "yes, I'll be in shortly if you'd like to get started."

"Sure thing," she said, and shut the door as she left.

"I have *so many* questions!" Jess giggled.

—

I met Isabella in the conference room as soon as I could get Jess out of my office. The last thing I wanted to do was explain my relationship with a subordinate to my cousin, yet Jess dragged it out of me anyway. She loved hearing about my new romance, which did help ease my worries just a bit. At least someone was on my side, unlike whoever left the note.

Jess also tried to help me figure out who left it although we didn't get very far with our guesses. What didn't make sense to me was that whoever left it, called June 'Aunt' purposefully, and they had to have had access to my office, which was always locked. The two points didn't add up, so Jess and I tabled the guessing game so I could get some actual work done with Isabella.

"Sorry sweetheart." I said after I closed the conference room door behind me. In the back of my mind I wondered if anybody in the office could read lips... I should be more careful.

"Are you alright? There were some weird vibes in your office earlier."

Isabella cocked her head at me and I couldn't help but chuckle. "Vibes?"

"Yeah, vibes. Like weird energy, ya know?"

"I know what vibes are, it's just such a Millennial word."

Isabella pursed her lips and rolled her eyes before pushing a fat folder across the table toward me.

"Here's everything we've gotten done." She then pushed a much smaller folder forward and smiled, "and here's what we have left! We're making good progress."

"Oh thank God, I don't think I can take much more of this event planning!"

Isabella and I split up the last few tasks and spent the morning tying up loose ends. I had just finished up a phone call with Rachel from Crave Catering to confirm her arrival time when my cell phone buzzed in my pocket.

Jess: AUNT JUNE ALERT!!!!!!

As I looked up from my phone and out the windows, I could see June walking down the hall toward us. She looked prim as ever in a navy blue pantsuit, her gray hair pinned into a pile on the top of her head. Aunt June knocked twice on the conference room door before letting herself in.

"Hello Fall Ball crew!" She crooned. "How is everything going in here?"

I stood up and offered her an old lobby chair where she sat and promptly folded her hands in her lap. If she knew about Isabella and I already she was certainly doing a great job of hiding it. But judging by her demeanor, she had no idea. Aunt June was a no-nonsense woman and would have given Isabella the ax immediately.

"Everything's moving along swiftly," I told her as I sat back in my seat. "We've gotten most everything done besides the stuff that'll be taken care of the day-of."

"Great," June smiled. "What about RSVPs? Do you happen to have an up-to-date list?"

"Here you go," Isabella said softly as she passed her guest list spreadsheet across the table to Aunt June. I forgot how shy Isabella could be when interacting with other people and it took everything in me to stifle a smile at my endearing Izzy.

Of course, the name Aunt June would be looking for was not yet on the list. We hadn't gotten an RSVP from Charles Penbrook yet. I had it on my calendar to follow up with Aunt June's guests next week, including Mr. Penbrook.

June looked over the list, her eyes darting down the page, searching. "Ah, okay, thank you dear. Do you think you could email me an updated list each Friday until the event?"

"Yes, I can do that." Isabella responded.

I then took the opportunity to gas up my event planning partner. "Isabella has been instrumental in getting this ball up and running. She's really impressed me with her ambition." And it was true, Isabella was carrying the Fall Ball on her petite little shoulders. Despite my best efforts, I just couldn't keep up with her.

June smiled at me, already moving onto the next topic in her head. "That's great, Ben. I'm so glad to hear. Do you have time to talk about department budgets?"

"Of course. Isabella, why don't we resume after lunch." So much for getting to take her out today, June would be taking up the majority of my time this afternoon, I knew it.

"Sounds great," Isabella said as she scooped up the folders and hastily exited the room. Aunt June stood up, too, and I followed her out of the conference room back to my office. Time to figure out what she knows.

Chapter 22 - PULLING IT OFF (Isabella)

Nervous jitters rocked through my whole body. The Fall Ball was only four days away and I think we were about to successfully pull it off. I looked over my lists again and again, and one more time for good measure. Everything that needed to be done up to that point was completed; I was so proud of everything Ben and I had accomplished!

Things had been going well with Ben outside of work as well. We'd been spending our weekends together, as well as a lot of our weeknights, too. We had been dating for almost a month and I was absolutely over the moon. Even though it was still a fairly casual relationship, it was the most serious one I'd ever been in and my heart fluttered every single time I thought about Ben.

Since we had to lay low around town we spent a lot of time at each other's homes or out exploring other towns. We'd basically dined at every establishment in Lancaster, and had plans to visit Harrisburg in a few weeks. It was nice being together even when there was a huge part of me that didn't want to have to keep it a secret anymore.

I jumped in my chair when Jess popped her head around my cubicle wall, interrupting my thoughts. "Good morning Isabella!"

"Morning Jess!" I replied, trying and failing as always to match her energy. She looked as bright as ever in a royal blue pea coat that was buttoned up to the nape of her neck.

"I have to run over to The Steamworks Hotel, wanna take a walk with me?" She asked.

"Sure, I could always stretch my legs."

I shrugged into my jacket and followed Jess to the front door. Jess was a social butterfly so I didn't question why she wanted company on her walk. I simply went along, assuming she'd want to discuss the latest episode of whatever corny dating show was on last night.

It usually only took five minutes or so to walk over to the back entrance of the hotel, and while I was glad for the fresh air, I was also happy that it'd be a short walk because it was quite chilly out that morning.

As soon as we stepped outside, Jess began to make friendly conversation. "So, everything is going well with Fall Ball planning?"

"Yeah, we pretty much have everything buttoned up," I told her, wrapping my coat tighter around me.

She walked briskly with her hands shoved into the pockets of her coat.

"You and Ben seem to work well together. There's good vibes between the two of you."

Jess always spoke in a way that was as if she knew all my secrets, and it was quite off-putting. But there was no way she actually knew...

"He's a good work partner." I replied.

"He's also a really great guy." Jess said as she swiped her employee key card to unlock The Steamworks Hotel back door. We stepped into the narrow hallway that led to various administrative offices on the bottom floor. The hallway was empty and quiet, with office doors all closed and fluorescent lights buzzing above us.

"Yeah he seems pretty nice."

Play it cool, Isabella.

Jess stopped walking and turned to look at me. Hushed, she said, "I know about you two, Isabella. Ben spilled the beans a little while ago now."

My mouth dropped open at the same time Jess swooped in for a hug. She squeezed tight before backing up, still holding onto my arms. "I can tell he really likes you." She said, smiling broadly.

For the first time in a while the blood crept up into my cheeks and burned hot. Suddenly my coat felt too warm and I wanted to be back outside in the autumn air.

Hearing someone else talk about my relationship seemed to solidify it. It was a tangible thing now, not just something that hid in the shadows. My heart thudded heavily and a sense of validation settled over me in that tight, dim hallway.

Jess was the most genuine person I knew, and to hear her say that about Ben confirmed the feelings I'd been having, too. She could have easily given me endless crap for dating someone so much older than me, especially her cousin; instead she authenticated our relationship and that was more than I could have ever asked for.

This time *I* pulled *her* in for a hug and held as tight as I could for I knew she wasn't just my supervisor, she was a true friend.

On the morning of Saturday, October 15, I woke up in Ben's bed with my head buzzing and my stomach turning. Today was the day we were going to pull off the Fall Ball, hopefully. I rolled over to find Ben already awake, scrolling through his phone. When he noticed I was up he greeted me with a kiss on the forehead.

"Morning Sunshine."

"Ready to host a ball?"

"I'm ready to do something else first." He mumbled into my hair.

The only thing better than starting your day with a good breakfast was starting your day with good sex. I tilted my head up so our mouths brushed and channeled my jittery energy into a passionate kiss.

I was wearing nothing but an old t-shirt of Ben's and he cupped my breast over the thin cotton. He ran his thumb over my nipple until it was hard with pleasure. He switched to the other breast and the building sensations began to drive me wild. I twisted myself so I was straddling Ben, his erection straining against his boxers between my legs.

I ran my hands over his chest, taught and covered in dark hair. Somewhere in the back of my mind I wondered why the silver hadn't creeped its way down yet, to match the silver sprinkled throughout his hair.

While Ben continued to tease my peaks, rolling them in between his thumb and forefinger, I slid his member out of his boxers and positioned it so I could lower myself onto him, slowly. Ben released a low, guttural groan as I took him in, inch by inch. Impatience got the best of him and his hands finally left my breasts, instead grabbing onto my hips and pulling me down onto him, hard.

I pressed my forehead against his and allowed him to set the pace. It was fast, hard, and oh so pleasurable. My orgasm came on quickly, blinding me with sensation rather than creeping up and exploding like it usually did. Ben thrusted into me one more time before his own eruption overtook him.

After Ben and I had rocked each others' worlds, I got dressed and drove myself home to get freshened up. I showered and threw on jeans and a comfortable sweatshirt, my staple weekend wardrobe. I was due to meet

Ben at The Kettle Inn at 10 am to begin setup for the event that had brought us together.

I walked out my front door to find Ben's truck idling outside of my house. The passenger window rolled down and he yelled out, "get in loser, we're going to put on a ball!"

I had shown him the cult classic movie *Mean Girls* a few days ago and he was still quoting it, much to my amusement. I bounded across my lawn and hopped into my seat in his truck. Ben had also chosen to go casual in faded jeans, an old hoodie, and sneakers that looked older than me.

"You're not worried about us showing up together?" I asked.

"Nope, not today, partner. There are too many other things to worry about and eyes won't be on us."

Things were already bustling at The Kettle Inn when we pulled up. Rachel's catering van was parked near the front door and a small crew was unloading silver trays of pre-prepped food. The decor from Shaw's Nursery looked amazing, with looming corn stalks standing tall against columns on either side of the door. We walked into the front doors and straight back to the event space, where even more moving and shaking was happening.

Tall high-top tables were already spattered throughout the room, and a small stage was being erected in the far corner. I could see out the windows that our mobile bar had been set up and a bundled up Dandy was there stocking the cart with alcohol for his signature drinks. String lights were being hung all around him in the courtyard and I was excitedly awaiting the moment the sun would sink below the horizon so we could switch the twinkling lights on.

"Well," Ben said, taking it all in next to me, "I don't want to jinx it but it seems like everything's right on track."

"I just have to call the musician to confirm he'll be here around one for a sound check," I told him.

"Great, I'll go check on Dandy while you do that."

I stepped out into the hall while Ben turned in the direction of the courtyard. As I held my cell phone up to my ear and spoke with the band's singer, June floated past me adorning yet another colorful pantsuit, tossing me a thumbs up before disappearing into the ballroom.

I finished my call and went back into the ballroom, where through the windows I could see Ben and June talking out in the courtyard. June's back was to me so I couldn't see her face, but whatever they were talking about was making Ben's twist into a most perturbed state.

"Isabella?" A familiar voice echoed throughout the room.

I turned around to see Jess strutting toward me. I almost didn't recognize her in her casual attire of joggers and a matching sweatshirt. Her long brown hair was plopped on top of her head in a voluminous messy bun.

In a few hours we would all head home and change into our twenties-inspired outfits. I helped Ben pick his out last week on a trip to the King of Prussia Mall in Philadelphia, where we had a ton of fun playing dress-up together in the high-end stores. I had taken a different approach to finding my costume, scouring thrift stores to find my own rendition of a flapper dress.

"How's everything going here?" Jess asked. Her smile didn't quite reach her eyes like it usually did, but I was so distracted by everything going on around me that I'd barely noticed.

"So far so good!" I responded.

"That's great! Is Ben around? I wanted to talk to him about something."

"Yes, he's out in the courtyard talking to June."

"Oh, she's already here. Okay then!" Jess clasped her hands in front of her as her eyes darted toward the windows. She was acting quite nervously and it was starting to fray my own nerves.

"Is everything okay?"

"Everything's fine, you're doing a great job!" She reached out and squeezed my arm before vacating the ballroom, leaving Ben outside with their Aunt June.

Well that was weird. But I didn't have too much time to think about it because Rachel needed my assistance with arranging long tables for the serving station. The next few hours flew by without a hitch as Ben and I bounced around the Inn helping to get everything ready. When we left shortly after two, the place was in good shape to be ready for the six o'clock event.

On the drive back to my house Ben held my hand over the center console and we drove in silence. I was buzzing from the excitement of the day while Ben seemed to be off somewhere else, staring out the windshield with a glassy gaze. I hoped it wasn't stress that was affecting his mood.

I squeezed his hand and asked, "is everything okay? You and Jess both seemed off this afternoon."

Ben shook his head. "Just family stuff."

"Ah, okay." I wasn't one to butt in to family drama, as curious as I was. I dropped the subject and figured if it were important enough Ben would tell me eventually.

Ben pulled up in front of my house and leaned over to plant a kiss on my forehead. "I'll see you at the ball."

"You're not picking me back up?"

"If it's okay with you, I think we should arrive separately. I have to get back soon anyway to help greet some of the guests that are checking into the hotel for the night. But you take your time getting ready, and I'll see you in a few hours."

He leaned across the cab and planted a second kiss on my forehead, but this one seemed to be saying 'goodbye.'. My feelings were slightly hurt that he was making me drive by myself, but it was a work function after all. I had to keep my wits about me and trust Ben or I could lose both him and my job.

"Okay," I replied, "I'll see you this evening then!"

As I walked up my front lawn I heard Ben's truck pull away behind me and I felt a tug of sadness. Hiding a relationship was hard, especially in the beginning when you feel like you're constantly floating in the clouds. You want to shout it from the rooftops, not sneak around. I didn't want to have to go to far away towns to get dinner with the man I was dating. But that yearning was constantly butting heads with the level-headed side of me that told me my job was amazing and I should do anything in my power to protect it.

My mind bounced back and forth as I got ready for the ball. Guests were encouraged to dress in costume and I really hoped they all would! I imagined walking into the decorated ballroom, dressed in my twenties garb, and feeling like I was stepping back in time. That was the whole goal for this event; to have the guests step back in time for just one night.

I had a few hours before I had to leave still so I decided to try my hand at some finger waves around my face. My hair was way too long for most of the twenties hairstyles I'd found online but I was determined to make something work.

After an hour or so of fidgeting with hair clips and a ton of hairspray, I had something reminiscent of finger waves happening, and it was going to have to be good enough. I went to look at my ensemble in the full length mirror.

I'd chosen a white satin shift dress from the thrift store and, one night last week, I'd hot glued tassels to the bottom so it would swish and sway like a flapper dress when I walked. I had a silver headband to wear across my forehead and, my best thrift store score to date, short kitten heels in a beautiful emerald crushed velvet.

It was a bit of a modge-podge of pieces, but all together it worked. I completed my look with a faux fur wrap and bright red lips. When it was time to go I gathered up my event planning folder and tossed it into my car's front seat before heading toward The Kettle Inn.

As I arrived at the Inn shortly before six, the sun was low in the sky, shooting orange rays up above the horizon. The front of The Kettle Inn was lit up with the same twinkle lights that were in the courtyard, and the corn stalks shuddered in a slight breeze. I took a deep breath, inhaling the crisp fall air. The smell of leaves and dampness helped calm the butterflies that fluttered around in my stomach.

I walked in the front door and I could already hear faint music coming from the band on stage. As I got closer to the ballroom doors, which were propped open, I could see inside that the lights were dimmed, and tealight candles sat on each high top table creating a moody ambiance. I stepped into the middle of the room and watched the band finish the song that they were playing, taking in the whole atmosphere around me. Before the last note of the song struck I felt a presence behind me.

"Good evening, Isabella."

I turned around to face Ben, who loomed over me looking sharp in a navy blue pinstripe suit and patent leather dress shoes. He'd even tucked the silk scarf I'd picked out into his lapels. He'd slicked some kind of gel into his hair and he smelled of pine and cloves, the scent of his beard oil that made it soft to the touch.

"Hello, Ben. You look dapper."

He grinned and I thought I saw the faintest hint of red creep into his cheeks.

"You don't look so bad yourself." He said.

"Thank you. Is there anything left to do before our guests arrive?"

"Nope, we're all ready for them. We just sit back and relax until people start arriving. Did you see the courtyard yet?"

Through the windows I could see lights twinkling against a purple dusk sky. Ben held out his arm and I paused.

"It's fine, partner," he said softly.

I wrapped my arm through his and he led me outside into the cool evening.

Pumpkins were stacked around on top of hay bales and twinkle lights were strung across the sky like hundreds of stars. Dandy stood manning his bar, prepared with sparkling high ball tumblers and martini glasses. He almost didn't need a coat anymore thanks to the two tall space heaters flanking him, glowing red with heat radiating against the chilly air.

"So what do you think?"

Breathless, it took me a moment to respond. "It really all came together, didn't it?"

"Thanks to you, Isabella." Ben said.

The cool breeze nipped at my cheeks and bare legs, but between Ben and the heaters, I was warm as could be.

"Dandy, could you give us some privacy for a moment?"

Dandy silently nodded at Ben's request and disappeared into the ballroom. I felt like we were the only two people in the world, despite the wall of windows behind us that gave us away to anyone passing by.

Ben leaned in and kissed me slowly, with one hand finding its way under my wrap and onto my waist.

"Ben!" I gasped. My head whipped toward the windows where I could see a few bodies mingling inside already under the dim lights.

"The jig is up," he murmured, still leaned in close. "Aunt June knows about us."

I stepped back, breaking away from Ben's grasp, almost tripping over my own heels on the pavers. "What do you mean?"

Ben straightened up and mindlessly adjusted his silk scarf. "Someone tattled on us and June came today to tell me."

"Jess knew…"

"It wasn't Jess, believe me. I still haven't figured out who it was, but I will."

Suddenly I felt the cold all around me. No amount of heat could thaw the ice that settled into the pit of my stomach. I pulled my wrap tight around me and stammered, "my job?"

"Aunt June didn't flat out say anything about a decision, but it came across a lot like an ultimatum."

Ben stepped toward me and offered his hand but I shrugged away. How could he be so calm?

"What ultimatum?"

"We end the relationship or she terminates your employment."

Ben's words cut through me like a knife, and without responding I found myself moving toward the ballroom. I didn't stop until I was down the hall, inside the women's bathroom, locked in a stall. My head spun and my stomach churned so I closed my eyes to stop it all from moving.

It took me several minutes to steady my breathing before I could actually think about what had just happened. I always knew something like this would probably happen, but I hadn't anticipated how it'd feel. And it was an extra slap in the face that Ben seemed so nonchalant, probably because the ultimatum affected me more than him. His job wasn't threatened, mine was.

And if I chose the job I worked so hard for then I would lose Ben, the one person on this planet who made me utterly and hopelessly happy.

How could someone do this to me? And why was June such a curmudgeonly old bat? Ben and I made an amazing team, I mean, look at this beautiful event! Why *wouldn't* she want us working together? None of it made any sense and I felt my breathing quicken again as my thoughts swallowed me up.

Just as I thought I was going to pass out from lightheadedness, a pair of shoes peeked below the stall door and a knock accompanied a familiar voice. "Isabella?"

I stayed quiet, hoping the voice would go away.

"Isabella I know you're in there. Please come out."

"Go away Jess."

"Isabella, as your friend I want to tell you this will all work out. I know Ben is all torn up about it, too, even though it doesn't show on the outside. I get how upsetting this situation is. But as your supervisor, and I hate to pull this card, I have to tell you to push the personal stuff aside just for tonight. There's someone very important here this evening and I think the fate of *all* of our jobs rests in his hands. We just have to get through tonight, then we'll figure out the stuff with Ben."

I steadied my breathing as I listened to her talk. What did she mean, *the fate of all of our jobs?* I stood up and pushed open the stall door, standing toe to toe with Jess. She enveloped me in a hug and held on for quite some time.

"Thanks, I needed that." I said.

"I'm here for you both, don't think I'm picking sides just because Ben's my favorite cousin." Jess winked. "Are you good to go back out there?"

I glanced in the mirror to make sure nothing was out of place before nodding. Rational Isabella was back in control. Suddenly, I hated that I had made even the tiniest bit of a scene; I worked hard to put the event together and I didn't want this hiccup to ruin all of my efforts. I smoothed my dress and stood up straight in my heels as I marched out of the bathroom and toward the ballroom, Jess following behind me.

The band music was in full swing now, and even from down the hall I could hear the rumbling of happy voices. Late arriving guests were still flowing into the room through the big wooden doors; I followed them, trying to take in the scenery as if I was an attendee myself. Warm lighting illuminated the band on their small stage and bodies stood around them bobbing to the jazzy beat.

People mingled with drinks in their hands around the high top tables, and others held small plates lined with hors d'oeuvres, the delectable aroma of which filled the small space. As the band ended their song our guests clapped lightly, and the hum of conversation grew louder for the few seconds of silence before the next song began.

Jess stepped up next to me, taking in the scene herself. "I've got to hand it to the two of you, this is amazing."

"It was all Isabella." Ben said, walking up to us from wherever he'd been hiding. "I'm sorry," he began.

"We can talk about it later. For now, we are working." I said, without looking at him. I felt my heart envelope itself in a suit of armor, blocking Ben and all of the emotions out. It hurt, but it felt necessary.

Jess smiled and patted my arm before floating into the crowd to mingle. Ben took her place and stood next to me.

"So who is this important guest?" I asked. I deserved to be in the know if this person was so important.

Ben side-eyed me, surprised that I knew about their special guest. His gaze moved across the room and I followed. "The man dressed in a brown suit by the windows."

I glanced over and saw a tall, skinny man, who had to have been in his early fifties. He held an empty highball glass and even from across the room I could hear his laugh as he talked to a small huddle of people. He didn't *look* very important, but looks could be deceiving, I supposed.

Reading my thoughts like he tended to do, Ben said, "Charles Penbrook. He's a developer that Aunt June invited, but Jess and I have yet to figure out why."

"So go talk to him," I said, with a bit more attitude than intended. "You're good at talking to people, I'm sure he'd love to schmooze with the Senior Operations Manager."

He smiled and nodded, glossing over the tone of my voice. "I suppose you're right. Time to go figure out what this man's up to."

Ben left my side and moved through the crowd. I watched as his head bobbed around people until he was spit out onto the other end of the room. He walked right up to Charles Penbrook and held a hand out. As content as I was to watch the event unfold from a distance, I sighed and figured I should probably mingle as well.

The only problem was that I was still me, and 'me' was still terrible at small talk and, really, any basic human interaction. I grabbed a small sampling of food and chose an empty table to stand at, hoping I'd fall under the radar for the next few hours.

Within a few minutes, though, a tall man close to my age stepped up to my table and placed his drink down. He was wearing a slim fitting suit in a dark plum color with a simple white button up beneath his jacket. His dirty blonde hair was combed and slicked back, and I hoped for his sake he didn't wear his hair like that every day.

"Mind if I join you?" He asked. He shot me a smile that oozed with confidence, his light blue eyes shining even in the dim atmospheric lighting.

"Sure," I said, before shoving a deviled egg in my mouth.

Smooth, Isabella, I thought to myself.

The handsome man in front of me waited until I was done chewing before he asked me my name.

"Isabella. And yours?"

"Tyler, since we're only using first names." He winked at me and asked, "what brings you to this ball?"

I realized that Tyler must assume that I was a guest like himself. I briefly contemplated making up a backstory to make myself seem more interesting, but eventually decided to go with the truth.

"I work for the hotel, I helped plan the Fall Ball this year."

Tyler slid around the table to stand closer to me. "Well I must say, you put on a great event. I've attended this ball the past few years with my father and this is by far the nicest one I've been to," he raised his glass, "so props!"

I felt my face flush red and I hoped the lighting hid it. "Thank you. What brings you to the ball? It doesn't look like somewhere a guy like you would usually spend his Saturday night. Not that you look like you'd spend it anywhere else. I'm just saying…" *Dammit Isabella, shut up!*

Tyler chuckled and took a sip of his drink. Judging by the clear liquid in his glass, I'd bet he was trying the Whiskey Sour.

"My dad owns a couple restaurants around here and we always come to network." He leaned in closer until I could smell the whiskey on his breath. "Besides, I heard a certain developer was going to be in attendance tonight, and he's always a good contact to have in your back pocket."

He had to be talking about that Penbrook guy that had Jess and Ben all nervous! Maybe Tyler could give me a little more insight into why this developer was so important.

"What's the deal with that guy anyway?"

Tyler backed up and looked down on me, as if he was sizing me up. He must've decided I was no threat because he eventually answered. "Charles Penbrook. He's a big developer guy who builds a lot of properties in this part of the state. But the thing with him is that every project he takes on is successful. He's the guy to go into business if you want to make bank."

Why is June wanting to go into business with a developer?

He continued, "I heard through the grapevine that he's currently looking for a new project to take on. If you have an idea, now's the time to pitch it because that man will make it happen."

"You said he builds properties, any particular kind?"

"No, he's done everything from shopping centers to hotels, the only thing they have in common is that they're high-end and attract a very affluent clientele."

"That makes sense. Will you excuse me for a moment?"

I stepped around Tyler, leaving him dazed and confused, and weaved toward the back of the room where I'd last seen Ben. Through the windows I saw him standing out in the courtyard with Jess, huddled close to one of the heaters. I rushed out to join them and tell them what I had learned.

"Pretty Izzy," Ben said as I approached, "let me get you a drink."

I shot him a glare at the use of my nickname in public and Jess let out a long, drawn out '*awwwww.*'

"No thank you. Listen, I was just talking to some guy--"

"I saw you two getting close." Ben frowned.

"He's not my type. But seriously, I think I know why June may be interested in," I looked around to make sure no guests were around to hear, suddenly hyper aware of how loud and fast I was talking. Lowering my voice I continued, "I think I know why June may be interested in impressing Charles Penbrook."

"Let's hear it." Ben said, crossing his arms across his chest.

"He builds high-end properties, *like hotels*, and he's looking for his next project. June has been all about attracting more upscale guests lately, like with the room upgrades, so I think she might be buttering him up for a pitch."

"A pitch for a new hotel." Jess echoed.

Ben ran his hand over his beard. "Isabella, I think you might be onto something."

Chapter 23 - *PROHIBITION ERA* (Ben)

We'd done it, we pulled off the 2022 Fall Ball. Isabella was absolutely instrumental in making that night a success, and everyone was still buzzing from the event. If only there hadn't been so much damage done, as well.

Isabella was wrought with worry over her job and she had shut me out for the rest of the weekend. Not the healthiest way to deal with a challenge, but I understood she was upset and needed time. It still hurt, though.

I was hoping that we'd get some kind of resolution today, now that the ball was over. I couldn't stand not talking to Isabella and I needed this all to be past us. At least June had the common decency to allow us to get through the event; she could have fired Isabella right then and there. So, there was that.

I was sitting at my desk the Monday after the ball waiting impatiently for my Aunt June to arrive. She'd called me on my cell early that morning to let me know that she intended to stop in to talk about the event. I also knew that she'd want to talk about myself and Isabella, and I was absolutely ready to plead our case. Hell, I'd leave and go take some other job, I didn't care as long as Isabella was happy.

Even though Isabella wasn't talking to me, I'd left flowers on her desk this morning as a little thank you for being such a great planning partner. The one benefit of this clusterfuck was that I didn't need to hide our relationship anymore, so I had no issues walking right up to her desk and plopping the vase down. I'd heard some of the women in the office cooing over the flowers, so at least someone liked them.

I didn't know what else to do. The situation sucked, there was no way around it. But in a way, this whole mess was inevitable. An office romance was never going to survive June's strict policies, even if I was her favorite nephew. I just hoped she'd have some compassion after seeing how well the event turned out.

Maybe I should have just let Isabella be, I thought.

If I hadn't pursued her in the first place none of this would have happened. She could still be the awkward Isabella hiding in the back of the office, hunched over her beloved computer working away. I did this to her, so I needed to make it right.

My thoughts were interrupted as they were most mornings by my cousin. You'd think I had a standing appointment with Jess the way she strolled into my office each morning, but today I actually welcomed her company. Today she was my only ally. At least, I hoped she still was.

"Good morning Ben, how is everything going today?" She asked as she sat in her chair. I should write her name on it since she utilized it so often.

I leaned back in my own chair and stroked my beard. "So far? Not great."

"Aunt June or Isabella?" Jess asked, with pity in her eyes. She knew today wasn't going to be easy for me no matter how it shook out.

"Both." I replied flatly.

"I saw the flowers you got Isabella, they're beautiful. Did they not work?"

"No, they didn't. I'm not sure what to do about her." I looked down at my desk, feeling the weight of her rejection. "I just want her to talk to me."

Jess reached forward over my desk and put a comforting hand on my arm. "Don't worry about her, that will all work itself out. I know she'll come back to you. What's going on with Aunt June though?"

"She's coming in today and I don't know--"

"Good morning nephew and niece!"

"Hi Aunt June." "Good morning Aunt June." Jess and I both said at the same time.

Our elderly aunt stood in my office doorway, prim and proper as always. Today's pantsuit was a mossy green, and she wore a sparkling brooch to match. Sometimes I felt like my aunt was a character on *The Golden Girls*, at least that's the feeling her style gave off. Her silver hair was tucked into that signature pile on top of her head that didn't move as she walked into the room.

"How are you doing today, Jess?" She asked, smiling at her only niece.

"I'm doing well! And with that, I'll leave you two to your meeting." Jess dashed out of the room back to her desk. June took her seat because, unsurprisingly, nobody liked utilizing the plastic chair next to it.

Aunt June crossed her hands in her lap as she usually did. "And Ben, how are you?"

I knew she only asked out of courtesy. She damn well knew how I was doing. When she came to talk to me before the ball began, I made it clear how I felt about Isabella. But that was the thing with June Simmons, she had been such a stern business woman for so long that I think she forgot how to *feel*.

I responded to her, struggling to mask my emotions, "I'm fine today, and yourself?"

"I'm really great, Ben. You pulled off the Fall Ball quite successfully, so congratulations!"

"It was mostly Isabella's work." I had to give credit where credit was due.

But she brushed me off. "Regardless, the event was a success. And I have some good news to go with that success if you're interested."

Was she finally going to tell me what this was all about? Or maybe she changed her mind about Isabella? She didn't wait for me to respond before telling me her news.

"I'm going to have the board give you a nice bonus for a job well-done."

Not what I was expecting. I didn't need a bonus, I needed Isabella to be happy. I was about to say so when Aunt June continued talking.

"You see, I needed this event to go well so I could impress a developer."

"Charles Penbrook?" I asked impatiently.

"Why, yes, he's the one. He's looking for a new project and I had a pitch for him, which I delivered to him just before coming here."

"What were you pitching?" I was ready to finally get this out of her because it had been tearing me apart inside for weeks on end. I noted in the back of my mind that I had to give Isabella props for her spot-on detective work, though.

"A new hotel." June said.

A new hotel? Isabella was literally spot-on with her prediction. Only my Aunt, at the age of 71, would want to build a brand new hotel. I was starting to think that maybe she'd jumped the gun on retirement.

I was still looking to get more information out of June, though. "I'm just curious, why couldn't you tell me this before?"

"Call it superstition but I didn't want to talk about the idea until I knew it could happen."

"I see. Well I'm glad it's all working out."

June nodded. "Yes, it will be good for all of us. You don't have to answer me now, but if you're interested, this project is yours to oversee."

That was a lot to think about, but for now it was time to broach the subject that had turned my life upside-down the past couple of days. I was hoping that, while June was still high on the success of her pitch, she'd be more forgiving of Isabella and myself.

I took a deep breath and leaned forward in my chair. "So about Isabella…"

"You know I want you to be happy, Ben." Her tone told me all I needed to know but she continued anyway. "I thought the last one was it for you, but obviously not and that's okay. If you're happy with this one now, then I'm truly happy for you. Regardless, I have to do the right thing."

She stood up and straightened her jacket. "Rules are rules, Ben. I'll be instructing Jess to let her go at the end of the day. I'm sorry.

And without another glance, she turned toward the door and left.

I hadn't heard from Isabella all day. She ignored my texts and emails, and I didn't want to embarrass her by going over to her desk, so I sat with the radio silence and festered. She and I both knew what was coming and it killed me that she was going through this all alone. I wanted to be there to comfort her, to tell her it'll all work out. Actually, I'd said as much in my texts and emails that she was ignoring, but I hoped it all offered at least the tiniest amount of solace.

Shortly before five, Jess came into my office. Instead of the cheerful stride she usually rocked, her movements were slow and somber as she lowered herself into her chair. She was wringing her hands and she looked like she was about to cry.

"Welp, I did it."

I had considered offering to do the deed myself, maybe I could dampen the blow somehow. But the responsibility fell on Jess as Isabella's direct supervisor, and as June said, *'rules are rules.'*

I felt bad for Jess, she felt emotions *so hard* and I knew this was a difficult task for her.

"How did she take it?" I asked, desperate for some kind of update on my Isabella.

"I think she'd been preparing for it because all she said was 'OK,' and when we went back to her desk, her things were already packed into a box. A very small box, at that. And she didn't seem to want the flowers." Jess dropped her face into her hands. "Ben, I feel *so bad*. And we're never going to replace her! This sucks."

"This does suck, Jess. Did she already leave?" I glanced at the time on my phone wondering if I could catch up to her.

"Yeah, I walked her out to her car. Are you gonna go after her?"

I shook my head. "No, I have something else to take care of first."

Chapter 24 - HEARTBREAK + UNEMPLOYMENT (Isabella)

I stared down into my glass, swirling the pale yellow liquid aimlessly, and took a swig. The glass clinked as I sat it down on my counter a little too hard. Drowning your feelings in fermented grapes was never a good way to cope with your problems, but it had only been an hour or so since I'd been fired and I needed the escape. Kendra, who was standing next to me in my little kitchen, wrapped her arms around me.

"You don't need them Izzy. You can go anywhere, you're so talented!"

I'd called Kendra on Sunday evening after everything from the weekend finally sunk in. Between relationship issues and all of the stuff going on with June and Simmons' Hotels, I had been an absolute mess when it all hit me. Like the best friend she was, Kendra took off from work early today and was in my house waiting with wine and chocolates when I got home from being fired. I hadn't given her a key but I knew better than to ask how she'd gotten in.

I couldn't believe that I didn't have a job anymore. I knew it was coming, but that didn't take away the sting or the embarrassment. Jess had been real nice about it, taking me into one of the conference rooms so no one would overhear. Not that it mattered, since everyone in the office knew what was happening by the time Jess actually did the deed.

Jess looked so sad when she told me, I felt bad for *her*. She was never meant to get caught up in all of this. I felt like I'd let her and the company down; had I not started dating Ben I wouldn't have been forced to give up my job. It was all my fault. Why did I have to have a crush on my stupid boss?

I was also upset that after everything, I hadn't heard a single thing from Ben since I'd walked out of the building. Did he even care? Or was I just a fling? He didn't even bother to show up here to comfort me, not that I wanted to see his face at the moment.

I rested my head on Kendra's arm.

"What's the next step?" she asked.

"I think I'm going to go stay with my dad for a little while while I figure out my next steps."

"Where does he live now? I know he's moved around a lot for his work but I can never remember where he ends up."

My dad worked for an electrical company and traveled all over the state repairing lines, installing new ones, and whatever else electrical contractors did. When my mom was alive he was just an electrician, but after she passed and I moved out, he took this job with the state and moved to a new location every couple of years. He was currently staying a few hours from here in the northeastern part of the state.

"He's up in the Pocono Mountains." I reminded her. "I think it'll be good for me to get away and spend some time with him."

She patted my hair. "I'm going to miss you though!"

"I'll come back, I just need some help figuring out what I'll do when I *do* get back. I'm going to have to find a new job pretty quickly if I want to keep paying rent here, so I can't be gone too long."

I glanced around at the house that had been my home for over two years. I loved having my own space that I worked hard for, and I couldn't stand to lose it. How embarrassing would it be to lose my job, my boyfriend, *and* my house?

Out of the corner of my eye I caught a glimpse of Ben's painting, hanging up on my wall next to pictures of my family and friends. Seeing it made me sad and angry so I squeezed my eyes shut to stop the tears.

"You'll get back on your feet in no time, I'm sure of it." Kendra said.

She was always a good friend to me, despite her flaws. And she was really the only one who knew about this from the beginning; she'd been my confidant from the start. I wasn't mad at her for pushing me to explore my feelings for Ben. It was quite the opposite, I was so glad that, even if this was all over, she'd given me the confidence to go for it.

I finished off my glass and put it in the sink. I wasn't even in the mood for wine, which is how I knew I was in a real funk.

"When are you leaving? I can stay with you for a couple days if you need." Kendra offered.

"Thank you, but that's okay. I'm going to call my dad tomorrow and hopefully I'll be with him by dinner time. But I'll definitely keep you updated."

"Okay Izzy, whatever you need."

This sucked. Everything sucked. I hated feeling like this, sad and uncertain.

I didn't feel like eating so Kendra left around dinner time. I may have been in a slump but that didn't mean she should also skip the meal.

After Kendra left, I shut off all the lights, slinked into bed and pulled the covers up around me. I pulled out my phone and mindlessly scrolled through all the texts Ben had sent between Saturday evening and this afternoon. He had tried reaching out to make things better but I wasn't ready to talk to him. But now that I was an absolute wreck, it was nothing but silence.

It was probably all my fault, I probably shouldn't have ignored him because now he was done trying. Why did I keep messing things up?

I opened the photo album on my phone where I kept photos of Ben and I. There were less than ten pictures all together, but each told a story of our budding relationship. Like the picture I'd taken of the appetizers at Crave Catering, just before we'd devoured them on what I consider to be our first date. That photo brought back the feeling of fluttering butterflies and awkward chattering. The beginning of our relationship, where neither of us was really sure what was happening, we just knew that it was exciting and new and forbidden.

Then there was a selfie I took on the ride to our second date at the French restaurant. Ben was in the background, scowling at a bit of traffic that we'd run into; he was sure it was going to make us late for our reservation. This one reminded me of our first time being together; my first time with a real man. That was a night I'll never forget.

Next was a selfie of the two of us in bed, swathed in wrinkled sheets after one of our 'romps in the hay.' Then, a picture I had snuck of Ben during one of our planning sessions. It was a slightly blurry snapshot of him at the conference room table, concentrating on a form in front of him. Next I had a picture of myself and Mollie playing in his yard, one that he'd snapped and sent to me thinking I might want to make it my profile picture on Facebook. He said the sun shining around me made me look angelic and that everyone liked a good dog pic.

And the last one in my camera roll was of Ben and I, just a couple days before the Fall Ball. We were dressed up nicely at a restaurant, waiting to be seated at our table. There was a mirrored wall that we stood next to and posed for the impromptu picture. Ben was beaming, teeth peeking out beneath his mustache, and his arm was wrapped around me. We looked so happy, so carefree.

Tears strolled down my cheeks. I let the dark thoughts take over and told myself that I was done for. Simmons' Hotels dumped me and now Benjamin Simmons no longer wanted anything to do with me. I'd screwed it all up and now I had nothing.

I put my phone down on my nightstand and pulled the covers up even further. Curled into a ball, I allowed myself to sob for the first time, letting all my emotions wash over me. I cried and cried late into the night until no more tears would come, at which point I drifted into a restless sleep, alone in my bed for the first time in a long time.

Chapter 25 - CONFRONTING THE DEVIL (Ben)

I wracked my fingers through my hair the whole drive; I was starting to think it was a nervous habit of mine. My mind kept going back to something Aunt June had said in our meeting today that gave me an idea of who may have tipped her off about Isabella and myself. It all made sense, really. There was only one person who wanted to see me suffer, and she was now living in an apartment above a Chinese restaurant on Main Street, getting ready to move to Indiana.

I'd considered foregoing this confrontation and heading straight to Isabella's house after work, but I had a gut feeling that she wanted nothing to do with me right now. *I* didn't even want anything to do with me right now. I felt like this whole situation was my fault, like I could have been more careful to protect her. I didn't even know how to begin to fix things with Isabella. So instead, I was going to channel all of my frustrations into one big bundle and take them out on the woman who ruined the best thing I ever had.

I parked my truck down the street a bit and walked to the old iron door that was set back into the wall next to the Chinese restaurant. At this time of year it was already dark, and this unlit door seemed a bit sketchy for a woman to be living there alone.

I looked up; lights seemed to be on up on the building's second floor, so there was a good chance that the she-devil was home.

From the sidewalk I texted Brinley.

Ben: I'm outside. Can I come up?

I didn't receive a response, but within a couple of minutes I heard the lock clunk on the other side of the door, and it creaked open to reveal Brinley standing in the dingy stairwell swathed in pink scrubs. Her hair was swept back into a ponytail and her face was void of any makeup.

"Well hello, Ben. Have you decided to take up my offer?" She leaned against the railing a few steps up, looking down at me.

"Am I allowed in?"

Her mouth twisted into a wicked grin that made me want to turn on my heel and march right back to my truck. I didn't need to deal with her warped games right now. But I was there for a purpose and I needed to keep that in mind, so I decided to play along just for a little bit until I got what I needed.

She stepped aside. "Sure."

I'd actually helped her move into this apartment; carrying her furniture and boxes up the stairs was a real bitch but it was the least I could do to help. I had offered to help her find a better apartment outside of town but she wanted to do it on her own, so I didn't feel bad that all of her stuff now permanently smelled like lo mein.

At the top of the dark stairwell was the door to her apartment, sitting ajar. I pushed it open and stepped inside, standing just inside the doorway to make it clear that I had no intentions of staying long. Brinley followed me in, clicking the door shut behind her and plopping down on her secondhand couch.

A few cardboard boxes were scattered around the apartment, reminding me that she'd be moving out of state very, very soon.

Good, be gone with ye witch. Maybe that was a little harsh, but this woman had been causing nothing but trouble lately. I'd be happy when she was finally gone and could no longer cause havoc on my life.

"Have a seat hun, what's on your mind?" She patted the cushion next to her and crossed her ankles.

"I'm good right here. I did want to talk, though."

She narrowed her eyes. "I won't talk unless you get comfortable. It's the least you could do."

I rolled my eyes and sat next to her, as far away as the small couch would allow. Unfortunately the witch was sitting in the middle of the couch, so even pressed all the way up against the couch's arm, our thighs were still touching. She knew what she was doing, and so did I. Her tricks weren't going to work on me.

"Alright, time to talk."

"Would you like a drink?" She asked, motioning to the kitchen and ignoring my prompt, drawing out my visit as long as she could. I'm sure she was happy to finally have me as a captive audience.

"No."

She shrugged. "Suit yourself. So what is it you'd like to talk about?"

"How did you get into my office?"

Her eyes went big and she stuck out her bottom lip. "What do you mean?"

She was already frustrating me. I knew that she knew exactly what I was talking about. She had to get into my office somehow to leave that note, and I wanted to know how she did it. Probably bribed a custodian or something.

I took a deep breath to calm myself. This conversation wasn't going to get anywhere if I lost my temper; that's what she wanted. So instead, I decided to try another angle.

"Isabella was fired."

Brinley picked at an invisible string on the couch's arm. "Oh, who was that? Was she the one who cleaned the bathrooms? Always a dedicated worker."

"You know damn well who she is. She was fired because of you."

"No, she was fired because of *you*." She stated matter of factly, turning to look me in the eyes.

She was pretty much right, and those words stung to hear, but at least we were on the same page finally.

"You're the one who tattled, like a whiny little child."

She rolled her eyes. "I simply informed the boss of your company that there was a violation of her policies happening right in the office."

Heat bubbled up in my core and I struggled to stifle it. This woman really knew how to push my buttons better than anyone else. I did not like being messed with.

"You used your relationship with my family to ruin Isabella's career." I was shaking with anger and my voice began to get louder. "June doesn't even work there anymore! She wouldn't have known, and we could have figured out some way around the policy! You just couldn't stand to see me happy with someone else."

Brinley put her hand on my knee and I jerked my leg away.

"Ben, I'm not worried about anyone else. The fact that you're here right now tells me that you're always going to come back to me, because even on the worst day of your little girlfriend's life, you came here."

I jumped up from the couch, tired of biting back my words and sick of her twisting reality to fit her narrative. "I'm never coming back to you. I'm here to ask why you keep insisting on meddling in my life! *You* dumped *me*, which I'll admit wrecked me for a while, but I moved on because I realized that you were never worth my time or energy. You are toxic and I'm frankly glad to be rid of you. But then you had to come slithering back into my life and ruin the one thing that made me truly happy, my relationship with Isabella! You are utterly insane if you think I will *ever* come back to you."

Brinley shot up from the couch and stood toe to toe with me, anger and rejection radiating off of her skin. "No, Benjamin, *you're* insane if you think dating that young bimbo was ever going to work. I'm sure she was a great rebound for your ego but face it, that relationship wasn't meant to last. If I didn't end it, something else would have. Really you should be thanking me for giving you an easy out."

All I could see was red. Did she really think she was doing me a favor by ratting me out to my elderly, retired aunt? Brinley was absolutely out of her mind. It was time for me to go before I did something I regretted.

"Whatever you say. I'm leaving." I scooted around her toward the door. I was reaching for the knob when she tried one more attempt at luring me back. Her voice was calm again, sweet and sultry which I could now see was a trick she'd pulled on me for a long time. There was nothing sweet or sultry about that woman.

"I leave in a week, you know."

I stopped without turning to face her, my hand resting on the doorknob ready for my escape. "So?"

"You can still come with me."

"In your dreams."

Chapter 26 - **NEXT STEPS** (Isabella)

The three hour drive up to the Pocono Mountains was quite peaceful; I'd taken mainly back roads, winding through the rolling Amish fields of Lancaster and eventually into the dense woods that dominated the northern part of the state. Most of the leaves on the trees had turned and fallen, leaving only the green pines and Rhododendron bushes in between bare gray branches.

It was a cool, damp fall day, mirroring my mood as if Mother Nature knew my struggles. My wipers dashed away the raindrops that hit my windshield as I did the same to the occasional tears rolling down my cheeks.

I should have been sitting at my desk, not pulling onto my father's street. I should have been chit chatting with Jess or grabbing lunch with Ben, yet there I was, hours away from them and my problems.

And why hadn't Ben reached out yet? It was like he didn't care; maybe it was only fun when we were sneaking around, and now that we were caught I was old news. Who knows. All I knew was that I felt like I had gotten the short end of the stick, and I had no sense of what was next for me.

I pulled into the driveway of my dad's rental home and shut off the GPS on my phone. I'd been to this house once before when he'd just moved in. I didn't let myself grow attached to the homes he lived in because of how often he moved for his job. Instead, I treated them like little vacations, popping in and out of new places and discovering each town he passed through.

This A-frame style home he was renting reminded me of a quintessential rustic cabin in the woods, with its high beams and wooden slat exterior. I expected to peek around into the backyard and find deer grazing on patches of grass, or a black bear roaming through the trees. My dad had seen bears there before, and I was secretly hoping to catch a glimpse of one before they all hid away for winter's hibernation.

That's what I wanted to do, hide away. In a sense, that's what I was doing by coming here. Escaping my problems in Strasburg and distancing myself from the one who hurt me.

I stepped out of the car, zipping my down jacket up to my chin. I walked up the slick black driveway to the front door, where I hit the doorbell and waited. Not even ten seconds went by before my dad threw open the door and grabbed me in a bear hug that probably rivaled the local black bear's grip.

"Izzy. How are you?"

He smelled of aftershave and Irish Spring. He must have just gotten home from work and jumped into the shower to clean up before I got there. My dad was happy to have me come visit so I'd timed it so I would arrive just after his workday ended. He took the next few days off to be with me and I was really looking forward to it.

"I've been better." I said into his shoulder. He pulled back and looked me over.

"Fair enough, that was a stupid question. Come in and get comfortable."

I had to admit, for someone as nomadic as my dad, he sure did have a comfortable space. Brown worn leather furniture filled the living room and framed a large stone fireplace which was crackling with a small fire. There was a wooden coffee table sat on a plush rug that looked like it had probably come with the rental, definitely not my dad's style. He even had a few family photos sprinkled about, including one of my mom who had passed a few years ago from Breast Cancer. I could sure use her advice right now, but my dad was a good second choice.

I kicked off my boots at the door and shrugged out of my coat, which my dad took and draped over the back of a chair. I followed him into the kitchen where he had an empty mug set out on the counter for me.

"Coffee, tea, or hot cocoa?" He asked, opening a cabinet above the stove.

"Ooh, cocoa would be nice… you know how to make hot cocoa?" I joked.

"Har har, of course I do. You don't get very far in life not knowing how to make powdered hot chocolate."

My dad had a sweet tooth just like me; actually, he was probably the reason I craved sweets as much as I did. I remembered his go-to late night snack would be warm chocolate chip cookies and cold milk for dunking. My mom's cookies were always his favorite. Years ago I had gotten him a pair of Cookie Monster pajamas for Christmas as a joke and he'd worn them religiously until they were nothing but rags.

I watched my dad as he warmed milk on the stove. He looked older than the last time I'd seen him, which scared me. I'd noticed that he'd given up on maintaining the few hairs he had left and had just shaved his head bald. It was a good look for him but it accentuated the deep lines that ran across his forehead.

My dad was an avid runner and still looked like he was in great shape, but he moved slower as if his joints needed some oil; like the Tinman, I imagined. He was dressed in lounge clothes, ratty sweatpants and an old company sweatshirt. His hands and face were still tanned from the many hours he logged outside each day.

"So," he said, turning away from the stove while the milk heated, "ready to talk?"

"I guess…" When I called my dad yesterday I hadn't told him what had happened, just that I needed his help dealing with some problems. Like the awesome dad he was, he didn't ask any questions besides, 'when will you be here?'

"Did you drive all this way to guess or did you come for help working through the problems?" He used his stern dad tone, one that used to make me shake in my boots when I was in trouble. I knew that this time, though, he was just trying to help me.

"I came for help." I replied, looking down into my empty mug.

"Alright, then let's start at the beginning."

He turned back to the stove to take the pan off the burner. He dumped two packets of hot cocoa mix in and stirred while he waited for me to begin.

"Well, I was dating this guy--"

"Boy troubles!" He exclaimed while he grabbed another mug out of the cabinet. He poured himself some hot cocoa then emptied the rest into my mug.

"Dad!"

"Okay okay, sorry. Continue. No more interruptions from me."

I took a sip before continuing. "The guy I was dating, uh, happened to be my boss--"

"He just so happened to be your boss?" He asked incredulously.

"You said no more interruptions!"

He eyed me over the rim of his mug while he took a sip of the steaming mix, obviously not ready for whatever boy troubles I had to tell him about. "Fine, proceed."

"He was my boss, and technically it was against company policy for us to date, but we did it anyway. We were put on this big project together and we were just spending so much time together and it just kind of happened. Well anyway, we thought we were being sneaky but someone found out and told his Aunt, who like owns the whole company, I think. Well, she's retired but she's still in charge, if that makes sense. Anyway she found out and she had me fired, and now I haven't heard from Ben and I lost my job which I loved…"

I looked down into my mug again, tears streaming as I said everything out loud.

My dad walked around the counter and put his arms around me. "Oh, Izzy, I'm sorry about the job." He paused, "and the guy, I guess."

"I'm not sure what to do about either, now."

My dad took a gulp from his mug while he pondered. A drop of hot chocolate clung to his gray goatee until he swiped it away with a finger.

"Well, that kind of job you had, I feel like you could work anywhere. You can find another office, or probably even find something remote. You could work *from* anywhere! No need to tie yourself down to a desk if you didn't want to."

"That's true, and I know you're right, it just stings having been fired. How do I even put that on my resume?"

He shrugged. "We'll worry about that another day. Just whenever you're ready, take a look at some job listings. Get a feel for what's out there, even if you don't apply to any right away. In the meantime if you need any help paying your bills you let me know."

"Thanks dad, I should be good for a little while."

"And about this Ben guy... tell me about him." He squinted his eyes at me. Despite his reluctance, I know he was trying hard to help. I'd never had to come to him with 'boy troubles' before, so this was new territory for both of us.

My dad motioned toward the couch and we both moved to sit near the fire with our cocoa. I let the warmth of both wash over me and calm my nerves a bit.

"Well, he's always really upbeat and nice and really good at commanding a room, which is why I liked having him as a boss. His work ethic reminded me a lot of yours, the way he always made sure things got done. But while we were planning the Fall Ball I got to see the sensitive side of him and, I don't know, I guess I kind of fell for him."

"What's a Fall Ball?"

"Exactly what it sounds like, a ball held in the fall."

He chuckled. "Alrighty then. So where exactly did things go wrong?"

"Well at the ball he found out that someone had told his Aunt about us--"

"The Aunt who owns the place but is retired?"

"Exactly. So he found out that she knew and he told me, but like he didn't seem bothered at all by it, which made me upset."

"And why would that news have upset him?" My dad sounded like a detective in an interrogation room, trying to get every detail of the story before he came to a conclusion.

"Because we both knew that if his Aunt June found out, she would fire me. The fact that I was losing my job because of the relationship should have upset him!"

My dad paused for a moment and scratched his scruffy chin as he mulled over my words. I appreciated how much thought he was putting in to his responses. Not every dad would drop what he was doing to help their grown daughters with 'boy troubles.'

"Now, I don't like taking the side of some strange man dating my daughter, but what if he was hiding his emotions for your sake?" His voice softened, "when your mom was sick I felt so many emotions -- anger, sadness, frustration, but I never let her see any of it because I knew she was fighting her own battle; she didn't need to share the weight of my emotions, too. Maybe that's what Brian was doing."

"Ben." I corrected.

"Right. But do you get what I'm saying?"

"I do, and I see your point, but then why haven't I heard from him yet?"

"That I do not know."

We sat in silence for a bit drinking our cocoa and staring at the flames dancing in the hearth. I missed talking to my dad every day. I had moved home after college when my mom was sick and spent every evening with the two of them. Despite the challenges of that time, it was a chapter of my life that held some of my fondest memories. Being back with my dad made me feel like we were a family again; like my mom might be laying in the bed upstairs if I went up there to look.

It also made me sad to be there with him, too. I moved out shortly after Mom passed and I still felt guilty, like I'd left my dad to live and grieve on his own. It was a guilt I carried with me every day and that's the one thing I would do differently if I could go back. I know my dad could have used my support.

Regardless, it was nice to be with him now.

"How did you know Mom was the one?" I asked after a while.

Still staring at the fire, I saw my dad smile. "Easy, she was a good cook."

"Really? That's all?"

"At first, yeah. I fell for the Italian food and obviously for the Italian woman behind it all, too." He laughed, "she cooked for our first date and I swear that was all it took. She was funny, and smart, and I knew she was the one I wanted to spend forever with." My dad side-eyed me. "Why do you ask?"

"I was feeling like maybe Ben was 'the one' before all of this happened."

"Okay, well does he make you happy?"

"Yes, incredibly."

"Does he treat you right?"

"Very much so."

"Do you love him?"

I answered instantly. "Yes." Then I paused for quite some time. I'd never said that out loud before and it felt weird, but right at the same time. Heat flushed my cheeks and the fire suddenly felt very hot. My dad chuckled at my reaction to my own realization.

"He must be some special guy if he's making my Isabella blush like this!"

I laughed despite myself; it was just like Ben to make me blush from over a hundred miles away. "Yeah, he's something special, alright."

"I'll have to take that man out for a beer." My dad exclaimed. "He is old enough to drink, right?"

"Yeah er, that's the thing, dad, he's forty-five."

"*He's what?*"

Chapter 27 - *MOUNTAIN RETREAT* (Isabella)

Early Thursday morning I awoke in my dad's guestroom to the sound of a loud thud. I peeked at my phone; it was almost 3 am. A couple of seconds went by before I heard another identical thud, coming from somewhere outside.

Half terrified and half curious, I wrapped myself in the throw from my bed and padded quietly down the hall. Descending the staircase, I moved slowly in case there was someone in the house.

One more thud and some scraping led me to the kitchen, to a large sliding glass door that overlooked the back and side yards of the house. I slowly approached the door and peered through the glass, pressing my nose against the icy cold surface. Suddenly, out of the corner of my eye, I saw a large figure moving in the shadows, causing my heart to jump into my throat. I was frozen in fear.

My breath fogged up the glass and I swiped away the condensation to squint into the dark. I saw the figure move slowly into the backyard, activating the motion sensing flood light that my dad had installed for security. When the yellow light flashed on and washed over the grassy space, I could see an enormous black bear, lumbering away from the house and toward the woods on the edge of the property. His bum swayed with each heavy step and his little nub of a tail bobbed up and down behind him.

"Damn it was that a bear?" My dad called out from the top of the stairs. He was shirtless and half asleep still, rubbing his eyes with balled up fists.

"Yeah, a huge one!" I replied, in awe at the creature.

"Did he make a mess? I don't want to clean that crap up again." My dad grumbled.

I looked back outside and noticed the trash cans that were laying on their sides. That would explain the thumping I heard up in my room. A couple trash bags had been pulled out of the cans but they weren't torn open, meaning my dad would have a painless cleanup in the morning. I guess nothing in the bags was appetizing enough for Mr. Bear so he decided to move on without any altercations.

"No, it's not bad. Just have to pick the cans up." I told my dad.

He mumbled something unintelligible before disappearing back toward his bedroom.

I peered out the door one more time, scanning along the dark tree line where the bear had wandered off to. When the flood light shut off a few minutes later, I pulled my blanket tight around me like a cocoon and went back up to bed.

At 6 am I woke up again, light just beginning to peek through the tree branches outside. My room was filled with a pale gray light that made the room feel peaceful and still.

My body was still conditioned to wake up for work and even without my alarm, I had been getting up around this time each morning. It was like a slap in the face, my circadian rhythm mocking me since I no longer had anything to wake up for.

I sat up in bed and looked out the window, wondering if I had really seen such an enormous animal last night, or if it had all been a dream. It had been huge and cumbersome yet quiet and graceful at the same time, the perfect example of opposites colliding.

I watched as the sun slowly rose into the sky, painting it with streaks of orange and pink before popping up over the horizon. Tree branches sat like black veins against the pastel sky and I took it all in, imagining myself capturing this view in oils. *Maybe I could paint more now*, I thought.

That idea set the tone for my day, I decided. I was going to look at the bright side of things instead of focusing on all the negatives. For example, I wasn't at work today but I *was* spending much-needed quality time with my dad. That was for sure a positive.

By the time I wandered downstairs, the sun was shining bright in a blue bird sky and my dad was already downstairs in the kitchen cooking breakfast. Bacon and eggs, his specialty.

I settled onto a stool and watched him cook.

"What would you like to do today?" He asked, hearing me sit down.

My dad was dressed in faded jeans and a thermal top, with worn-in house slippers on his feet. He used a pair of tongs to grab some bacon out of the pan and place it onto a paper towel lined plate to drain. Then he turned to me and smiled.

I certainly took him by surprise yesterday when I told him how old Ben was. There were a lot of questions and pointed glares as I tried to explain that what we had was special, and not at all a sugar daddy situation. It took a lot of convincing, but eventually I was able to plead my case. In the end it came down to the fact that I was in love, and happy, so my dad accepted that he could be happy for me.

Now if only I could get a phone call from the man I loved. Or a text, or *something*.

"Oh I don't know, what is there to do around here?"

"I've got an idea of something you might enjoy," he said as he plated the eggs and the rest of the bacon.

He brought two full plates of food over and we sat and ate while discussing potential activities for the day. Apparently my dad had just installed some new lines at a ski resort not far from there. While there was no snow yet, the resort was currently running their ski lifts for people to ride and take in the view. The mountain still had beautiful fall colored leaves clinging onto the trees that made the ride breathtaking, so my dad told me.

After breakfast I went up to my room and got dressed, bundling up in layers to stay warm in the crisp October air. Despite the shining sun, there was an icy breeze that would chill anyone to the core.

I was looking forward to this time with my dad. I was hoping that the quality time would help ease the nerves that had become bundled up inside of me. Spending time up in the mountains was starting to make me realize how tightly strung I had become. It was time to unwind.

When we were both ready, we got in the car and my dad drove us to the ski resort not far from his house. I took in the sprawling mountain as we pulled up and parked. I could already see the fall colors clinging to the branches of the trees that lined the trails. My dad bought us tickets to ride the lift and soon we were waiting to catch a chair to the top.

There weren't many people around since it was a weekday, so we practically had the place to ourselves. A man attending the lift helped us both slide onto a narrow chair and pulled the bar down into our laps before we began ascending up the side of the steep mountain.

The lift moved slowly yet swiftly, and up on the mountain it was quiet and serene. My dad was right about the leaves, they were still brilliant shades of gold and orange. Occasional gusts of wind yanked handfuls of the leaves off of their branches each time it blew, making it look like the trees were throwing confetti as we rode past.

"So how are you doing today?" My dad eventually asked, breaking the silence of our ride.

"I think I'm doing better today. Talking with you really helped, so thank you."

"Any time." He looked out over the grassy trail below us. We still hadn't reached the top and I was okay with that; I wasn't quite ready to vacate the lift and get back to real life.

"What are you going to do when you get back?" He prodded after a few minutes more. Another cold breeze nipped at my bare face and caused a shiver to run through my body. We were nearing the peak, where I could just see the horizon as we crept up on it.

"I don't know."

"Are you going to talk to Ben?"

"I guess I have to, huh?"

We lurched up over the incline and slowly moved around the top of the lift tower before facing out over the Pennsylvanian slice of the Appalachians. From the top of that ski mountain we could see for miles and miles, across rolling Pennsylvania hills that eventually met the smooth ridge of the Kittatinny Mountains. Now *that* view was breathtaking.

My dad brought me back to reality as we began our slow descent. "You probably should. You've got to tell him how you feel, even if he ends up not feeling the same way."

The thought of Ben not loving me back hurt more than anything I'd ever felt before. It was a physical lump in my chest that caused my breathing to quickly become ragged. My dad realized that I was having a panic attack and he swiftly changed the subject.

"I'm so glad you came to visit, Izzy. I missed you."

I took a few deep, calming breaths before responding. "Thank you for letting me come here. I'm sorry I don't do it more often."

The hard lump in my chest was replaced with the heavy weight of guilt from leaving my dad alone.

"It's okay, really. You're an adult and you have a life that you're living in Strasburg. That's where you belong right now. Although you could call more often." He joked, elbowing me over the lap bar.

We crept toward the bottom of the mountain and I thought about what my dad said. I also felt like I belonged in Strasburg; it was my home and it's where I needed to go back to. But for now, I needed a few more days to build up the courage to go back and say what I needed to say to the man I loved.

Chapter 28 - *I HOPE THIS WORKS* (Ben)

Working in our little office building wasn't the same when I knew Isabella wasn't back in her corner cubicle. That desk sat empty now, with all design projects put on hold for the foreseeable future.

It had been a week since she was fired; Jess had a few interviews lined up for the position but we both knew we'd never be able to fill Isabella's shoes. No one else would be as efficient or as detail-oriented as Isabella was. And certainly, no one would be as cute as her.

Aunt June had been in a good mood lately because of her new partnership with Charles Penbrook and it was a bit of a slap in the face. She didn't even care about Isaebella, there was no remorse to her, just business. I tried once a few days ago to talk to Aunt June about bringing Isabella back, but she would hear none of what I had to say.

"Rules are rules," she'd reminded me. I was sick of hearing that.

I'd heard from Jess that Isabella had gone up to visit her dad, which was a blessing in disguise, giving me some time to put together a secret little project outside of work. I kind of felt like a major ass because I hadn't reached out to Isabella yet, but I had a good reason! My secret project was for her, and I wanted it to be perfect.

I'd had this idea for a while, pretty much since we'd started dating seriously. I knew that eventually, if our relationship progressed, one of us would have to leave the company since *rules are rules.* Assuming it'd be her having to leave Simmons' Hotels, I'd started working on a contingency plan.

See, Isabella is so incredibly talented that she could easily run her own freelance firm and do design work for companies all over the globe. But once I saw what she did with the Fall Ball, I thought about the whole picture. What if Isabella ran an event planning company? She'd be amazing at it. The company would utilize both her extensive design knowledge and the leadership skills that she clearly possessed but never used. It seemed like the perfect idea and would solve our little problem.

So when Aunt June shot down my plea to hire Isabella back, I put my plan in motion to kick start this brand new business so it'd be there if Isabella was interested in it. And if she wasn't interested? Well, I was really counting on her to be.

I wanted everything to be done for her so all she had to do was say 'yes.'

I'd put together a proposal for Isabella, complete with the perfect office location in town, just five minutes from The Steamworks Hotel. Close enough that we could grab lunch together but far enough away from me so that she never felt smothered.

I had preemptively signed a lease agreement on the building and had spent the last few evenings fixing the place up, giving it a new paint job and taking care of some general maintenance. I was confident that Isabella would love the idea so I worked hard to make the place feel like a space that could be hers, and whenever the doubts creeped into the back of my mind I shoved them away by throwing even more of myself at this business.

But really, the idea was fool-proof. With Isabella's design portfolio and newfound event planning experience, along with my business plan proposal, I'd made sure that she could get a small business loan from the bank in town without an issue. And I already knew who her first client could be; Simmons Hotels. We were never going to replace Isabella, so why not bring her on as a partner? Besides, it wasn't against any policy for business partners to be in a relationship with hotel employees; I had HR check to be sure.

It was all perfect, just as long as Isabella was okay with it. And that was the tricky part, as confident as I was, those thoughts wondering if she'd actually be okay with running her own business kept popping up. What if I was way off the mark on this one; what if she wanted nothing to do with the business, or me?

Regardless, I was excited to be able to offer her this opportunity. I just had to set up a meeting with the bank and then I was ready to call her and try to get her back to Strasburg.

I just hoped I hadn't waited too long.

This past week I had Jess checking in on Isabella and keeping me updated, and from what I could tell she still seemed pretty upset with me. I was really hoping this grand gesture would make up for it all.

Besides the bank, I just had one more loose end to tie up. Brinley was moving today, off to some far away state where she couldn't bother us anymore. I had to make sure she was gone for good, so I was going to help her load her boxes into the moving truck she'd rented for the trip. I was planning to make quick work of the move so I could get her out of Strasburg once and for all, and get my Isabella back.

I took a half day off of work and drove into town. I pulled my truck up behind the small box truck that was parked in front of the Chinese restaurant. The door to Brinley's stairwell was propped open, ready for us to move boxes and furniture for the next hour or so. I walked up the stairs and into the apartment which looked much emptier than it did last week.

"Brin?" I called out, using a nickname that I hadn't used in a long time.

"In the bedroom, be right out!"

I stood in the living room waiting for her to emerge. Brinley was wearing leggings and a tight fitting jacket, showing off her tall, slim figure. I took a moment to really look at her and I wondered, why did it take me so long to get over her?

Sure, she was the textbook definition of attractive, but her personality was never that great. I overlooked outbursts, jealousy, and childish behavior because I was blinded by what I thought was love. I let out an audible sigh of relief when I realized that I was finally over her. It felt great.

"If you're just going to stare at me all day then you might as well come move away with me," she purred.

Brinley had been absolutely ecstatic when I'd called her to offer my help with her move. She must've thought she finally had me on the hook but I was going to make my job very clear.

"Nope. I'm good, just here to help you pack a truck."

Brinley huffed. "Well the place is all packed up, grab a box and start loading."

She crossed her arms and walked back to the bedroom, obviously disappointed in my disposition. As I scanned over all the things that needed to be moved, I wondered why *I* was the one helping her today, and not one of her new boy toys. I guess it didn't really matter, did it?

I grabbed the first box I saw and hauled it down the stairs to the truck. I did that at least ten times before Brinley joined me back in the living room. I had gotten a lot of the boxes moved and was about to start figuring out how to get the furniture back down the stairs.

"Do you want something to drink?" Brinley asked.

"I could use some water if you happen to have a cup still unpacked."

She moved into the kitchen and I heard the faucet turn on and off. She came back with two glasses and handed me one before sitting down on the couch. I gulped my water down and sat next to her. She looked annoyed as she stared into her cup.

"Aren't you happy to be moving? You never liked this town much."

"Yes, I'm *so* glad to be getting out of here. It'll be a much needed fresh start."

"So why do you look so displeased?"

"Because I don't understand why you're here, helping me. You don't like me anymore, so what gives?"

I couldn't tell her that I was there to make sure she was really actually leaving, so instead I said, "I'm here helping because, despite our recent history, you were still a big part of my life. You needed help today so I showed up. Consider it my olive branch."

And I realized that I really meant that. As much as this woman got under my skin lately, I did love her at one point. Hell, I was going to marry her. I didn't have those feelings anymore but I was tired of carrying so much anger toward her. It was probably a good thing to bury the hatchet and send her off on a positive note.

Brinley set her cup down on the floor and turned toward me. "I'm sorry things turned out the way they did. I'm going to miss you and Mollie but you're right, this move is going to be good for me. I just hope you'll let me come visit some time."

"Of course you can come visit."

She smiled, like a true genuine smile with no ulterior motives behind it, and I felt at peace, finally.

It took us another couple of hours to get all of her stuff into the moving truck. Boxes were stacked up taller than me and furniture squeezed in between them like a giant game of Tetris. When we were done, all of her belongings, less one suitcase of necessities, were locked into the back of the truck. I stood on the sidewalk and watched as Brinley climbed into the front seat, cranked the engine on, and pulled out into the slow Main Street traffic, heading west.

That was it, she was gone. I felt good, and it was finally time to focus on the most important thing in my life. Isabella.

Still standing on the sidewalk, I tapped Jess' number on my phone and waited for her to pick up.

"Hi Ben!" She answered.

"Hey, how's it going?"

"I heard from your estranged girlfriend this morning." She teased.

"Oh?"

"She's coming back tomorrow."

"That doesn't leave me a lot of time but I can work with it. Are you still OK with the plan?"

"I feel kind of icky luring her to you but I suppose it's for the better good. So for the sake of love, yes."

Love. I hadn't thought much about that word when it came to Isabella, but it felt right. I did love her, and that was becoming more and more apparent each day.

"Alright, then if all goes well, I will see you tomorrow."

I hung up and walked back to my truck. I had a lot to get done before tomorrow.

Chapter 29 - *Four Letter Word* (Isabella)

There was still another hour left of driving before I was home. Today's sunny weather matched my disposition and the new positive approach I was taking home with me. My dad had made me feel a thousand times better over the few days I'd spent with him, and I was ready to get back to Strasburg and pick up the pieces of my shattered life. Maybe that was a bit dramatic, but that's definitely how it felt.

I checked the clock on my dashboard. I'd timed it so I would be driving during lunch time because I wanted to catch Kendra on her break, and be able to fill her in on my week with my dad.

I used my phone's voice command to connect to my car via Bluetooth, and dialed Kendra at exactly 12:01 pm when I knew she'd be having lunch. She picked up on the first ring.

"Izzy! I thought I was never going to hear from you again!" Her voice boomed through my car's speakers and comforted me instantly.

"I know, I'm sorry, but I was totally taking advantage of the poor cell reception that I had up there. I barely kept in touch with anyone while I was at my dad's and it was nice to be disconnected for a while."

"Does that mean you're home?" She squealed.

I smiled to myself; it was so nice talking to my best friend. "I'm headed home now, I'll be back this afternoon."

"We have to get together!"

"Actually, Jess, she was my supervisor at Simmons' Hotels, has asked me to grab a drink tonight. But let's meet up tomorrow!"

Kendra paused for a beat. "Wait, isn't she Ben's cousin?"

"Yes, but she's also a good friend. She had been checking in on me and I just want to assure her that I'm fine."

"Ah, I see. And have you heard from Ben yet?"

That question stung. I don't know why I hadn't heard from Ben yet. If I wasn't meeting up with Jess later I would probably have driven myself right to his house and demanded an answer. I tried to keep positivity front and center, but it was hard when that piece of the puzzle was still missing.

"...no." I responded.

"What the hell? Forget him, Izzy, you deserve someone who will fight for you!" Easily agitated, Kendra's frustration with the guy radiated through the phone. But as much as I was also frustrated, I couldn't give up on him just yet.

"Well, that's the thing, I can't forget him. Kendra, I love him."

The line was silent for what felt like an eternity. I'd have killed to see Kendra's face at that moment, to know what thoughts were flashing across her features. Finally, she spoke.

"So... what are you going to do?"

"I've got to go talk to him and figure out if he feels the same way."

"I wish you luck with that, Izzy."

Kendra and I chatted for a while longer until she had to go back to work. It helped pass the time for me while I drove and before I knew it, I was pulling into the driveway of my rental home. I'd missed this place, more specifically this town. I love spending time with my dad but Strasburg was my home.

I had just finished unpacking my small suitcase and begun a load of laundry when my doorbell chimed. Without checking the camera I walked into the living room and opened the door. Jess stood on my porch dressed in her usual colorful work clothes.

She beamed and swooped in for a hug. "Izzy! I'm so glad you're back in town."

"Thank you, Jess. Um, did you leave work early to come greet me?"

An unapologetic grin spread across her face. "Yeah, but I know the boss, so it'll be okay. I just couldn't wait to see you!"

Jess and I were pretty good friends but she seemed a little *too* excited to see me. I imagined her camped out in her car outside my house, watching for the moment I got home like she was a spy in a movie. I was curious if she was up to something but I was also secretly elated to have someone that cared so much.

"Do you want to come in?" I asked.

"Actually, are you ready to go grab a drink? I know it's a little early but we can just get a glass of wine or something, nothing crazy."

"Yeah we can go now, let me just grab my purse."

I ran back to my room to throw a coat on and sling my purse over my shoulder, and met Jess back outside.

"I'll drive!" She said as she climbed into her huge SUV.

I walked around and hopped into the passenger side. As we headed into town Jess asked about my dad and my trip upstate. She loved the black bear story and as I told it, I still wasn't sure if it had really happened. Regardless, it was nice having a friend like her that showed genuine interest in my life.

We drove past The Steamworks Hotel and I felt a pang of sadness and rejection. I missed working every day and the fact that I still hadn't figured out where to go next in my career made me feel lost. Luckily, I had enough savings to hold me over for a month or so while I thought about the next step, but I was still anxious to get back out there. I had planned to spend the afternoon job hunting online, but that would have to wait until later now.

Jess pulled into a small parking lot at a building I didn't recognize.

"Is there a new bar in town?" I asked. I had assumed we were going to one of the hotels or even to the dive bar that Brinley worked at.

"Uh, not quite." Jess said, looking past me out my window.

I followed her gaze and saw Ben walking across the gravel lot toward the SUV. My heart started pounding like a drum and my stomach twisted into knots. It had only been a week since I last saw Ben but after everything that had happened, it felt like it had been years. He was dressed for work, slacks and a button up with the sleeves rolled up to his elbows, looking as sexy as ever.

I whipped my head back toward Jess. "What's going on?"

Her face softened and her voice came out as hardly more than a whisper. "He's been working on something really important, that's why you haven't heard from him."

"What's so important that he can't even send a text?" I shot back, allowing my frustrations to break free of the dam I'd built and flow over me. I was fired from his company over a week ago and I hadn't heard from him once since then. I didn't mean to take it out on Jess, I know she was just trying to help, but my emotional state was an absolute mess and she just happened to be the closest person to me at the moment.

Luckily Jess was good at keeping a level head. "Why don't you ask him for yourself?"

Ben stood a few feet away from the SUV, waiting patiently for me to get out. I didn't know if I wanted to yell at him or run into his arms, so for the sake of my frail emotions I decided to do neither of those. I opened the door and walked toward him, waiting for him to talk first.

"Isabella." He breathed, and just like that my anger was absolved.

All I wanted in that moment was to be held by him, I didn't care that we were in the middle of town in some random lot. I just wanted him.

But first I had to figure out what was going on. "Why didn't you call? Or text, or email, or *something*?"

"I know, I'm so sorry. I should have done something, you're right." He ran his fingers through his hair. "I'm not denying that, but I'm really hoping this makes up for it."

"You're hoping *what* makes up for it? I don't know why we're here."

"Come with me." He said as he held out a hand.

After a moment of hesitation, I took his hand and he led me back toward the street and onto the sidewalk. He stood and faced an empty building that I recognized as a boutique that had gone out of business a year or so ago. There were no lights on inside the building so all I could see were our own reflections staring back at us.

I almost giggled, I looked quite ridiculous standing next to Ben. He had almost a foot on me, and even in the smudged glass I could see the physical signs of our age difference. But instead of feeling weird or embarassed about the way we looked together, I felt comfortable. He was my person, no matter how many years were between us.

"So what do you think?" Ben broke the silence.

"About what? Are you going to explain what's going on?"

"Let's step inside and I'll explain." Ben walked up to the door of the abandoned boutique and pulled a set of keys out of his pocket. One of them unlocked the door and he held it open, waiting for me to enter.

This was it, he was actually going to murder me this time.

Despite everything in my body telling me I probably shouldn't walk into the dark, abandoned building, I did so anyway. I stepped in and my eyes slowly adjusted to the dark before Ben closed the door behind us and switched on an overhead light.

In spite of its appearance from outside, the inside was fairly clean. It had a large empty front room with what looked like maybe an office or storage in the back. The wood floors looked recently polished and it smelled faintly of fresh paint, which explained the bright white walls. After I took it all in, I turned toward Ben for that explanation he'd been promising.

"If you want it, this place is yours."

I narrowed my eyes. "For what, exactly?"

"Isabella's Events & Design. Or whatever name you'd like, really, that was just the working name for the paperwork." He paused, trying to gauge my reaction. "It's a studio for you to use to do freelance design and event planning. You're so talented, I know you can be successful running your own business. I even got you a client!"

"A client? Freelance design? Event planning?"

I heard Ben's words but they weren't clicking in my mind. I was suddenly feeling extremely overwhelmed, my head spinning like a top on my shoulders. I sat on the window ledge and took a couple of deep breaths to calm myself.

I tried to collect my thoughts as Ben looked at me, concern creasing his brow. Was he serious? Did Ben really start a business for me? I didn't know how to run a business or manage clients. I was starting to get worked up again, so Ben placed his hands on my shoulders.

"I know it's a lot but I also know you can do it. The way you took charge of planning the Fall Ball showed that you have what it takes to be a leader, and an efficient one at that. Did you know we came in over three thousand dollars under budget? *Somehow,* the most successful ball of all time came in under budget. That was all you! So now it's your time to show this town what you have to offer. And besides, when you run the place, you make the rules." Ben winked and ducked his head down to my level to plant a kiss on my lips.

It was true, no one could fire me from my own company. For a moment I got lost in Ben's kiss; I forgot how much I loved kissing him. My arms wrapped up around his neck and he chuckled, breaking the kiss.

"Well, maybe keep in mind the giant windows behind you." He straightened up and motioned to the space around us. "So, *what do you think?*"

"Is this all for real?" I still couldn't believe it.

"There's a little bit you have to do on your end, but if you want to, this space is yours. And of course I'm here to help you in whatever way you need."

I stood up and walked around the front room, beginning to envision it set up as an office space. I could see a large desk for myself, comfortable *matching* chairs for my clients, and my art hung on the tall white walls. It was actually becoming real to me.

I turned to Ben, "why did you do this?"

"Because I love you Isabella, isn't that obvious?"

He wrapped his arms around me and I finally felt whole. This is what I wanted all along. The business is cool, but Ben was the missing piece. I buried my face in his chest and choked back tears. All I could manage was a breathless *'thank you.'*

We stood there like that for several minutes before Ben started laughing. I unburied my face to see what could be so funny. Ben was shaking his head, looking out the large front window. I turned to find Jess peeking in, with her hand above her eyes so she could see through the glass that her breath was fogging up.

"Shall I let her in?" Ben chuckled.

"Yes!"

Ben walked over to the front door and opened it, letting Jess in out of the cold. She ran up to me and hugged me while squealing like an excited toddler.

"Are you doing it Isabella? Are you starting your own company?"

I couldn't help but to break out in a grin so wide my cheeks hurt. "Yes, I am."

More unintelligible squealing came from Jess while Ben silently fist pumped behind her. It felt so nice to have these two humans on my side. From the pocket of her coat, Jess pulled out three small bottles of some kind of liquor shooter and handed one to Ben and myself.

"I'd like to propose a toast to -- Isabella, what are you naming your company?"

I only paused for a moment before answering, "Artistry Events."

"Oh that's perfect," Jess crooned. "Okay, then let's toast to Artistry Events."

We all raised our tiny bottles and toasted each other before drinking whatever was inside of them. And then I remembered something Ben had said earlier.

"Wait, did you say you have a client for me already?"

Ben and Jess looked at each other and smiled, before both turning to me.

"What do you think of taking on Simmon's Hotels as your first client?" Ben asked.

"Are you serious?"

"Is that a good or a bad 'are you serious'?" Jess asked.

"How would that even work?"

"Simple," Ben said. "We need a designer, you now own a design company. We host events, you plan events. I can have Cindy reach out and be your official contact and onboard you as one of our business partners. It's no different than one of our linen suppliers, or the local distillery that we partner with to stock the bars. You'd be a business partner of Simmons' Hotels and we'd have you handle everything you were doing for us before. If you'll have us."

"And June?" I asked, perplexed by the whole situation.

"She can't take any issue with our relationship now. I followed her rules and you no longer work for her company." Ben huffed, obviously still angry about the way I'd been fired.

Had I known he felt that way, maybe I wouldn't have run off for so long; all I needed was his support this whole time. Better late than never, I supposed.

"And he cleared it with Aunt June this morning." Jess finished for him.

"Okay…" I mulled, "let's do this then!"

Ben high fived Jess before scooping me into a hug.

Chapter 30 - *New Horizons* (Ben)

I walked toward the conference room for my weekly staff meeting. It had been about three weeks since Isabella had come back and accepted my apology, and the job proposal. She had been doing really well with getting the business up and running. The bank approved her loan and she was using it to get her space furnished and ready for clients. As soon as the shock wore off she had taken control of the situation like I knew she would. I was so proud of her.

It was also a lot of fun seeing Isabella thrive like this. I was thrilled to even be just a little part of it all and jumped at any opportunity to help my favorite blonde. Just last weekend I spent what felt like forever assembling the furniture for her office. Isabella was so cute, arranging everything just the way she wanted it. I had to admit, I was a bit jealous of her brand new, coordinating furniture. So much so that I was now considering upgrading the stuff in my own office.

I had been a little nervous about Isabella handling the finances of her company since she would be billing as an independent contractor, but I foolishly underestimated her determination. One evening in bed she had been leaned over her laptop furiously tapping away. When I finally asked her what she was doing, Isabella had informed me that she'd just signed up for an online class on business finances. I should have known that this woman could do anything she put her mind to.

Isabella had also been busy meeting with myself and Cindy, who was a major help in getting Isabella set up as a partner. Onboarding was easy and it was nice to have Isabella back in charge of her own projects. Even Aunt June was on board with it all. I had sat down with her a couple weeks ago to hash it all out and once we did, I felt much better after our discussion.

"Isabella is going forward with her own company," I'd said to her while she was sitting in my office one morning.

"That's wonderful, I know she's going to do well." Aunt June looked sincere, with her hands clasped in her lap.

"She's really good at what she does."

"I know that."

"Then why did you let her go?" I asked, still longing for closure on the situation. I was tired of June's aloofness.

"Ben, I built this company from the ground up. Each rule that is in place is there for a reason, because somewhere along the way, I learned my lesson by not having a rule to protect the business."

June stared off at the wall behind me for a moment, before continuing. "Back in the eighties I had a hotel manager named Jim. He was very good at his job but he fell into a very, er, *passionate* relationship with one of the housekeeping women.

Now at that time we were hosting some kind of government meeting. It was big for us, our first large-scale event. The hotel was packed with all sorts of important people. The day of the event, a state senator ended up walking into his room to find my hotel manager butt naked on his bed, with the housekeeper on top of him. Can you imagine the backlash I received because of that? Luckily I was able to keep it out of the press and I spared the company's name. But it was all my fault really, I knew how sex-crazed those two were but I didn't do anything about it for the sake of love.

That day I learned my lesson, and a company-wide policy was put into place immediately to ensure that something like that would never happen again. I trust you, Ben, and I know you would never do anything on purpose to harm the company, but people do crazy things when they're in love, and you are obviously in love with this girl. I just needed to protect us, was all."

I nodded. That made sense... I couldn't imagine having to deal with a situation like that. I couldn't be mad at my aunt for wanting to protect everything she'd worked so hard for. My conversation with Aunt June had finally put everything to rest, and I felt a rejuvenated passion for my work now that the layer of resentment was gone. Add in this new partnership with Isabella, and I was feeling great!

Everything seemed to be back on track: work life, personal life, it was all working out for me. As cliche as it sounded, I felt lighter these days and there was a pep in my step that hadn't been there for quite some time.

"Good morning everyone!" I bellowed as I stepped into the conference room.

All of Simmons' Hotel's finest staff sat in the room in their hodge podge of chairs, looking up at me. It was a great feeling and a perfect team, or at least it would be very soon. We were all set to start sending work Isabella's way, we just had to let the rest of the team know to make it official.

"I have another short one for you today," I began, fully aware that one one actually wanted to be there. "Our properties are seeing massive spikes in bookings beginning next week with Thanksgiving, and already through the whole holiday season up until January. Everything is looking good for ending this year with a bang."

I paused for a few seconds of mild, mostly uninterested applause. At that moment I really missed Isabella's passion.

"But before I let you all go, I do have some announcements. The first is a big one." I paused for dramatic effect, much to everyone's annoyance. "June just finalized a deal with the developer Charles Penbrook, which means that Simmons' Hotels is going to gain a fourth property in 2024!"

My employees started murmuring amongst themselves; some looked excited while others looked worried about the change, a hurdle we would navigate over the next few months. I had no doubt that the people in front of me could handle this thrilling change. I looked at Jess, who was practically bubbling over with enthusiasm. Most likely because she knew she didn't have to keep this secret anymore.

I raised my voice just a bit to settle the room. "It'll certainly be a change for all of us but I know we can handle it. Once June gives us the 'go-ahead,' Jess will be sending out a press alert and I'd expect a lot of excitement from the community about this project."

Clark looked like he was going to keel over at that news and I chuckled to myself. He and his department would manage just fine, he's been at it for this long and there was nothing he couldn't handle.

"That does bring me to one more bit of news," I looked over at Jess who once again looked so giddy that I was certain she was going to vibrate right out of her chair. "As you know, due to company policy, we lost our designer, Isabella."

Someone cleared their throat loudly at the mention of my lover's name.

"Well, I'm happy to report that we finally have someone to fill that role. A company, actually. We will be contracting our design work out to Artistry Events, a new local business that opened up just a few miles down the road."

Only a few faces showed mild interest, not what I was hoping for but it was expected out of this group.

"Isabella owns the company!" Jess blurted out.

The murmurs began again and I motioned to Cindy. "She's been welcomed on as a partner, and for those of you wondering, yes it was approved by June. Isabella will also be handling our event planning moving forward, since she did such an amazing job with the Fall Ball."

"People are still calling about the ball, they can't get over it!" Clark chimed in from the back of the room.

"I ran a report, and about fifty percent of the people who attended the ball have since booked a stay at one of our properties. That has never happened." Brenda, our CFO, added.

"That's right," Aunt June's voice joined us from the doorway. Everyone turned to greet our head honcho. "It was the most successful event we've ever had, thanks to Isabella Morgan. We should all be excited to have her back on board."

June turned to me and smiled. I felt validation wash over me at the realization that I never needed to convince Aunt June of Isabella's talents or worth. She already knew. That old woman was sharper that I'd realized; maybe it was time to start giving her the benefit of the doubt.

After a round of questions and answers about the new hotel and our new business partner, people seemed to feel a smidge better about the onslaught of change. The meeting dissipated until it was just us Simmons left in the room.

"This will all work out." June said to myself and Jess.

"I am so, so excited for everything, Aunt June!" Jess replied.

"So am I, dear. And I just wanted to tell the two of you that I'm really proud of everything you've done here. I never had time to start a family of my own, but the two of you are like children to me." June said, then added, "don't tell your brothers, Ben!"

"They'll never know," I joked.

Jess herded us in for a group hug, which I reluctantly joined. It felt corny, but deep down inside I knew it was the beginning of a fresh, new chapter in all of our books, and I was looking forward to it.

Chapter 31 - *My Boyfriend, Ben* (Isabella)

My doorbell chimed from the app on my phone and I ran to the front door. I swung it open and threw myself into my dad's arms.

"I'm so glad you came!" I said, as he enveloped me into a hug.

"Anything for you, Izzy. Are you ready to go?"

"Yes." I stepped back and smoothed my silky emerald green dress. The cold December air chilled my legs through the sheer tights I had on, and caused goose bumps to run up my arms under my cardigan.

Today was the soft opening of Artistry Events, and I was throwing a small soiree at my new office for friends, family, and a bunch of prospective clients that Jess had helped me snag with some light marketing. With Ben's help, I had gotten the space looking exactly how I wanted and I was ready to get the business up and running with some new business. My heart was pounding out of my chest at the thought of having to mingle with so many people this evening, but I was slightly comforted knowing I would have my dad and Ben by my side.

Which was another thing that had me sweating bullets; Ben would be meeting my dad tonight and the thought made me so nervous that I started swaying a bit as I stood on my front patio.

"You okay?" My dad asked, reaching a hand out to steady me.

"Yep, just a little overwhelmed. I'll be okay in a sec," I lied. I wasn't going to be okay until this was all over.

I locked the door behind me and followed my dad out to his truck. As he drove us into town I started to give him directions on how to get to my office until I remembered that he used to live here too, up until mom passed. That felt like a lifetime ago rather than only a few years, but he did know the town just as well as I did.

As my dad pulled into the small lot next to my building, I saw that Ben's truck was already there and I felt the anxiety start to take over again. I took a few steadying breaths before I hopped out and walked with my dad through the lot. The sun had set a couple of hours ago, and the dark evening was broken up by pale yellow lights that shone over the lot.

I peeked over at my dad to gauge his mood; he'd never formally met a boyfriend of mine, mainly because there haven't really been any to meet. I had no idea how this was going to go. I did have to give him props, though, since he had dressed up nicely for tonight. He was wearing the heck out of dark jeans and a button up shirt underneath a leather jacket that screamed 1995.

I wrapped my arm through his and led him toward the front door. Through the large picture window I could see Ben moving around inside, starting to set up for me. I took one more deep breath to ground myself. Just before we pushed open the door, I whispered, "be nice."

"I'm always nice."

I opened the door to my brand new office space. I had kept all of the bright white walls that Ben had painted except for the one directly behind my desk, which I had painted a sunny yellow. I chose sleek, white furniture for the consultation area, and accented the wooden floors with a plush throw rug.

I had lush green plants filling the spaces where bright light shone in through the front window, and despite my hesitation, Ben had helped me hang my own artwork that I'd had hidden in a closet for years. And of course, just behind my desk in the center of the yellow wall, was the painting that Ben had done on our date so many weeks ago now.

"It looks great in here Izzy!" My dad exclaimed while taking in the space. "It looks just like Isabella Morgan works here."

I felt a smile tug at the corners of my mouth despite the jitters still running through me. He was right, this office was the perfect representation of me. Neat, clean, organized, and a little bit eclectic.

Ben walked in from the back room where he had most likely been stashing food and wine for the event that was meant to start in less than an hour. When he saw me and my dad standing by the front door, he squared his shoulders and I noticed him immediately put on his businessman smile, something that I'm sure no one else would have noticed. I'd seen Ben do that plenty of times when preparing to enter a meeting or meet a new business partner. It was like he put on a mask of confidence that helped him face any problem or situation, regardless of how he was feeling inside. I knew now that it was all a charade, a way for Ben to protect his vulnerable self.

He rolled his sleeves up as he walked over to us, and held his hand out to my dad. "Hi, I'm Ben. It's nice to meet you."

My dad looked him up and down for a whole thirty seconds before grabbing his hand and shaking it firmly. He didn't smile, he only kept a straight face that showed no hint of emotion while he looked Ben directly in the eyes. I knew it was all a tough-dad act, but even I was scared standing there next to him. *I* wouldn't want to date me if that was how I was received.

"Hi, Ben." He finally replied.

There were a few minutes where an awkward silence hung heavily in the air between us as my dad dropped Ben's hand, and we all just stood there looking at each other. I knew I should probably say something to fill the quiet, but the uncomfortableness of the situation had me at a loss for words.

Ben ran his hand through his hair, and I noticed the tough businessman charade shrivel away. At that moment, he was just a man who was meeting his girlfriend's dad for the first time, and it was actually making him nervous.

Thankfully, Jess burst through the front door and broke the weird tension.

"I'm so excited for you Isabella!" She squealed as she ran up to me, waving a bouquet of flowers. She scooped me into a hug and my dad cleared his throat beside me.

"Jess, this is my dad, Mike." I wriggled out of the hug and motioned to my dad, who looked amusedly at the grown woman who was sporting a grin that stretched from ear to ear.

"Hi Mike! I see you've met my cousin Ben already. He's so great for Isabella, don't let the tough exterior fool you." Jess spewed.

"Cousins, you say?" My dad looked back and forth between the two of them.

"Uh, yeah." Ben replied, "we don't have much in common besides the shared bloodline." He chuckled nervously.

"We're like yin and yang!" Jess chimed in.

Finally, my dad cracked a smile. "I'll say. Well it's nice to meet both of you. Izzy, what do we need to do to help you set up?"

I breathed an audible sigh of relief. We'd cleared one of the hardest hurdles of the night, now I just had to host a building full of people without barfing from nervousness.

Between the four of us, we had the room set up with a few minutes to spare. Ben had snagged some high top tables from one of the hotels, and we'd set them up around the room. I had designed tent cards for the tables with my company's information, and I had a stack of bold new business cards in my cardigan pocket, ready to hand out.

Ben volunteered to greet everyone as they came in, while Jess would be making sure that guests' glasses stayed full. The first few people strolled in, which I recognized as a couple local business owners. I felt the nerves rock through me as I started to step toward them to introduce myself.

"You've got this, Izzy."

I felt a hand on my shoulder and turned around to find Ben. He opened his arms up for a hug and I fell into them.

"I'm scared." I whispered into his chest.

"I know you can do it." He let me go and nodded toward the people that Jess was currently chatting to while handing them glasses of champagne.

I can do this. This is my business, and I've got to put myself out there. Here we go...

I took a page out of Ben's book and squared my shoulders. I pasted a smile on my face and walked toward them.

"Hello, welcome to Artistry Events! I'm Isabella Morgan."

Made in the USA
Middletown, DE
11 February 2022